Compass North

By
Stephanie Joyce Cole

Duncurra LLC

Copyright Stephanie Joyce Cole

ISBN-13: 978-1-942623-18-2

Cover Art by Earthly Charms
Produced in the USA

Praise for Compass North

"This debut novel is an intricately woven tale of recreating self in an austere Alaskan setting...The plot twists and revelations kept me guessing throughout. I highly recommend this novel."
– Jan T, an Amazon reviewer

"Appealing characters, a crisp writing style and evocative emotions...Be forewarned....if you haven't visited Alaska yet, it will make you want to.....and if you already have, it makes you want to go again." –Dan Douglass, an Amazon reviewer

"The plot of Compass North moves quickly with plenty of suspense. The characters are well-developed. They are folks with interesting histories who would be fun to meet. Ms. Cole's book displays a genuine knowledge of Alaska and its often quirky inhabitants. If you've booked the cruise for next summer, read this first! –Akchck, and Amazon reviewer

"Compass North is a must read book for today's generation of women (and men), defining their role in a complex and fast changing world." – GM, an Amazon reviewer

"Such a smart, fun book! I was quickly immersed in this story about starting all over-- haven't we all imagined that at some point? Lush with gorgeous scenery and a page-turning plot, it kept me flying through to the end. Can't wait to read the next one!" –MJ, an Amazon reviewer

Dedication

For Mark.

There must have been the sound of the plane coming, buzzing low, dropping out of the sky. When the plane hit the bus, there must have been a blinding, massive flash and billowing smoke, and the shock wave rattling over her, then the taste of hot metal and ash. But when she tried to remember, to picture herself where she had been standing at the edge of the long, black parking lot, all she could recall was the boom and rumble, then the wall of flames.

One

It was a small tour group, mostly older retired couples. They were first-time visitors like Meredith, most fulfilling a lifelong dream to see Alaska. After everyone had made their introductions at the Anchorage airport, Meredith realized she was the only single traveler. As they settled into the pattern of long days on the bus, ending with casual dinners in roadside lodges, fragments of their life stories emerged. Meredith listened, but she didn't offer any information about herself.

"We've been around the world, but we've been saving Alaska until now." Jonas Browning had smiled at Meredith, while his wife Angela held his arm. He stood tall, gray-haired and rangy, a retired engineer; and she was a tiny, plump, red-haired homemaker. They looked nothing alike, yet to Meredith they seemed to fit together like matching puzzle pieces, the way couples sometimes do after years and years of marriage. She felt a tightening in her chest now and then, watching them. But she still sat with them at meals, since it was immediately obvious that Angela's habit of talking in a continuous monologue usually made two-way conversations unnecessary.

Meredith found everyone friendly, but some seemed a bit too curious about her. At dinner one night, Peter had asked her outright why a married "youngster" of forty-two would choose to take a solo, late-season whirlwind bus tour around south-central Alaska. Of course, she didn't tell them the truth. "Oh, just a whim...had some time on my hands...the real estate business is so slow right now...always wanted to see Alaska." Well, the last part was true. For her, photographs of Alaska always depicted a fantasy world of pine forests and glaciers, so different from anyplace she had ever been. She didn't add, "And it seemed the farthest place I could go from Florida, away from my cheating husband and the rest of my miserable life."

No, she didn't complain, but she couldn't engage either. She'd realized almost immediately that the trip was a mistake. She had taken her body to a different place, far, far away, but her shell-shocked mind was numb and only had the energy to chew at the images of the mess she'd left behind. She'd sat with her fellow travelers at dinner and on the bus, and she smiled and chatted about whatever they were discussing, but all the while, so far from home, Meredith had only been able to think about going back and what would come next.

On the final night of the Land of the Midnight Sun Overland Tour, the bus pulled into yet another rustic Alaskan lodge. After nearly a week on the road, Meredith was hard pressed to distinguish one moss-covered log structure from another. Each of them was plopped into the middle of a pebble-strewn lot, right on the edge of the narrow highway, and as the bus bumped to a stop, scruffy mutts always greeted it with an enthusiastic chorus of barking. The travelers stretched and yawned as they strolled inside. The beaming ruddy-faced landlady in a bright blue apron distributed room keys, while Marty, their driver, hauled their bags from the bus and dumped them on the lobby floor in a jumbled pile.

Meredith dropped her suitcase next to the bed and stared at the cell phone in her hand, her knuckles clenched white against its shiny, black case. Footsteps thumped down the narrow corridor right outside. Then a greeting, a hoot of laughter. Her fellow travelers were already gathered for the evening.

Her hands shook as she dialed Ellen's number. "Be there," she whispered as the phone thrummed once, twice, three times. She envisioned Ellen walking through her kitchen, reaching for her black vintage phone as it shrieked out its shrill clanging ring, not unlike a fire alarm. "Please be there."

"Hell-o," Ellen lilted in her usual two-tone greeting. Meredith closed her eyes. "Ellen." Her voice rasped as if she hadn't spoken in a long time. She paused and swallowed. "Ellen, it's Meredith."

"Meredith, oh, so good to hear from you, but is everything okay?" Ellen's voice moved from bubbly to panicked in mid-sentence.

"I'm fine, just fine." She exhaled slowly and let the phone lie smooth and cool against the hot skin of her cheek. "I know it's late there. I...well, I just wanted to say hello." The words tumbled awkwardly to a stop and she pictured Ellen, so many miles away in Florida, frowning, searching for the truth beneath her words. Meredith swallowed and started again, forcing her voice into more cheery tones.

"The tour is going fine. We just checked in for our last night. I've seen so much. You wouldn't believe how big the world is up here. Nothing like Florida. Miles and miles of untouched wilderness." She paused. "How are you? How are things at home?"

"Oh, we're all fine here. I miss you, of course. I've been rushing to finish the staging for the Madsen contract, because they moved the open house up a week. Crazy timing, but I guess Nora Madsen insisted."

Meredith nodded, her unblinking eyes staring, unfocused, at the window. Rain spit and pattered against the pane. More footsteps paraded down the hall. She glanced at her watch. Almost time for dinner. She pulled in a deep breath.

"Ellen, I just was wondering...have you seen Michael?"

She heard Ellen's quick intake of breath, then silence. When she spoke again, her voice was measured and careful.

"Meredith, you took this trip to get a break from everything here. I didn't think it was a good idea at first, but maybe it was the right thing to do. You needed to give yourself some time to think, away from Michael and all the mess here. And that's the best thing you could be doing now, I think. Enjoy yourself. Put Michael out of your mind until you get back."

Tears pricked at the back of her eyes. Ellen was right, of course. That had been the whole point of the trip. "I know, I know, but..." Her vision blurred as her eyes filled with tears. "Oh, Ellen." She took an unsteady breath and pressed the palm of her hand into her forehead. "It's just so hard. I can't get away from the pain. I can't make it stop."

Ellen's voice tried to cut in, but Meredith rushed on, talking over her.

"What's wrong with me? This kind of thing happens to lots of people, lots of women. Worse things happen, and they get over it. They deal with it and go on. But for me, every day is a fresh cut. I wake up and remember and ache all over again. I don't know how to handle this." She was almost panting, breathless, and she felt the heavy beats of her heart thumping in her chest.

Ellen's voice was soft. "Meredith, it's only been a few weeks. And everyone's different. You've always been so calm and steady, so dependable for everyone else. After all that's happened, you're better off without him. But I know you, and even after everything he's done, you just don't want to see him as the creep he really is. I think you've forgotten how to take care of yourself."

The creep he really is... The truth of Ellen's words echoed in her mind. But now that she was away from Michael, it was as if he had been split into two separate people. One was the rage-filled man who had loomed over her and slammed his fist into the table an inch from her hand, sending her glass of water spinning to the floor when she'd told him she was going on the tour. "Let's just get this over with now, Meredith," he'd said, almost spitting the words. She had started to shake as she looked into his eyes, so cold and cunning, inches from her face. A stab of fear had coursed through her, a physical fear of a man she'd shared her life with for fifteen years. She shuddered. But there was another Michael. The Michael who had rushed home from work in the early years of their marriage, eager to see her, regaling her with funny stories about his day at the office. The Michael who walked to the beach with her on Saturday mornings, his hand caressing the small of her back before he darted into the crowded coffee shop for two cups of steaming dark coffee that they'd sipped while sitting on the edge of the sunny boardwalk. That was the man she loved. That man had been gone a long time. She knew that. But grief for his loss enveloped her now that she was far from home.

Meredith muffled the sob that pushed upward from deep in her throat. I won't cry. I won't. She pictured Ellen, worried, pacing the floor, casting about for the right words to help her. She blinked and tipped her head up, willing the tears not to fall. Down the hall, the dinner bell clanged, and more footsteps hurried along the corridor.

"I've got to go in a minute, Ellen. It's time for dinner here, but I really want to know...have you seen Michael at all?"

She heard the reluctance in Ellen's answer. "Only once. Two days ago." Another pause, as though Ellen was taking the time to weigh her words. "I was driving by your place. He was with two guys in a truck. They were moving some stuff out of the townhouse." Ellen hesitated again. "I'm not sure, but I think they were carrying out your lacquer cabinets."

Meredith's eyes widened. Why would Michael be moving anything before she got back? And the antique Chinese cabinets belonged to her. They were the only really valuable possession she'd inherited from her mother. What possible reason would Michael have for moving them? It didn't make any sense. She shook her head.

"Ellen, are you sure?" She frowned at her reflection in the dark window. "We didn't talk about the stuff in the house before I left, and besides, those cabinets are mine."

Ellen waited a moment before answering. "I'm not sure. I was in the car, and I just got a quick glance, so maybe it was something else. But you know what, Mer? You can figure all this out when you get home. You'll be back soon enough. For now, just enjoy the rest of your trip."

She jumped at a loud knock on the door. "Meredith, time for dinner. Are you coming?" She recognized Paul's booming voice.

"Yes, coming, be right there, Paul." She knew she had to go. No one sat down and started dinner until everyone was present and accounted for. She pressed the phone hard into her cheek.

"Ellen, I miss you." Her voice was soft and full of longing. "I'll be home tomorrow." And then what? her bruised mind shrieked. What will you do then?

She murmured a quick good-bye and clicked off the phone. She had hoped for comfort, but talking to Ellen had only made the hurt and yearning worse. Hurt for the horrible turn her life had taken. And yearning, but for what? Escape. She mulled over the word that rose unbidden in her mind. Trap doors, parachutes, trash chutes, wormholes. Yes, means of escape, but where did they lead? When you walked through the magic mirror, what was on the other side? She glanced at herself in the lodge wall mirror, then swiped the mascara that had smeared under her eyes. God, I look half-dead. Like a ghost.

~ * ~

The next morning, when Meredith woke up, bleary-eyed and her throat dry, she buried her head in the soft pillow. Going home. She probed the thought gently, thinking about opening the townhouse door, sensing the silent whispers. Was it even home anymore?

On their way to the Fairbanks airport, someone yelped, "Look, a bear!"

Even though it was the last day of the tour, the bus

still shuddered to a stop when anyone shouted out a sighting. Meredith rushed with everyone else to the left side of the bus to squint at the distant-moving speck on the rain-drenched green expanse in Denali National Park, all the time thinking, Will he be at the airport? No, of course not. I didn't even tell him my flight information. But he could ask Ellen. But no, he won't be there. Unless he wants to talk about the divorce right away...

"Wow, look at those fall colors!"

At a scenic viewpoint, they had all huddled together against the whistling wind and stared at the rolling tundra outside of Fairbanks, with its late summer greens, scarlets, and browns pocketed by hundreds of tiny lakes shining a deep navy blue in the weak afternoon sunlight. The stiff breeze carried the scent of trampled evergreens, wet earth, and the suggestion of still, boggy water. The bite of the wind made her eyes water and blurred her vision. She murmured some words of admiration, but her thoughts were far away. What will I do next? How could Michael do this to me after fifteen years?

Meredith had found her fellow travelers to be a contented and congenial group, solicitous and moderately interested in their only single, and rather withdrawn, slightly nervous fellow traveler. They must have found her odd, she realized, her slender frame swaddled in layers of Florida cotton, while they had prepared for this trip for months, fortifying themselves in down parkas and carrying brightly colored backpacks. She was at least two decades younger than most of them. But they had been kind to her, and after the first few days they realized she preferred to be left alone.

It was one of the last tours of the season, and though the sun often offered a bit of pleasant warmth midday, the nights drew in sharp and bitter. On the road to Fairbanks, they had driven through vistas splashed with streaks of red and gold stretching to a far horizon, and they could see that a fine new layer of snow had already dusted the lower slopes of distant, craggy peaks. The brief Alaska autumn had arrived, and winter had already announced its intentions. But Meredith might as well have been traveling in the vast expanse of some flat, monotonous desert, for all that the magnificence of the country registered with her.

~ * ~

Low dark clouds descended and blanketed the Fairbanks airport when they arrived in the early afternoon. ,The tour company had touted their brief sightseeing flight from the Fairbanks airport to circle Mount McKinley as the trip's final crowning event . The mild weather was degrading, and even heavier clouds were threatening to move in, so everyone had hustled quickly onto the small plane. On the bumpy ride, the others "oohed" and "aahed" as they circled the giant snow-covered mountain, so close that the dark fissures in the massive white-and-turquoise ice fields threatened to reach out and swallow the plane. Meredith just held on tight to the back of the seat in front of her, thinking about the hours to come, the bus ride to Anchorage, then the long flight home.

After the flight, everyone hurried to the bus idling on the edge of the long parking lot, already pointed at the highway that would carry the twenty-one weary passengers back to Anchorage, its tailpipe spewing gray smoke into the wet, heavy air. She felt a simple relief as she climbed the bus stairs. She settled into her seat, hoping she could doze on the drive to Anchorage, that the heavy weight of her fatigue would finally overpower her gnawing dread of what awaited her at home.

Then she needed to visit a bathroom.

Marty probably didn't see her leave, but she was only planning to be one little minute, and she knew he always did a final head count right before they departed. Marty started every day with a scowl and ended every day with a frown, and she hoped he wouldn't glare at her from the driver's seat, furrowing his brow under his wrinkled gray uniform cap as she rushed back up the steep steps onto the bus. She didn't want to blurt out that she had to go to the restroom one more time, just to be sure she wouldn't need to go again until the next scheduled stop. If only the bathroom on the bus wasn't broken. Which was worse: holding up the bus now, or asking Marty to stop just for her somewhere on the road between here and Anchorage? The closer they got to the departure time, the more she was convinced that she had to get off the bus one last time. And so she had bolted while Marty was running through his daily ritual of adjusting the mirrors and checking all his gadgets and dials.

As she rushed back toward the airport terminal, Meredith scanned the horizon. The parking lot stretched in front of her, a vast expanse. She took a deep breath and clutched her travel bag, preparing to move fast, maybe even to run. She didn't want to make the others wait for her, especially when their thoughts were likely turning to the final segment of the bus trip and their long flights home from Anchorage.

And that was all it had been, only a minute or so. She'd rushed into the chilly metal stall, fumbling in her lumpy bag for a tissue because there was no toilet paper. She'd bent over the sink and splashed cold water over her hands, giving herself the briefest of looks in the wavy restroom mirror. Tired hazel eyes in a puffy face that clearly hadn't had enough sleep blinked back at her. She quickly turned away. The ordeal this trip had become would soon be over, but going home offered no respite.

~ * ~

Meredith had booked the tour impulsively, wanting to get away from Michael, anywhere away from home, so she could have some time to clear her head and think. A few mumbled words into the phone, a credit card number, and airline reservations and packing instructions had materialized almost instantly. The luxury bus would be waiting when her flight arrived in Anchorage, and there she would join her fellow travelers for the weeklong trip showcasing the sights around Anchorage, Fairbanks, and points in-between. Her open suitcase had gaped on the bed, waiting.

For the two weeks before the she left, she had been alone in their townhouse, and panic waited for her around every corner. The lump in her throat had become a permanent and painful obstruction. Comfortably familiar photographs and mementos whispered betrayal. She was a feral animal trapped in a cage, obsessed with the idea of escape.

The day before her flight to Anchorage, she'd sat in Ellen's kitchen, pressing her fork gently against the side of a square of apricot coffeecake on a tiny plate. She couldn't even bear to bring the fork toward her mouth. She wanted to eat it, to please Ellen, but all food tasted like cardboard.

Ellen had leaned over, spreading her hands flat over the tabletop. "Okay, so he's a jerk, and maybe your marriage is over." She settled back in her chair and picked up her coffee cup, staring at Meredith over the rim. Without looking up, Meredith had felt her friend's eyes searching her face, trying to find a way inside, a way to help her through this. "But come on, what are you going to accomplish by running away? To Alaska? It's not even the right time to go to there." Ellen frowned and shook her head. "It's too late in the season. Stay. There's still time to cancel. I'll help you figure this out."

Meredith had rubbed her fingers along the edge of the kitchen table. She understood it was an honest and caring offer. Ellen knew her better than anyone, and she would talk with her or not talk with her, whatever Meredith needed. Ellen had held her close when at first she could only sit and rock back and forth in silent agony. But not even a friend she loved and trusted could understand. No one could understand how time had contorted itself so that minutes in the house seemed like hours, how the quiet objects in her home, each resting in its proper place, now taunted her with their order and purpose.

And she couldn't explain, even to Ellen, the shame that plagued her, along with the unrelenting pain. Her devastating conviction of failure, of being somehow at fault, lacking, and her constant revisiting of memories of Michael, looking for evidence of deceit, the clues she should have seen all along. I'm a fool, a fool, a fool. If she went away, maybe she could breathe again. Maybe the ache in her chest wouldn't wake her up every night, when she slept at all, to start the endless loop of panic and despair. She couldn't stand it anymore. She'd go crazy, totally insane, if she had to endure it much longer.

"I don't know if it's the right decision," she had said slowly, avoiding Ellen's eyes, "but at least I won't be looking over my shoulder for a few days." I'm a fool, a fool, a fool. Always the same mantra. She heard the voice aloud sometimes, taunting her. She paused, staring out the kitchen window at the clear blue sky beyond. "At least I won't be wondering if I'm going to see...them..." she gulped down a sob, "every time I leave the house." She had squeezed her eyes shut, trying hard not to cry again. I'm a fool. It's all such a damn cliché.

~ * ~

The restroom door squeaked open and a woman bustled in, dragging an oversized piece of luggage in one hand and a wailing child in the other. Meredith stepped around her, giving her a small smile as she hurried out the door.

And then, as she exited the airport and stepped onto the curb, her travel bag held tight under her arm, her lungs breathing in the cool, crisp air, the bus looming ahead of her, the sound of a plane deafeningly roaring, coming closer...

Later, she would wonder if she had seen the plane crash into the waiting bus. She didn't think so. All she remembered was the noise, the terrible boom, then the fiery mass where the bus should have been.

Screams erupted then, and voices wailing. Meredith

couldn't absorb it at first, that the bus heading back to Anchorage—the bus she should be on—had just exploded at the far end of the airport parking lot.

She dropped hard onto the concrete curb in terror, sprawled, sitting with her legs awkwardly splayed in front of her. She watched in confusion and horror as people streamed out of the terminal. The crowd pushed a few feet ahead, shouting and pointing and holding their hands to faces that wore masks of shock and horror, but the heat and flames kept them at a distance.

Oh my God, that's our bus, everyone is on board, everyone is there...

Jonas and Angela were right behind me. And Carrie and John were across the aisle...

Oh my God. I should be on that bus. I should be dead.

But I'm not.

Two

Nothing could be seen of the bus except a wavering shadowy outline behind the mass of fire. Flames leaped upward and roared. Around her, shouts and screams raked through the air, but the voice of the fire, the voice of the explosion, poured over all other sounds, diminishing them. Sirens shrieked, coming closer. People ran toward the fire, but then retreated, shading their eyes, as the furious heat pushed them away.

Meredith stayed where she had fallen, on the pavement curb of the parking lot next to the terminal. People swept by and around her. Her eyes stung and teared from the smoke that whipped away from the fire.

Hands shoved underneath her armpits, lifting her from behind. She wanted to stand, but she had no strength, no way to make her legs work. She coughed with deep, gasping breaths as she realized that someone was dragging her inside the terminal and away from the chaos in the parking lot. The stranger's hands were suddenly gone, and she collapsed on the floor against a wall.

Through streaming eyes she saw a puckered, brown face staring at her, just inches away. A tiny birdlike woman in a pink polo shirt grabbed her hands.

"Dearie, can you hear me?"

Meredith nodded, unable to speak. The shouts and screams continued all around her. She was shaking so hard that her teeth had started to chatter.

"Ned, I think she's all right, just in shock, maybe."

Another face peered closely at her, this one ruddy and wrinkle-lined underneath a bristle of thin, black hair.

"I think you're right, Abby, just in shock. And maybe a little scratch from the explosion, on her forehead there." The man patted Meredith's back carefully and continued to eye her face.

The woman glared at him. "Well, then, let's get her some tea with sugar. That's what they told us, didn't they, about what to do for shock? I'll help her over to the others. And get some of those blankets we keep behind the counter." Abby frowned at Ned's back as he scurried away, dodging the firemen running through the lobby to the parking lot.

Meredith huddled in a heap where Abby had settled her on the floor in a corner of the lobby. Several other people were crowded into the small space, all sitting with their backs to the wall, some with their heads on their bent knees.

"Yes, dearie, a terrible shock, we just can't believe it. A terrible thing to see. Tell me, dearie, did you know anyone on the bus?" Abby bent over and wrapped an arm around her shoulder. Meredith grabbed hard at Abby's other arm, almost pulling her over, but she couldn't seem to let go. Know anyone? Well, really know anyone, not really... Meredith shook her head to say no, no, but...was that right? No, of course, she did know them, all of them, Arnie and Peter and Alice... Meredith felt heaving sobs take over her body. "I-I did...I was supposed to be..."

A young Alaska Native woman sitting next to her started to shake and retch. Abby grabbed a nearby wastebasket and held it under the woman's downturned face. Without thinking, Meredith stretched her arm around the shuddering figure and pulled her closer. Did she lose someone? Someone on the plane? Meredith shook her head, trying to clear it. Her mind refused to focus, as if her brain was enveloped in a thick fog. Abby helped the young woman to her feet and guided her toward the nearby restroom.

Meredith leaned against the wall and put her hands over her eyes. Her gritty palms scraped her cheeks, and she rubbed her hands together, knocking away the tiny embedded fragments from her fall in the parking lot. Her chest was tight and sore, and it was hard to breathe. She looked up a few moments later. Abby was back.

"I understand, dearie. It's such an awful thing. You just let Ned and me take care of you for a bit. Such an awful thing to see. Look, here's Ned with your tea."

Ned bent over and handed her a warm paper cup. Abby clicked her tongue and helped Meredith move the cup to her mouth. She forced herself to take a sip and felt her throat close. The tea, tasting like liquid sugar, left her gagging.

"Come on, dearie, sweet tea will help, really it will."

Meredith managed a half mouthful. Ned carefully draped a blanket over her shoulders.

A fireman sprinted by, slowing for a moment as he passed them, turning toward Ned and Abby. "You two from Traveler's Aid, get them out of here. If they didn't witness the crash and they're not hurt, get them out of here." He gave the small group against the wall a brief glance, then he muscled his way through the door to the parking lot.

Every time the door opened, smoke billowed inside. Abby grabbed Meredith's arm and turned to Ned. "He's right, they've got a bigger job to do. We should get out of their way. We need to move and take care of these poor people."

Meredith opened her mouth, trying to find the words to explain that she had seen the crash and she should have been on the bus. But the words wouldn't form. They just garbled and fragmented and made no sense. "I...the bus...I saw..." No one paid any attention to her. Abby nodded to Ned, and they grabbed at arms, pulling everyone upright, then herded them toward a door at the back of the lobby. Ten or so people were walking on their own, though Meredith saw that three leaned against others in the group as they shuffled forward. Abby hovered over a heavyset man in a business suit who limped and pressed his hand to his thigh.

Abby led them into a windowless space deeper inside the terminal that seemed to be a hallway to some offices. Through the door that closed behind them, Meredith could still hear the turmoil beyond, but sounds were a bit muted here. And the noise outside had changed. It seemed to have taken on a purpose. No more screams, just voices yelling curt orders, the quick pounding of feet, the shrill tire squeals of heavy vehicles, the rasp of hoses dragging over the ground.

Meredith and the rest of the group dropped into white plastic chairs lined up along the wall. Most of them sat hunched forward, holding their hands over their faces, some resting their heads on their crossed arms in their laps. Ned helped a limping man walk through another door. Abby moved along the small group, stopping to talk to each person in turn. Meredith concentrated on trying to breathe, because somehow her breath wasn't coming, wasn't filling her lungs. What just happened?

Abby was in front of her now. Meredith looked up into her kind, anxious face. "Dearie, tell me your name."

"Mere..." she could barely whisper. Her throat was closed, dry.

Ned joined her. "How is she doing?"

"Her name is Mary. Mary, where is your home?"

Home. Where was home? "Home? Home...er..."

"What did she say, Abby?" The noises from outside rose and fell. Meredith shuddered as she imagined what was happening outside the door. All gone. Everyone on the bus gone.

"Mary says she's from Homer, Ned. You got that darned hearing aid turned off again?" Abby patted Meredith on the back. "You're fine, dearie. You were probably waiting for the peninsula shuttle, I'll bet. Well, no shuttle into here tonight. They won't let it in, for sure. But stay here, drink some more tea, and let me see what I can do for you."

Abby sidled away and bent over to talk to a man who was holding his head and rocking back and forth. Meredith gulped another half-cup of the sweetened tea, and leaned her head back against the wall. She licked her lips. They tasted like smoke. All dead. They're all dead.

Abby returned minutes later, leading a young couple who were holding hands and whispering to one another, their faces pulled tight into expressions of worried confusion. Meredith was still sitting with the stunned group of bystanders, trying to sip the now-cold tea from her paper cup, but her hands shook, and the tea sloshed over the rim when she put it to her mouth. Her head pounded, and everywhere she looked, objects had a painful, sharp-edged quality. She should call someone. Who? Michael? Her stomach quaked. No. Maybe Ellen? She had no idea what to do next. Images flashed over and over through her mind in a horrific closed loop. Whenever a door opened, shouting voices and sirens bellowed from the parking lot.

"Quickly, dear, please. We have to move out the people who aren't injured. Jan and Evan here," Abby glanced back at the young couple in faded jeans and rain jackets, looking to be in their early twenties, "are heading out to Homer. Their car is just a little ways away. They'll give you a ride, get you out of here and on your way home."

Meredith looked up at Abby, not understanding. The relentless pounding in her head almost drowned out Abby's voice. Wh-what? Homer? Why would she go to a place called Homer? Where was Homer? Meredith opened her mouth to try to form a question, but Abby was already edging away, not paying attention to her, scanning the room. Abby frowned at Ned, who had just come back with cups in each hand. He put his head down and started to scuttle more quickly across the floor.

Abby turned to face Meredith with a puff of

impatience. "I'm sorry, dear, but you have to go. Now. There is too much going on right now, others who are really hurt. The firemen want everyone not involved to leave. Let's get you out of here and on the road and safely on your way home." She raised her voice to carry over the sounds of the commotion as she pulled Meredith to her feet. "You'll be fine, just fine. Do you have any other bags?"

Meredith looked down at the small travel duffel she was somehow still clutching, the bag she had carried off the bus to the restroom. Whoever had pulled her inside must have grabbed it too. She shook her head. "No, but..." She swallowed hard and tried to speak, but Abby was already looking past her, to the three bystanders who still remained stiff and huddled in the plastic chairs.

"Good, then, off you go. I'm sorry, dear, I hope all goes well with you, but it's best that you leave here as quickly as possible."

Abby patted her arm and turned away. The young man—Eric or Evan or....Evan, that was it...pointed toward the side exit door. She stood still, staring after Abby, trying to understand what was happening. Jan reached over and grabbed her arm, turning her toward the door, and she trailed behind the couple as they hurried out the other end of the terminal. As soon as they left the building, the shouts and sirens drowned out all other sounds. Every face that flashed by was grim and hard. One fireman yelled and waved his arms at a white television station van. "Move back. You have to move back. You can't be here." Other firemen rushed by them with stretchers. For whom? No one can be left alive. No one.

She realized Jan was shouting at her, trying to get her attention over the din. "Over here. It's not far."

In a few moments, she was sitting in the back of a scratched and dented old Suburban, clutching her bag to her chest. Next to her, a smooth-coated black mutt stood and studied her with alert liquid-brown eyes before sniffing her arm, curling down into a tight ball on an old towel, and sighing. Jan called back from the front seat, "That's Dixie. She's really old and mostly deaf, but she's friendly."

As they pulled away from the horrific plume of black smoke and the insistent wail of sirens, Meredith closed her eyes and pressed her head against the back of the seat.

They are all dead.

Three

She fell into a fitful sleep as soon as they left Fairbanks. When she awoke, her throat dry and her head aching, she heard Jan and Evan talking in the front seat. She couldn't make out all the words, but she could tell they were talking about the accident. "Dead. All dead. How many? Tragedy."

Tragedy.

Meredith crossed her arms over her chest and leaned against the car door. They were all gone. Angela and Jonas, with their blurry pictures of the grandkids by the pool; Donald, with his feeble way of flirting with her after his third glass of wine; and grouchy Marty. All dead. Tears pushed through, stinging her eyes. In one instant, they were all dead.

In the seat next to her, Dixie stirred, yawned, and sighed. She stared over at Meredith, then settled down in a new position with her nose between her front paws, her side firmly planted against Meredith's leg. Meredith tangled her fingers in the dog's silky fur, feeling the rise and fall of its steady breathing. The car's rattles and clatters limited conversations between the front and back seats to Evan's occasional call of, "You okay back there?" and Meredith's raspy reply of, "Yes. Fine."

The headlights cast a tube of light in front of them, exposing the stark monochromatic outlines of trees flying by on either side of the highway and little else. They drove in a tunnel bored through darkness. They barreled away from Fairbanks and down the Parks Highway, passing through the bright, harsh lights of Anchorage quickly, stopping only for gas and to stretch their legs. After they turned south from Anchorage, signs of the city fell away.

Meredith sensed an expanse of water to her right, a suggestion of a shoreline, but the moonless night revealed little. Tiny bright outposts of restaurants and motels materialized from time to time on the edge of the highway. The Suburban crawled over a high mountain pass. Its engine groaned and protested, and the headlights flashed over traces of ice, cracked and white, on the edges of the road.

Now it seemed that they were far into a wild country, though they still passed clusters of ramshackle houses and stores from time to time. Most of the buildings looked patched and weary, cobbled together haphazardly. Occasionally they spun by a brightly lit mini-mall or a huddle of businesses, lodges, camps, and diners, but most often they were in a small, dark world, limited by the beams of their headlights. What had they said? Ten hours to Homer? Where was Homer anyway? South, she thought. South and near the water.

Somewhere in the darkness, she rolled her wedding band around her ring finger for a few moments, then pulled it off and dropped it into the inside pocket of her jacket. There will be fewer questions if it's not on my finger. Her mind was foggy, as if her brain had gone numb, as if this were some sort of very bad and confused nightmare. She knew she needed to do something, to say something to stop all this, but that seemed an insurmountable task. She had no energy to say the words, and she couldn't conjure up her next steps in any direction. She dozed in and out of consciousness, gasping awake as images of the crash flashed into her head.

She squirmed, half-asleep, trying to find a more comfortable position. Michael...Michael will be so angry when I'm not back on time. She flinched, watching Michael's face in her mind's eye, seeing the wave of rage sweep over him. She pushed the image away. She'd known from the beginning that Michael had a bad temper. She saw it for the first time when they'd returned to his parked car after a late Italian dinner at a restaurant she loved, only about a month into their seeing one another, to find a deep, ugly scratch along the side of his prized BMW. In an instant, he was enraged, screaming obscenities, though there was no one around to hear him but her. His face flared red, his hands curled into tight, hard fists. When she got into the passenger seat, he slammed her door shut. The car rocked from the force of the impact. Then she heard a loud dull thud, and another, and she realized in horror that he was kicking the side of the car next to them, even though there was no indication it had anything to do with the damage. She had pressed her hands over her mouth and wondered what she should do. When he got into the car, still flushed and breathing hard, she hesitated, then put her hand gently over his. His head whipped around to stare at her, and for a brief moment she was almost afraid, but his expression softened and he looked sheepish. He even chuckled, dropping and shaking his head and apologizing.

"You have a gift." She could hear her mother's voice from so many years past. She was only nine, leaning against her mother's legs in her aunt's kitchen. "It's a gift," her mother had said. On that day, her mother stroked her hair after she had stepped between her two older cousins who were poised for one of their seemingly endless brutal battles. They fought over everything, bashing each other and jumping into fights with terrible intensity, routinely resulting in black eyes, bruises, and blood. Meredith had gently pressed an open palm on each of their chests and quietly said, "No." They moved apart, a puzzled look on both their faces, but they hadn't fought again that day. The gift to soothe, her mother said. "Not many people have that, Meredith," she had said, carefully pulling apart the snag of twisted hair Meredith had unconsciously tangled against her check. "You know how to be quiet, how to comfort people. You're a peacemaker. You can make a bad situation better, not worse. It's a blessing."

Huddling into a ball in the corner of the back seat,

she muffled a sob, missing her mother, missing a childhood filled with the sure knowledge that she lived in a family where she was cherished and had value. Missing too, the man she had married, who had somehow become an entirely different person. So many years had passed. Her mother was gone, and when Michael's temper flared, so often now, when she saw his eyes narrow and shoulders tense and his face curve into hard harsh lines, her quiet touch and air of calm only seemed to inflame him. Her gift had failed.

Jan abruptly swerved into a sharp left turn, and the car rumbled down a long dirt driveway toward a dimly lit building.

"Mae's Diner," Jan said. "I really need some coffee."

The air in the diner was heavy with the smell of cooked onions and hot grease. Rivulets sweated down the inside panes of a bank of windows near the door. Battered red vinyl booths snugged together on both sides of a narrow center aisle. Evan made a beeline to the cash register and jumped into an animated conversation with a stocky bearded man in a food-stained chef's apron.

He's talking about the crash.

Jan and Meredith dropped into a vacant booth next to a window. Half circles of bruised fatigue hung under Jan's eyes. She's driven all night. She's exhausted. There had been long silences in the front seat during the drive, and Meredith now realized that Evan had probably slept while Jan steered them all safely through the long night. Meredith looked up at Evan, who was leaning against the front counter, still talking. She's the responsible one. She takes care of both of them. Jan pulled a cell phone out of her pocket. "Got to let our friends know we're close. We can get some bars here."

Meredith nodded. Her brain was so very fuzzy.

The clouded window glass revealed nothing but the blackness of the night outside. A short, plump waitress with spiky black hair and a nose ring brought them mugs of steaming coffee. Meredith looked around the room. Men dressed in heavy pants and sweaters filled a few other booths, their thick, dark jackets slung over the seat backs behind them. Three men in one booth laughed and talked in loud voices, but most seemed to be in a state of quiet exhaustion, not saying much, nursing cups of coffee, and stabbing at plates of eggs and toast. A couple of banged-up red toolboxes in the aisle threatened to trip the waitress as she shuttled around the room to refill coffee cups. Meredith stared down into her mug, holding it with both hands. The coffee smelled metallic and a little burnt, but the heat from the cup was comforting.

"Just a couple more hours," Jan murmured.

Meredith nodded back at her. She couldn't muster the energy for any sort of small talk, and she was at a loss to know what to say anyway. She had no idea where she was going or why. She was traveling to a place she didn't know with people she didn't know. She looked down into her cup and shook her head. This was all just some strange mistake, a misunderstanding that she should have corrected right away.

Her silence didn't seem to bother Jan, who finished texting and was rubbing the back of her neck as she sipped her coffee. Jan didn't appear to expect any conversation. She and Evan seemed quite content to have her tag along. She supposed that they saw her simply as some middle-aged transient traveler caught in the turmoil at the airport, needing a ride to where they were going. As far as she could tell, they didn't mind that she had been thrust on them. They hadn't asked her any questions, maybe because they could tell how tired and upset she was, or maybe, she thought, because they just weren't very interested in her. Either way, it was a godsend, because Meredith didn't have the answers to any questions. Not even the simple ones like, "Where are you headed?"

Evan joined them and shrugged off his jacket,

moving with the gait of an adolescent puppy, loose and awkward, not quite sure of where its body ended. The reek of old sweat drifted over the table. He looked up and waved. "Joyce, coffee?" The waitress headed over with another cup, and Evan wrapped his hands around it. He nodded toward the man behind the cash register, who sat in a chair hunched over a dog-eared paperback, and he grinned at Jan and Meredith.

"Ron said he got a scare the other day. Someone came in who looked just like his ex-wife. Thought he'd been found out for sure."

Evan and Jan looked at each other and snickered. Evan turned to Meredith.

"He took off from someplace, I think it was somewhere in Oklahoma, years ago. Left his family. I'd guess running away from child support. Not a good story, really, though maybe his reasons were good. Who knows?" Evan shrugged and spooned sugar into his coffee.

"Took off?" Meredith didn't understand. Her voice creaked and broke, out of practice after the long hours of silence, and she coughed. "How can anyone do that in this day and age? You need a social security number, you need an ID to go to the doctor, to use your bank account..." Her voice trailed off. She was so very tired. She didn't think she had ever been this tired before.

Evan laughed again. "Well, yeah, you're mostly right. That's the way it would be in most places. But Alaska is different. At least some parts of Alaska are."

Evan gulped his coffee and lifted his cup to salute two fishermen walking by. He stretched his arms above his head, one at a time, groaning.

"Lots of people here get by off the grid. They barter for food, work in exchange for getting what they need, no records, no government, no Big Brother. They hunt and fish when they can. It's not always easy and it's not always pretty, but you can do it."

Meredith leaned back against the sticky vinyl seat.

The clanking of dishes in the kitchen and the rise and fall of voices from the other booths flowed around her, comforting in the normalcy they evoked. She gripped her coffee mug tightly and rubbed her finger over a tiny chip in the rim. She closed her eyes and felt a prickle of cold air from the drafty window slip down under her collar. Alaska cold. Alaska, where things are different.

Off the grid...

I'm off the grid.

Her head swam from the fatigue, the heat, and the unrelenting memory of the crash. I should be dead. They all think I'm dead.

She ran her tongue over her sore chapped lips.

Maybe, at least for just a little while, I don't exist.

The thought buzzed through her body like an electric shock. Out of the raging whirlwind of her life, the tiniest tendril, the most slender thread of steadiness emerged. I can make a choice.

Everyone at home would be reeling from the news of the crash, but that had already happened. She couldn't change anything about that now. If she didn't reappear for just a little bit of time longer, it really didn't make a difference. She shook her head. These ideas were crazy. Of course it made a difference, but even a few more hours, maybe a day or two, of being a different person...

Since she'd discovered Michael's betrayal, overpowering forces had buffeted her back and forth. But even before she found out what a lie she'd been living, the signs had been there, signs that powers outside her control were in play. She had just turned away, not wanting to read them. Months before the damning evidence that her marriage was an empty husk had been thrown at her feet, she should have known. She should have taken charge of her life, stepped forward instead of letting Michael bully her into submission. She should have stood up to him instead of trying so hard to find new ways to please him, to subdue his anger and the meanness. When she went back, it would all start again—his pressure, his insistence that their marriage end immediately, on his terms alone. Again, she would feel adrift, helpless, as a tidal wave of events and consequences washed over her, dragging her along, making futile any effort she made to exert even the smallest amount of control over her life.

I'm afraid of my own husband. The thought shocked her, and she wanted to deny it. He had never struck her. But she could remember the very first time, months ago, when she felt a first unsettled pang of anxiety. She woke after midnight and saw him in the faint light from the streetlight that intruded around the edges of the heavy bedroom drapes. Michael leaned against the far wall, staring at her with a blank expression on his face, his eyes so calm. Not with affection or longing or even curiosity, but analytically, as though she was a mystery. No, not a mystery, more a problem to be solved, an obstacle to be overcome. It had startled her, his standing there, and she had said his name gently, her voice still fuzzy with sleep. He said nothing in answer. He just turned and walked through the door. She didn't get up to follow. She lay awake with a lump aching in her stomach.

She rarely confronted him, even when his words or actions withered her. She hated conflict. She didn't want to argue with him. He had all the skill in that area, and he used his abilities to outmaneuver her, to imply that any position she took had no value. She saw the pleasure he took in winning, no matter what the cost. She wanted to keep the peace. She just tried harder to make him happy, to make their marriage a place where he could escape whatever personal demons were tormenting him.

She had lost confidence in her own ability to make decisions for herself. Even her trip to Alaska wasn't really a choice. It was more of a desperate grasping at an escape from the pain. And up to now, she had been carried by chance and mistake on this bewildering journey away from the airport and into this unknown country. But now she was making a decision. She claimed this time, this breathing space, for herself. She would stay dead, just for a little while.

There would be a price to pay in the end, a big price, and she knew it. But maybe there could be a little while, just a little bit of time, when the grim realities of her life weren't slapping her in the face. Maybe she could be someone else, just for a little while. Maybe there could be some small respite after all.

~ * ~

Light seeped into the landscape, and from the back seat Meredith glimpsed scrubby trees and high brush on both sides of the road. The rain had just stopped, but with no promise that it was going to stay away. The ground oozed wetness. Sorry-looking leaves in drab browns and faded yellows puddled in soggy hollows among the trees. Buildings, more plentiful now along the road, stood leached of color in thin predawn light pressing through the blanket of dark gray clouds overhead. Meredith inched away from the window and slouched closer to the warm mound of Dixie's sleeping body.

The sun had just begun to rise when Jan swung the steering wheel to the right and lurched the car to a stop at the far end of a turnout. Evan twisted around to face her. "We always stop on the way back in, just to look at the view for a couple of minutes." Jan and Evan sprang from the car and ran to the edge of the overlook, laughing and holding each other close as the wind whipped their hair against their faces. Dixie darted out with them, yipping and running in frenzied circles.

Meredith shoved her door open and heaved herself out of the back seat. Her body moved reluctantly, and her joints ached as she stretched. The heavy scent of wet mulch hitchhiked on the cold, brisk wind, and bushes whistled and hissed, whipped by the rushing air. They had been driving for a couple of hours since they left the diner, and she had been dozing on and off. She was numb from fatigue and from sitting in one position for so long. Then she caught sight of the view.

The overlook stood on the brink of a cliff, and the cliff opened to a vast bay, shining gunmetal gray in the growing light. In front of her, a long isthmus of land spun far out into the sea, and glimmers of light dotted the far end. Behind the water, mountains climbed, first black and rolling, but beyond that, impossibly tall and jagged. Their snowy peaks gleamed stark white in the early morning sun and framed the view like an enormous fantasy backdrop, from east to west as far as she could see. Dark rainclouds hovered over the mountains in the far distance. Glaciers— yes, they are enormous glaciers—poured through the mountain passes toward the bay. But was it right to call them mountain passes, she wondered, for surely no one could pass through a gap that high, that snowy, that wild.

The sheer size of the place took her breath away. As she stood in the icy wind, feeling the occasional raindrop sting her face, and hugging her jacket close around her, she felt dwarfed by the vast expanse before her. That there could be such a place. Never in her life had she imagined there could be such a place as this. It made her feel small, insignificant, almost invisible. But at the same time it made her feel free and vibrant, so alive, as if she were in the presence of something very primordial and powerful.

Jan and Evan dashed back toward the car, laughing and still holding onto one another. Jan fought against the wind to open the car door. She dove into the driver's seat and tucked her wind-tangled hair behind her ears.

"Ready to go?" Evan asked. "Cold, eh?" He plopped back into the front passenger seat. Dixie, smelling of wet, trampled grass, jumped into his lap then over the seat into the back of the car.

Meredith stood with her hand on the rear door handle. She was terribly cold and exhausted, and she didn't really even know where she was, but this landscape, this massive place of land and sea and ice, made all that seem inconsequential for the moment. Here was an expanse of splendor, of grandeur. Here was a place of light and water and cold and space so huge and wild it was almost beyond her comprehension, scrubbed clean by rain and wind and snow. In this place, she thought, who knows what might be possible. The light warmed and brightened as the sun crested over the horizon, and the lights on the isthmus faded away.

Meredith eased herself into the car, shivering hard, and nudged Dixie over to her towel. Jan cranked the heater up to high, and they rolled down the steep grade on the road to Homer. The view dropped out of sight as they descended toward town, but Meredith still felt the power of this place, and she sensed that she was now somewhere else entirely, almost in a new world, someplace completely cut off from her old life.

Four

Meredith sat squeezed against the wall behind the wobbly table with the plastic checkerboard cover. She pushed the last bits of her hamburger bun around her plate. With the long drive finally over, they had stopped to eat at a trailer-turned-diner on the fringe of town.

"So, can we drop you someplace before we take off?" Evan waved to the waitress, motioning for the check.

She took a deep breath and ran her fingers along the pattern in the tablecloth. "Well, I'm not sure...um, I haven't really decided where..." She looked up and saw Evan frowning at her.

"You don't have a plan? No place at all to stay tonight?"

Meredith shook her head.

Jan bit at her lower lip and stared at her. "Gee, we just assumed you had it all worked out. I wish we could offer you a place, but we're couch surfing right now until we can get back into our old apartment."

She saw Jan and Evan exchange anxious glances, and she felt a pang of shame. This wasn't what they bargained for when they offered a stranger a ride. They didn't expect to be responsible for me.

Meredith looked down at her hands. She took a deep breath.

"I...guess I thought there might be a cheap hostel. I guess I just didn't think..."

She didn't have any plan. She'd hardly focused her thoughts except when the memory of the accident raged back into her head, and when that happened, the terror and pain were almost too much to bear. So she'd tried to smooth out her mind, just letting the hours pass, letting the fatigue and the strangeness of all this wash over her.

No plan. But something had changed now. This was all crazy, but she felt like she was watching someone else, someone brand new sitting here in this rundown but cozy restaurant, and that new person was the one with no place to go. It was like play-acting, like being inside of someone else's skin. Here was a new someone, who didn't know where she was going to sleep tonight, but this new person wasn't stumbling around, lost, dragging a huge, black bag of mistakes and bad decisions. She lifted her chin and stared out the window.

"Wait a minute." Jan looked at Evan. "What about Auntie Rita? I saw her outside just a few minutes ago." She turned back to Meredith. "She's not really anyone's aunt— at least as far as we know—but my mom always made me call her that. I know she's got a bit of room. She was trying to rent out a spare room a while back, but she didn't get any takers, I guess." Jan shrugged.

Evan smirked. "Big surprise. No one wanted to live with Rita. How can that be?"

Jan glared and him and breathed an exasperated sigh. "Her place is out of town, but you should be able to get back tomorrow without too much of a problem. Rita drives in all the time."

"Rita, really?" Evan gave a low whistle. "You're really ready to go there, Jan? You know how she can be."

Jan pointed her finger at Meredith. "Look, it's past noon already, and she doesn't have a clue about where she's going to sleep tonight. Rita likes me. Well, at least I think she does. I'm going to find her."

Evan rolled his eyes up at the ceiling. "Rita...jeez..."

Meredith sipped her coffee and stared out the window. She tried to keep her thoughts steady. Now what? She did need a place to stay. She needed to be in a place where her new self might exist, just for a little while. She didn't want this new Meredith to disappear, not yet.

Puffs of dust bloomed as a brisk, stinging wind

whipped at the loose dirt in the parking lot. It was only late September, but the few people outside wore gloves and hats pulled down snug over their ears. Just beyond the rough lot, a greenish-black wall of spruce trees huddled close, their thick boughs knocking and bouncing in the wind. And behind them the tops of jagged and fierce peaks seemingly leaned forward, looming over the spruce. The wild world pushed back here, refusing to let the manmade world have the upper hand.

I am in a new place where I don't exist. The old Meredith doesn't exist here.

"Another storm coming in," Evan murmured.

She looked up to see Jan waving and mouthing "Come on" from the front door.

Outside, a hard-faced old woman with a black-beaked cane sat statue-still on a bench close to the front of the restaurant. The overhanging eaves buffered the full force of the wind, but tendrils of gray hair still batted against her lined and weathered face. She glared in their direction. The deep descending creases at the corners of her mouth looked like they had been there for a very long time.

"Don't be afraid. Her bark is worse than her bite," Jan whispered. She pulled Meredith forward.

Jan's words poured out in a hurried rush. "Auntie Rita, this is Meredith. She's drove in from Fairbanks with us. She really needs a place to stay, just for tonight. I'm hoping you might be able to help her out."

Meredith stood in front of Rita, hugging her arms around herself to keep warm. The air swept cold and damp through her thin jacket. Rita stared at her as if she was a loathsome creature that had just crawled out of the sewer.

"What am I, a charity house?" Rita's voice was gravelly and loud, and Meredith flinched. She had an almost irresistible urge to turn away.

I really need a place to stay. I have no other options.

But she knew, really, there were other options. Of course there were. A phone call home. Pulling out the

VISA card and finding a hotel room somewhere around here, making a reservation for a plane back tomorrow. Everyone would be astounded, amazed that she wasn't dead. Soon everything would be all right. They would wonder, of course, about these last twenty-four hours, but they would understand that she had been traumatized. She'd been through a horrific experience that had made her just a little crazy, for a while. She would go back, and after the dust settled, her life would return to normal.

Everything could be the same as it was; everything would be the same again.

She squeezed her eyes shut for a moment. Not that, not yet. Not yet. The thought of going back, being home, facing up to that future, released a thunderclap of dread.

"Hello, Rita," Meredith said as warmly as she could manage, holding out her hand.

Rita ignored her. After a few moments, Meredith dropped her hand to her side.

Meredith sighed. I really need to make this happen.

"Rita, I'm sorry to impose. You don't know me, and I don't have any right to ask. But I really just need a bed, a couch, whatever you've got, for one night. I don't have anywhere else to go."

I must look desperate. She cast around for something else to say, something that would persuade this total stranger to let her sleep in her home.

Her voice came out in a low whisper. "Please."

The sadness and need in her own voice hung in the air between them.

Rita's expression didn't change. She barely glanced at Meredith. Meredith stood there silently for what seemed to be a very long time.

Rita sniffed and leaned forward over her cane. "I have a room. It ain't much. For a night it'll cost you twenty bucks. Cash."

Rita snapped her mouth shut and stared out over the parking lot. Meredith watched Jan's eyebrows shoot upward. Her mouth opened then closed without saying a word. *Jan knows I need this. What choice do I have?*

She hadn't counted up her cash, but she knew there wasn't much of it left. Still, twenty dollars was a small price to pay for any room that wouldn't make her produce a driver's license and a credit card. At least she'd have a roof over her head tonight.

"Okay," her voice quavered. "Okay, Rita, that's fine."

"Come on then. I got to get back." Rita pushed herself upright, pressing her free hand against the bench seat. Her head dropped low as she stood motionless for a moment. She turned and started to walk, placing each foot carefully in front of her, leaning heavily on her cane. Meredith hugged Jan quickly, whispering a hasty thank you, and hurried after Rita. She followed her to a battered and scraped brown truck parked at an awkward angle near the corner of the parking lot. Rita reached for the door handle, then swiveled to face Meredith.

"I got some stuff I need to do first. Come back here at seven o'clock."

Meredith stood still, confused, as Rita hauled herself up into the driver's seat. The truck rattled and belched white tailpipe smoke as Rita rocked and banged her way out of the rough dirt lot. It was only early afternoon.

Maybe she's hoping I won't be here when she comes back, Meredith thought. *Maybe she won't even come back.* She turned back to the diner, but the sign on the door had been flipped from open to closed. She looked right and left and shrugged. *One way is as good as the other.* She drifted toward a cluster of buildings downhill.

For most of the afternoon, she huddled on a backless metal bench between a Texaco gas station and a coffee hut, her thin jacket buttoned to the very top and pulled tight around her, her hands jammed into the pockets for some bit of warmth. As squalls moved through, the wind blasted bullets of icy rain into her face, even though she tucked her head down as far as it would go under her jacket collar. The bottom half of her body felt frozen in place on the steel of the bench seat.

She felt herself dropping into a bottomless well of fatigue. Her thoughts swirled in broken, senseless fragments, and twice she felt herself nodding off, her body giving way, before she shook herself back awake. From time to time she forced herself to stand, stamping her feet and blowing on her hands, avoiding all eye contact with the occasional bystanders who hurried by, bundled in fleece hats and down coats against the cruel gusts. At one point, a state trooper patrol car cruised by, slowing as the officer leaned over and stared at her. She held her breath and focused her eyes on the ground in front of her, but he didn't stop.

When she trudged over to the hut buy a cup of coffee, a sandwich, and to use the restroom, she picked up some sections of the Anchorage Daily News scattered over one of the hut's little round tables. The front-page story of the crash began with an enormous headline, "Fluke Bus/Plane Collision Claims 28 Lives," but it was one of the smaller headers that caught her eye: "Coroner: 'Identification of Victims Doubtful.'" She clutched the front page with shaking hands and scanned the first paragraph. "The plane was heading north for the Cherry mine carrying several crates of explosives, which ignited on impact with the bus and magnified the explosion...fire consumed bodies to such an extent...may be insufficient material for full DNA identification..." She shuddered and dropped the page without reading any more.

A few minutes before seven o'clock, Meredith stumbled, stiff and clumsy from the cold, into the restaurant parking lot. Rita's truck was just pulling in, splashing through the muddy puddles. She climbed into the passenger seat, mumbling a quiet hello as she handed Rita a crumpled twenty-dollar bill. Rita pocketed the cash, harrumphed, and stared straight ahead. Meredith closed her eyes and felt her cheeks and ears burn, and her hands thaw and ache, as the truck's clanking heater pumped out a blast of gasoline-scented warmth.

Rita stayed silent as she drove, and Meredith's mind drifted through a sleepy, exhausted fog. They swung off the main road after a few miles, and the truck bumped and lurched down a dirt road that became ever more narrow and pocked with potholes. Rita steered the truck up a driveway to a dull dung-colored log structure that seemed to be sinking into the surrounding meadow. Three splintering steps led up to a rickety covered porch and a front door. Grass and moss were growing in abundance along the bottom edges of the pitched roof.

Rita slowly led the way inside, banging her cane against the floorboards with every step. Her mouth was still cemented in the same downward curve. As they entered a low-ceilinged room, Rita snapped on an overhead light. At one end, a counter and sink were blanketed with overlapping piles of dirty plates and cups, bookended by a stove and a refrigerator. A vinyl-topped card table flanked by three metal chairs, their seats topped with flattened, mismatched cushions, parked close to the counter. At the other end of the room, a sagging couch and a low, battered wooden table squatted under a metal pole light. The table was strewn with water-warped magazines and other crinkled papers. Two weary armchairs leaned close to the lip of a tiny fireplace mounded with gray ashes. Meredith shuddered as her eyes caught the motion of a fat, black spider skittering across a web high in the corner of the window over the sink.

"That there's the bathroom," Rita barked, her back to Meredith, pointing her cane toward a nearby door. "Over there, that's my bedroom." Meredith heard the unspoken message in that sentence: "Stay out of there."

"That's upstairs." Rita jabbed her cane toward a set of narrow stairs near the back of the room. "There's a bed up there—well, a cot—and some blankets and pillows too. There's an extra towel in the bathroom, I'm pretty sure." She barely glanced at Meredith. "I get up real early." Rita gave her a curt nod. "Switch the light off when you go up." Rita turned away and hobbled into her bedroom, pushing the door closed without a backward glance.

Meredith clicked off the overhead light and felt her way across the room and up the narrow stairs, trying not to think of the spider or what else might be ahead. She slid her hand up the wall to find the attic light switch, and pressed the door shut behind her. The room reeked of wet wood and old paper. The sharp pitch of the roof made standing in the tiny attic impossible, except in the very middle. She dropped her bag to the floor and collapsed onto the attic's one dusty chair, causing it to creak and shift under her weight. She heard Rita below, moving around, probably getting ready for bed. One triangular window looked out over the meadow behind the cabin, but she only saw blackness outside. Sharp splats of rain knocked against the windowpane. She looked at the pillow and blankets on the cot, waiting to be made up for the night. She was tired, so very tired, but she couldn't move. Not yet.

"What on earth am I doing?" she whispered. She wrapped her arms around her chest and bent forward, staring at the floorboards.

Her thoughts tumbled and tossed. Okay, okay, tomorrow I'll go back. I was in shock. I'm still in shock. Anyone would have been out of their mind after seeing what I saw. I'll go back tomorrow and I'll explain.

But even as she rubbed her face, trying to think clearly, trying to make some decisions about how to make her way back, Meredith knew, she just knew, that she didn't really mean it. Yes, she was going to sleep in this dingy attic in the home of a grouchy, old lady who didn't want her here. Rita would surely want her to leave first thing in the morning. And Meredith had no plan, no path to follow. But somehow, being here was better than going back. She had no idea what tomorrow would bring, but when she thought about going back, she could only see an abyss, a place so dark and painful that anything, anyplace was better than going home.

I'm a coward.

She slowly pushed herself out of the chair. Her hands shook as she unfolded a thin blanket and draped it over the cot. She grabbed the lumpy pillow, hugging it close, breathing through the deep thudding pain in her chest, thinking of the night ahead and expecting full well that the endless run in her mind of what she had done, and what she was still doing, would make any sleep impossible.

Five

The storm passed through overnight. When Meredith awoke from a fitful doze, with some surprise that she had slept at all, clear thin sunlight was probing through the grimy window. She untangled her legs from the blanket she'd cocooned around them, and cocked her head to listen. No sounds came from downstairs.

She looked at her watch. She hadn't expected to be here past early morning, but it was almost nine thirty. She dressed quickly, wrinkling her nose at the ripe meaty smell of her clothes worn too long without a wash, and eased herself carefully down the narrow wooden stairs.

Rita was gone. The front door was cracked open, and clean chilly air drifted into the kitchen. A paper fluttered on the kitchen table, held in place by a rock. "There's some bread for toast," was written in a spidery but steady hand.

"And a good morning to you, too," Meredith muttered. She crossed her arms and looked around the kitchen. The sink was crammed with dirty dishes, and dust bunnies floated back and forth along the plank floor in the breeze. When she opened the refrigerator door, she found half a loaf of bread, squashed on one side, and a brick of eroded butter in a smeary dish next to some jammy substance in a sticky jar. Meredith dropped two slices of bread into an ancient toaster she found sitting on the counter. She was very hungry, so even simple toast sounded wonderful.

She perched on one of the metal chairs and slowly chewed her breakfast. She needed to think about this crazy thing she had just done. The future presented itself like an impenetrable fog bank on her horizon. Even what was going to happen in the next fifteen minutes seemed unfathomable.

She eyed the kitchen. Well, she had taken advantage of Rita's hospitality, such as it was. The accommodations were marginal, even priced at just twenty dollars, but Rita had let her stay when it was clear she didn't want to. She could at least offer something in return. First, she tackled the dishes, after locating a bit of dish soap under the sink.

There was some soothing satisfaction in scrubbing the chipped plates in the hot, soapy water, some pleasure in seeing the stack of clean plates and cups climb higher in the drainer. Then she took on the countertops, with their accumulations of mystery stains and blobs. In some spots it was like descending into an archeological dig, crumbs on top of smears on top of spills. Next she attacked the floor, first running down the dust bunnies with a spindly broom, then mopping the floorboards with a sudsy solution of water and a little dish soap. Finally, she took several deep breaths and hefted the broom to knock away the huge dusty spider web on the kitchen window, feeling thankful that the spider was not in residence.

As the sun rose higher, the air warmed and she nudged the kitchen door further ajar. She heard the shush-shush of waves splashing somewhere nearby. It was so quiet here. Birdsong descended, dropping and then pausing, a plaintive refrain, and tree boughs rustled now and again, as puffs of wind blew through. When the breeze slackened, the only sound was the steady murmur of the water, but no car noise, no sirens, no city buzz.

She sat down at the kitchen table to take a break, leaning back in her chair, closing her eyes, settling into the moment. So peaceful.

Suddenly, the cabin darkened. Rita stood in the doorway, blocking the glowing stream of sunshine.

"What the hell do you think you're doing?" She bit off the end of every word as she glared around the kitchen.

Meredith stared at her, startled and confused. "I-I

thought I'd do some picking up to thank you for letting me stay. I only meant to offer a little help, to thank you..."

Rita's face was still fixed in a scowl. "You shouldn't touch things that aren't yours. It ain't right." Rita twisted around and banged her way back through the front door, whacking her cane against the floorboards with each step.

You'd think I'd taken the family jewels. What on earth is the big deal? She followed Rita outside. Rita stood at the top of the stairs, frowning toward the road.

Meredith pitched her voice low, trying to sound soothing. "Look, Rita, I'm sorry. I don't know you, and maybe it was presumptuous of me to think that you wouldn't mind if I cleaned up a little." She hesitated and searched for the right words. "But honestly, all I was doing was trying to thank you. You didn't have to take me in last night. I didn't have any other place to go, and I don't know what would have happened to me if you hadn't come along. If I've put some things in the wrong place or not done something the way you'd like it done, please just tell me and I'll make it right."

Meredith didn't know what else to say. She dropped down onto a rough wooden bench on the front porch and sighed.

Rita's stiff back softened just a little.

"I've lived alone a long time," Rita spoke gruffly, but there was less anger in her voice now. "I'm used to having things my own way." There was another long silence, then Rita turned halfway toward Meredith, absently tapping her cane in an irregular staccato rhythm against the splintered porch boards, as if the action was helping her to think. "I'm sorry, girl, you didn't deserve that."

Meredith nodded her head, but didn't speak. The silence was a little more companionable now. Meredith's tensed shoulders slumped just a bit, and she leaned back against the cabin wall.

"I guess I should be getting back to town." She

could hear the dark shading in her own voice, the overtone of sadness.

Rita peered at her, her cane still tap-tapping on the porch boards.

"Meredith, where are you going?"

Of course it was the question she had been dreading. It was also one of the many questions for which she had no answer. Her tears welled up, and she tipped her head back and tried to will them away. She shook her head. Where was she going? The tears escaped and ran down her cheeks, tears that, once started, seemed like they would never stop. Tears for those poor people on the bus, tears for the senseless tragedy that had happened, but tears that flowed from an older grief too, tears that meant I don't know where I'm going, but I don't want to go back now, I can't go back to what's waiting for me there.

Meredith realized that Rita had moved to sit beside her on the bench. "I'm sorry," Meredith said, her head bowed low. "Really, Rita, I'm sorry. I have some problems I have to deal with. It's nothing to do with you. I'm really sorry about this."

Rita sat unmoving and silent and let her cry. After a few minutes, Meredith wiped her face on the sleeve of her shirt and took a deep breath.

"You could stay here another night," Rita said. Her words sounded stiff, as though they were being pulled reluctantly from her mouth. "It's not going to hurt anything if you stay another night."

Meredith kept her head down and hugged her arms hard around herself, hardly daring to breathe. Another night.

Rita struggled to her feet, leaning heavily on her cane. "And I'll just charge you ten for tonight if you make yourself useful, girl. There're some groceries in the back of the truck. Pick them up and take them into the kitchen." Rita started to walk back inside. On the threshold she paused and said, "And you smell like you need a shower.

You can't have much of anything in that fancy, little bag of yours. Look in that there bureau in the attic. There're some old clothes in there. You can see if any of them fit you."

Meredith looked up quickly, but Rita wasn't meeting her eyes. She started to stammer another 'thank you', but Rita just shrugged, her back ramrod straight, her gait uncertain and wobbly as she hobbled inside.

Six

Rita disappeared into her room, so Meredith put away the groceries and took a shower. It was so wonderful to get clean, even if the water only dribbled off the showerhead and had an unfortunate brown, rusty cast. Wrapping the thin, gray towel around her, she tiptoed barefoot over to the splintery stairs, then climbed back to the attic. The top drawer of the battered bureau screeched when she wrenched it open, as if it hadn't been disturbed for a long time. She fingered the soft, faded jeans, the neatly folded T-shirts, and a couple of cable sweaters. It seemed obvious that they weren't Rita's. They belonged, she thought, to someone much larger and probably much younger. The jeans were too big, but she wore them anyway, hitching them up and in with a ropey belt. She gathered up a T-shirt with a "Grown in Alaska" logo and a heavy red cable sweater that came down close to her knees, and some threadbare but clean underwear that would have to do until her own rinsed-out clothes dried.

She didn't know quite where she was, other than that they had driven a fair way out from the little town yesterday, first on a small highway, then on a rutted dirt road through some dark spruce-filled woods, and past what had appeared to be a very wet bog.

The morning was cold, but the sunshine invited her outside. She stood on the porch bench to view the landscape beyond. Rita's cabin pressed close to the edge of a bumpy meadow near a shoreline, a few hundred yards or so from a cliff that dropped to the beach below. She followed the thread of a worn path across the meadow to the cliff, then slipped and stumbled her way down the short but very steep incline to the beach, grabbing at roots to keep from tumbling on the way down. She was gasping for breath by the time she reached the bottom, and only then did she see the rough wooden steps she could have taken from the cliff to the beach a few yards to her right.

Her breath settled and came more easily as she walked along the shore. The pebbled beach stretched in front of her, glistening wet from the overnight rain. Smooth gray rocks slipped and clattered under her feet, so she moved slowly. Seabirds swooped closer, calling out in thin, reedy voices, and in the distance a small plane buzzed, faint but steady. The air danced cool and damp over her face, and she was glad she had found some wool gloves in the bureau. When she filled her lungs with the clean fresh air, she imagined she was drinking in this new day, this new place.

She stopped for a moment and closed her eyes. Where am I? Everything about this place rolled in continuous flowing motion. The high bushes to her left rustled and hissed in the morning breeze, waving their branches in pale clear green patterns, punctuated here and there by patches of shiny reds and yellows where some had already felt the pinch of fall. The choppy steel-blue bay to her right tossed small whooshes of waves against the rocky beach. Meredith felt quite alone, but it wasn't an uncomfortable feeling. No, the stirrings and murmurings soothed and lulled her.

She walked the beach without any thought of a destination. Her mind drifted and settled, quieted by the pattering sounds from the quaking leaves and the steady, rhythmic splashes of the waves. The cliff all but disappeared as she walked farther along the beach, and now only a foot-high mound separated the beach from the seemingly impenetrable stand of heavy brush to her left. Rough-angled boulders and piles of driftwood logs blocked the beach ahead, so when she discovered a small path leading off through the bushes, she turned down it. Within a few feet the path narrowed, and to move forward she pressed aside the intruding alder branches reaching down from the bushes towering above her head. Raindrops plopped off leaves and dripped onto her head and sweater. She shivered.

From somewhere right ahead, a rumble arose, then a muffled grunting, a snuffling. Meredith froze as the head and torso of an enormous bear slowly rose from the bushes.

It reared up onto its back legs from about fifteen feet in front of her, towering above the alders. The bear was massive, probably twice as tall as she was. She could hear the huffing of its breath and the deep growl in its throat as it caught sight of her, a growl so low and terrifying that it seemed to vibrate through the earth toward her. Blood pounded in her ears, and she stopped breathing. She couldn't move. She couldn't think. An instant later, she heard the snapping of the bear's jaws as it dropped to all fours and charged toward her. She shrieked, turned, and began to sprint back down the trail.

A brutal push sent her sprawling into the bushes at the side of the path. The heavily built man who had shoved her aside dropped down flat over her, knocking the breath out of her. She heard the bear streak by, crashing through the alders, and it took her a moment to realize that the bear had charged but then had run right past them and away. It was over in an instant.

She lay where she had fallen and started to shake and gasp for air. She had just been attacked by a bear. No, not attacked, but it had passed so closely that the dank, musty stink of it hung in the air.

"Are you an idiot?" the man grunted as he pushed himself away from her and staggered upright. He glared down at her. "Walking here without making any noise? Running away from a grizzly? Could you have done anything more stupid?"

She gaped at him. He loomed over her, his graying ginger hair falling into his red face. She opened her mouth, but no sound came out.

"Come on, we have to get out of here before he decides to come back and make it real this time." The man grabbed her arm and heaved her upward.

She shook her head in confusion. "Leave me alone." She jerked her arm away and stared up at him, and he scowled back at her. Who was he? Where had he come from? He looked like he belonged in the woods, bundled up for a day outdoors, in heavy rain pants and a red vest over a bulky sweater.

She was shaking violently and her teeth chattered. She could barely speak. "Leave me alone. That bear could have killed me." She could hear the quavering notes in her own voice.

"Yes, and you certainly made that more likely when you surprised him and then acted like prey. Never run from a grizzly. Come on, we've got to get out of here now. He's probably protecting a kill someplace nearby." He shoved her back onto the path. "Clap your hands or whistle or make some kind of noise until we get into the clear. I don't want to sneak up on him again."

Meredith stumbled down the narrow trail toward the beach, still breathless. The man right behind her yelled into the bushes and clapped his hands as he walked. She was unsteady, still terrified, but she moved as quickly as she could on the uneven path. The bear could be anywhere, just waiting for them.

She swiveled to face him as soon as they emerged from the brush. He was still frowning, his lips twisted into a grimace. A deep bleeding scratch snaked down the left side of his face, probably, she thought, from the alder branches that must have whipped at him when he dove to cover her.

"Look, I guess...thank you...I'm sorry, I didn't know..." She knew she was babbling, and he just stood silently, his expression rigid and angry. He had a strong, plain face, with laugh lines crowding around his blue eyes, but there was no trace of humor in them now.

A faint "hello" echoed from far down the beach, and they both turned. Rita walked toward them, picking her way gingerly across the pebbles, scowling at the beach stones as she placed her cane with attentive care before she took each step. The man hurried down the beach, and Meredith wandered behind, still trembling.

"So, Nick, you've met Meredith." Rita looked up and called out to both of them as they came closer, but Meredith watched her expression sharpen as she scanned their faces. "What's wrong? Did something happen?"

Nick shrugged. "Meredith, is it? Well, Rita, Meredith here just about got herself killed by a grizzly back down on the river trail."

Meredith felt her face start to burn.

"A bear? Girl, are you all right?" Rita peered into her face, and Meredith felt tears sting hot behind her eyes. Her knees buckled, and she wobbled down onto a beach log.

"Look, Rita, I've got to get back to the boat. When Meredith here feels like herself again," Nick jabbed his chin in her direction, "you better sit her down and explain a few things to her before she goes wandering off on her own. It was pure chance that I was down on the river trail just now. And if I hadn't been there..."

He shook his head and slowly exhaled. "Just set her straight, okay? I'll stop by Fish and Game and let them know about the griz. It's probably the same one that was up by the Eddy place last week." He gave a brief nod and started striding down the beach.

Meredith hunched over on the log, still fighting back tears.

"What a rude and awful man."

Rita gave her a sharp look. "Nick? Well, that rude and awful man just saved your life. Come on, let's get back to the cabin. We can talk about this later."

They began to make their way back, not talking, moving slowly. The wind was rising, and Meredith was shivering and miserably cold. She shot backward glances at the alder thicket behind her, keenly aware that the bear could still be very close by. It was the same beach, the same shore, but now it had turned into a landscape of imminent danger.

She shuddered as they moved toward the safety of the cabin.

~ * ~

They sat side by side in the two small armchairs facing the fire, wrapping a couple of Rita's tattered throws over their knees. As Meredith's shivers subsided, she could feel the beginning of the deep, heavy fatigue she always experienced after being very cold. They watched the little fire sputter behind the grate.

Rita tapped her cane gently against the floor.

"Look, girl, it's plain to see that you're not from around here." Rita paused, squinting into the glowing embers of the fire. "This can be a dangerous place. It's not forgiving. You make one stupid mistake and..." Rita's voice caught in her throat and she shook her head. Her eyes stared into space as her fingers rubbed against the polished wood head of her cane.

Meredith forced herself to sit up straighter. She stretched and tucked the nubby throw to snug it close around her chest and arms.

"I made a mistake. I know that now, but I don't know anything about bears. I'm sorry, Rita, that I gave you a scare, and I'm sorry that man had to rescue me."

Rita chuckled. "Well, you certainly managed to get Nick's undies in a bundle. But running from a grizzly?" She shook her head again. Rita's voice became very matter-of-fact. "If you run from a grizzly, it'll give chase. They're hunters and they think you're prey if you run. If you play dead and you're lucky, the griz will just sniff you and walk away."

Meredith tried to imagine not running from a bear, but it was pretty hard to visualize. She didn't have any experience to help her understand the wildness of this world. In Florida, there had been occasional news stories about monstrous rogue alligators, but she had never encountered one. She'd been taught to watch for strangers who might threaten her, but the most dangerous animal she had to deal with was her neighbor's yappy and unpredictable Chihuahua. She hadn't really thought about running away from the bear. It just happened. Her feet had taken over, not her head.

"Well, okay…" She knew she sounded doubtful. "No running from bears, then."

Rita shook her head. "No, it's 'no running from grizzlies.' If you come on a black bear, and they're much more common round here, you stand up and try to make yourself big and scary. If that doesn't work and they come at you, running's probably your best bet. Them blacks, they're scavengers, and they'll just think you're a free lunch if you play dead."

Meredith turned and stared at Rita. She's not kidding. Meredith snorted, then started to laugh. She felt the hysterical giggles just bubbling up and out. Rita turned to her, her face quizzical.

Meredith pressed her hand against her mouth to muffle her laughter. "So you're telling me that I'm supposed to figure out what kind of bear is charging at me before I decide what to do?"

Rita's mouth squeezed into its usual frown, but then the corners lifted and she smiled, and for the briefest moment, Rita's face transformed and became softer and kinder. "Well, yes. And it's not that easy, because some grizzlies are dark and some black bears are brown. Grizzlies are bigger and have a hump high on their back."

Meredith threw her head back against the chair and started to laugh again. It was so absurd. "This place is crazy." She buried her face into her throw.

"Yes, a bit crazy and a lot dangerous, sometimes." Rita turned back to the fire. "Where are you from?"

Meredith froze. It was a perfectly reasonable question, but she didn't know what to say. It would have been easy to say, "Florida," or even to toss out another location, but whatever she said, more questions were likely to follow. Questions about why she was here and where she was going, and of course, who she was. Questions she couldn't answer until she had decided what she was going to do next. "Oh...here and there." Her voice cracked and stumbled and came out an octave too high. She knew she sounded just as evasive as she was trying to be. She didn't dare look at Rita. Instead, she kept her eyes on the fire and concentrated on keeping a blank expression on her face.

They sat together in silence for a few more minutes. Meredith was almost holding her breath, dreading Rita's next question, wondering how she was going to answer.

"Meredith," Rita said, then she paused and sighed. "This is a place where lots of people have secrets. They don't call the folks here 'end of the roaders' for nothing." She chuckled to herself.

Meredith held very still. A lump of panic grew in her chest. Was Rita going to press her about the past? She didn't want to lie. Rita was rough-edged, that was for sure, but in spite of her misgivings, she'd given Meredith a bed. But she couldn't tell Rita that she had run away from her life. She couldn't tell anyone.

Rita rose slowly and shuffled forward to put a few more logs into the fireplace. She looked down to watch the flames lick around the wood. She leaned closer to the fire, rubbing her leg.

"There are things I don't like to talk about either. Hell, there are things I don't like to think about." She knocked her cane against the wood floor, as if it was keeping pace with her thoughts.

She glanced at Meredith.

"Girl, keep your secret or don't. I have no idea what brought you here, and maybe it was a dark and terrible thing, but I have a feeling it was something, and probably something big." Rita paused again. "But it's hard keeping a big secret. Takes a lot out of you."

Rita fell back into her chair. Neither of them said anything for a long time. The fire warmed the room, and Meredith realized that she was drifting toward sleep. She heard the wind stirring through the trees, and she imagined how icy and sharp the night outside must be.

Rita banged her cane on the floor again, startling Meredith awake. "Here's the thing," Rita said brusquely. "Why don't you just stay here for another day or two?"

Meredith twisted in her chair to stare at her. What?

"Well, I'm sure you have a plan about where you're going next," Rita continued.

If only you knew...

"But it don't seem to me that you know where you're going to be tonight, or tomorrow night, and so it's okay with me..." Rita stopped and shrugged. "It's okay if you stay a day or two till you get your plan all together. You can help me out a bit, for your keep. Winter is coming on, and there's some stuff got to be done around here that's hard for me to get to now."

Rita's words trailed off as she looked into Meredith's shocked face.

"I know, I know, I was a bit hard on you this morning. I didn't like you getting into my stuff without asking. It was like you were throwing it in my face, how run-down this place has got. But now I'm saying, well, it's okay for you to stay for a night or two."

Meredith shook her head slowly. "Rita, I'm sorry, I would love to stay here, but I don't have enough money with me to pay you for rent or food or anything. I have a few dollars and that's all, and I'm not sure what I'm going to do after that."

"Who said anything about money?" Rita snarled at her with the prickliness that had been so evident yesterday. "I didn't ask you for money. I could use your help, if you're willing to do some work. If you'll help me with the winter firewood and some of the other things I need to do around this place, you can earn your keep. Just for a day or so more, you understand. I'm not looking for anything permanent."

Meredith stared down at her hands. She could stay here. Not forever, but she could stay here. For a few days. For a little while. She exhaled slowly.

"Th-that would be great. That would be really great. I'm really pretty strong. I don't know anything about getting ready for an Alaskan winter, but I can figure out, you can show me..."

Meredith knew that she was rambling, but she couldn't stop. It was such a relief.

"I can help you with cooking, too, you know. And I can take clothes to the Laundromat downtown too, I saw there was one—"

Rita reached across and patted Meredith's arm, just one quick touch.

"They'll be plenty to do, don't you worry about that. And as to secrets?"

Meredith looked back down at her hands, clenched in her lap.

"Your secrets are yours alone, girl."

Seven

Meredith leaned on the broom, eyeing the room. Her efforts to clean on her first morning here had barely scratched the surface of what needed to be done. She should find a dustpan and a few dust rags, and she'd probably have to run down some sort of window cleaner. It would be useful to have oil or furniture wax to use on the wooden coffee table that she could barely see under the stack of old magazines and newspapers. Furniture wax might help with the strange, musty smell, too. Every time she moved a pile of paper or nudged a piece of furniture, she expected to uncover a dead mouse or a desiccated bird. The room was compact, but almost every inch of it needed a good scrub. Well, she was up to the task. It felt so good to have a job to focus on. It would be comforting to do some mindless work and see results.

Rita disappeared early, barking out something about going to a gallery for the morning. Meredith now realized that communications with Rita were likely to consist of only Rita's gruff announcements that invited little in the way of two-way conversations. She shrugged. It didn't matter. In fact, it was better really, if she didn't have to talk. Less dangerous. A plastic jug of liquid soap and other supplies were stacked in a dusty corner deep under the sink, and she didn't need any guidance about how to approach the cleaning of this room. Any effort would make an improvement.

As she began picking up and stacking the newspapers, her thoughts turned, unbidden, to the mess she had created in her old world. She could tidy up the newspapers, but she knew she couldn't shuffle and neaten the broken pieces of her life back into place so easily. She stood still for a moment, staring into space, as she focused on what she had brought with her to Homer. It didn't take her long to catalog her assets. All she had on hand was what she had carried off the bus in her small travel bag. She knew that she had little more than one hundred dollars in cash, the rest of her travel money. She'd had no stomach for buying souvenirs or much of anything else on the bus trip, so she hadn't spent much. She'd bought some food and coffee on the way down from Fairbanks, and she'd given Jan and Evan money for gas. She wondered how long the rest would last. Not long, she suspected. She should figure out a way to give Rita a bit of money for food without offending her. Rita didn't seem to have a taste for fancy food or even balanced meals—dinner last night had consisted of canned soup and toast—but even that cost money.

Other than her wallet, her bag contained a little makeup, a half-read paperback book she had found profoundly dull, a cell phone that had long gone dead since the charger had been in her luggage, and (she smiled to herself), one pair of extra panties she had put in her travel bag in an abundance of caution in case her luggage had gotten lost. Of course there were credit cards in her wallet, but they were just useless pieces of plastic now. She couldn't use them. Besides, knowing Michael, one of his first acts would have been to cancel the cards "just in case" they had somehow fallen into someone else's hands.

She thought of Michael. Her chest tightened. What would he be feeling now? Grief? Or relief? Maybe both. He had been so cold, so very cold for months, even before she had discovered how he had deceived her and betrayed her trust. Certainly her death wasn't going to interfere with his future plans.

The duality in her memories haunted her. She could still conjure Michael and see him so clearly in those early years, the years when they faced life together, when her steadiness meshed so well with his tendency to be hotheaded and impulsive. But now she had to fight him at every turn, battles that she was ill-equipped to undertake. All Michael wanted was to get her out of his life as quickly as possible.

She dumped the stack of newspapers by the door and rubbed her hands over the front of her jeans. Everything had been moving a little too fast. She had a bit of hope, for a while, when she retained George Miller to represent her. George was in her corner. He would help her through this.

Michael had been livid when he learned she'd hired George. She'd told him when he'd stopped by the townhouse to pick up some of his sporting equipment. He rapped his fingers on the dining room table. His voice was hard and controlled, layered with an undercurrent of warning. "Syd could represent you for next to nothing, as a favor to us. Christ, you really don't even need a lawyer. Jake could take care of this for both of us. It's all straightforward. It's not like there's much to divvy up." His mouth contorted into a mean thin smile, as if their financial challenges were a result of her mistakes or stupidity, although he had always managed their accounts and kept all of their records. "It's not like your great house sales have been helping us out, Meredith. And George Miller, for Christ's sake! He's not even a divorce lawyer. He'll just cost us money that we don't have, and for no good reason. That's means less for us in the end." He slapped his palm on the table.

She tried to keep her breathing steady. Syd was a friend of Michael's, maybe not a close friend, but he was cut from the same cloth. She lifted her chin and met his eyes, startled by the fury in them. She swallowed and resisted an urge to look away.

"I'm happy with George." Ellen had recommended him. He normally only handled estates, and Meredith had liked him immediately. When she'd first met George, he grasped her outstretched hand in both of his, then they sat across from each other in comfortable cushioned armchairs in front of his desk. Photographs of his wife and son decorated his office walls, alongside his legal credentials. His expression grew sad and kind when she told him about her situation, and he didn't interrupt or hurry her while she told her story. He explained that he hadn't done any divorce work in a very long time, but since custody of children wasn't involved in her case, he felt comfortable assisting her. They would get all the financial records, he said, and then they'd have a better idea about how to proceed.

"I'm going to stay with George." She had said the words calmly, slowly, trying to keep some control.

He stared at her, leaning forward over the table, then straightening to stand in one swift motion, knocking his chair away from him. "You are making a mistake, Meredith. A very big mistake." He spit the words at her and she shivered. He stormed out of the house without another word, his face red and his hands curled into fists. The door slammed behind him, and she put her head over her crossed arms on the table.

If only George hadn't gotten sick. Sometimes it seemed that the entire universe conspired against her. George hadn't yet received all the financial documents he'd requested from Michael when he was rushed to the hospital, doubled over in pain. "They think it might have been an extreme case of food poisoning," his assistant had told her over the phone. "They're really not sure. But he's not getting better as quickly as the doctors had hoped, and his wife is insisting he take some time off to rest and recover."

So she would be passed off, not to an associate, because George was a sole practitioner, the assistant explained, "but to a very competent attorney who George has confidence in, who will be sure to take good care of your case." They'd given her a name and number, but she hadn't called before she'd left. She just didn't have the energy to start again.

She shook her head briskly, turning away from thoughts of her struggles with Michael. Who else? Aunt Barbara would be grief-stricken, she knew, though Meredith only visited her once or twice a year. Aunt Barbara always sent birthday and Christmas cards, and a letter now and again, but she had her own children and grandchildren to keep her busy. And she would lean on the support of her church to comfort her. She would believe that Meredith was now with her parents in heaven, and that God had called her home. And her cousins—well, she had avoided seeing much of them in recent years, as they married and built families of their own. Looking at all those new babies, bringing new joy... She shook her head again and turned her thoughts away.

Grabbing an old metal bucket, she maneuvered it into the sink. The frigid tap water took forever to get hot, but finally she had some warm, sudsy water to work with. She sloshed some onto the kitchen counter and stood back, tattered sponge in hand. Who else will even notice I'm gone?

The crew in the real estate office. Yes, they would miss her, and their feelings would be sincere, but Meredith didn't think it would take them that long to move on when she didn't reappear on schedule. The properties she was selling could easily be handled by another agent. Business had been very slow for everyone. She had only been working with two potential buyers. The first was a young couple who were hoping to purchase their first home. Meredith liked them very much and took them on, even though she did wonder if they had any hope of getting bank financing. Their enthusiasm for life was contagious, and she enjoyed listening to them chatter about their plans for the future when she showed them distressed low-end condos and fixer-upper cottages. She felt a pang of regret that they would have to start again with another agent. She rubbed her face. But what was she thinking? Ron and Carol would still be looking when she got back, when this was over. After all, this was just for a day or two.

There were her friends from the neighborhood, but she hadn't spent that much time with them recently. They were engrossed in baby showers and potty training and soccer games. Some even babysat grandchildren now— activities that she wasn't a part of. And Michael had no interest in socializing with them. No, she hadn't seen much of anyone lately, except for Ellen.

Memories of Ellen flooded her head on a very deep wave of grief. Ellen would be devastated. Meredith cringed as she imagined Ellen hearing about her death. Who would tell her? Michael, probably. How would Michael have done it? Just a phone call, most likely, if he even remembered to do that much. She could picture Ellen's horrified face, the phone handset frozen in her hand, the blow of the words stopping the world's turning, then the searing pain as the news sank in. Meredith bowed her head and squeezed her eyes shut.

Oh, Ellen, I'm so sorry. So very, very sorry. I'm not sure how this all happened, but I am so sorry that I've hurt you.

Suddenly, the reality of this situation rushed over her again, and Meredith bent over, feeling a sob rise from deep in her chest. This was all just crazy. They thought she was dead. They were all dealing with the news and the shock and the grief. And she was here, swabbing out a cabin in a remote part of Alaska. It was absurd, unreal. It couldn't be real.

She took a shuddering breath and stood up. It didn't make any sense, but here she was. She knew she wasn't thinking clearly, but the muddle of thoughts spiraling in her brain wouldn't settle. She had to go back. She had a life, a life in Florida, not here. But not today. She couldn't make those plans today. Her mind numb now, she felt exhausted again. She looked around from wall to wall. What did make sense, somehow, was to pick up the broom and start on this room. She could clean this room. She pushed the other thoughts out of her mind. Right now she had a job to do.

Eight

Meredith bounced along in the cab of Rita's old pickup. The gears screeched as Rita muscled the ancient stick shift through its paces. The truck rocked and slid through the deep puddles in the ruts in the road, breaking through their thin skins of ice, while heavy drops of water plopped from the overhanging cottonwood leaves onto the windshield. Hot air poured from the rackety heater vent, laying a reek of wet wool over the close air in the cab. Meredith balanced herself by pressing both hands into the bench seat, more than a little scared that she was about to be catapulted through the windshield. A seat belt would have helped, but Meredith couldn't see any sign of one, and Rita wasn't wearing one. The ride smoothed out as they left the dirt road and turned onto the main highway. Meredith exhaled and let her shoulders ease down away from her ears.

There had been frost on the ground this morning, and a film of frozen white had rimmed the inside edges of the kitchen window. Already, she thought. It's just early October.

She had been at Rita's for a week, but she barely registered the passing of time. She scoured the cabin from top to bottom, except for Rita's room, where she hadn't been invited. She stacked firewood in a humped pile close to the house, suffering a few painful splinters in her palms in the process. She cleaned out the neglected vegetable garden behind the cabin and covered what she guessed were perennials with straw from a shaggy bale she found nearby. Rita dropped her at the Laundromat, where she packed five washers with floor mats, curtains, towels, and the little pile of personal laundry that she and Rita generated.

It was mindless but satisfying work, and she was numb with exhaustion by the end each day. She shared simple meals with Rita, and they ate them mostly in silence, each reading from the newspapers, the Homer Tribune and the Anchorage Daily News, that Rita picked up from town. The Anchorage paper was still running stories about the crash, though the footprint devoted to them was less every day. Meredith didn't read those stories. She liked to pour over the Homer paper, filled with news about arriving oil rigs, city council meetings, and revenue summaries from the recent Kenai Peninsula Fair. The Soldatna community theatre was staging two plays by local writers, and the South Peninsula Hospital was welcoming three new doctors. The drugstore was having a sale, and The Twins restaurant published a recipe for making jam with flower petals. There were stories about controversies and accidents, too, but all in all she found the Homer paper and its recitation of the business of ordinary lives soothing, even lulling.

Every morning and every evening, Meredith waited to see if Rita would ask her to leave. Every morning after breakfast, when Rita trundled out to the truck, and every evening when Rita mumbled a terse "good night" before closing the door to her bedroom, Meredith let out a relieved sigh. She tried not to think about anything but the housekeeping tasks at hand. Sometimes she took short walks down the dirt road or through the meadow over to the beach, but she didn't stay outside for very long. She was still spooked by the memory of the bear. She kept looking around and behind her, listening for a huff or a growl.

This morning, when Rita told her she needed to be in town by ten o'clock for her "work in the gallery," Meredith asked to go along. The cabin was in good order now, and she was curious about the town. Rita agreed with a shrug.

On the way in, Meredith scrutinized the houses by the road and the ones she could see tucked away across meadows and in the woods. A few were modest and rundown like Rita's, but many looked spacious and modern, luxurious even, and could have been homes anywhere in the country, except, perhaps, for the line-up of snow machines she saw parked in front of many of them, awaiting winter.

When they got to town, they drove along the main paved road, passing a grocery store, gear outfitters, the volunteer fire department, bars, and bookstores. The road bustled with cars and trucks, many of them as vintage and battered as Rita's. Some of the other drivers and the warmly clad pedestrians on the sidewalks acknowledged Rita with a wave and a smile, and Rita gave a curt, jerky nod in reply.

This place is like a relic from the sixties. She remembered other towns with distinct personalities she had visited, like the laid-back mellow community near Big Sur in California. But Homer seemed to have its own special mix of roughness and sophistication. Hippies and hunters and who knows what else. Sagging, old bars nestled close to upscale outdoor clothing stores. An auto parts chain store sat next to a tall, narrow chapel welcoming visitors and offering redemption. Meredith saw signs pointing to a museum, a sea-life center, and a hospital. She wanted to ask questions about the town, but she kept quiet. Rita kept driving, eyes straight ahead, and she didn't seem to have any desire to talk.

Rita pulled into a wide, empty dirt parking lot in front of a two-story wooden building. It was not quite ramshackle, but it certainly looked a little tired. "Seaside Fine Art Gallery" was painted in bright blue-and-gold lettering on a sign over the door. Through the tall front windows, displays of souvenirs stacked high on tables huddled close together. There was no evident plan or order to the displays. It looked like a dollar bargain store.

She followed Rita into the store without thinking, but then she stopped abruptly, realizing Rita hadn't invited her inside. It was a store, after all, and she could be a customer. She smiled to herself. It wasn't very likely that she was going to spend the last of her few precious dollars on the crab-shaped napkin rings with threatening raised claws staring her in the face from the table in front of her.

"May I help you with something, dear?" Rita had disappeared, and a sixtyish slender woman dressed in a black pantsuit with enormous red hoop earrings stood in front of her. "Looking for something in particular? Something to take home from Alaska?"

"No, ah, thank you. I just came into town with Rita. I'm staying with her for a few days."

The woman's eyebrows shot upward. "Staying with Rita? Well..." She gave Meredith an appraising look and held out her hand. "I'm Moira. This is my gallery. Rita's already gone to the back to get started sorting the weekly receipts. Please do come in and make yourself comfortable."

"I'm Meredith." She thought she should say something more, but what? "You...have a nice place here."

Moira beamed back at her. "Thank you. We've been here for over thirty years. We carry a little of everything, because our visitors seem to like a variety of things. Why don't you look around while I check in with Rita?"

Meredith edged slowly through the narrow aisles between tables, looking at the mix of gaudy trinkets, postcards, and hand-painted gold pans. Much of the merchandise was covered in a thin layer of dust. A feather duster lay on the counter next to the cash register, and she was tempted to grab it and use it. But then she stopped short and stared.

An array of hand-thrown pottery was arranged on a table in the middle of the store. The pitchers, bowls, and cups were fashioned in swaying, flowing lines, as if they had been frozen while dancing to some lyrical music. Many of the pieces were huge and asymmetrical and swooped upward, straining to move into the sky. They were glazed in glowing bright colors, green bases blending subtly into bright yellow tops, whimsical lines of purple and black circling the sides of blood-red bowls. Meredith realized she was holding her breath. She had seen a lot of ceramics over the years, some in singularly fine collections. And she always paid attention to the art displayed in the houses she showed and viewed for clients. But she had never seen pottery quite this fluid and magnificent.

She heard Moira come up behind her. "I see you've found Cassandra Drake's work. We have a few local potters, and some of them are quite talented, but Cassandra's work...well, I think you can see. Her work is really in a class by itself."

Meredith nodded, not taking her eyes off the display. In the middle of nowhere, who would have thought she would find work like this? It was incredibly beautiful. To be able to work clay that way, to construct such wonderful pieces....

The front door bell jingled, and they both turned around. Nick pushed through, carrying a cardboard box. Just great. I can't get away from this guy.

He looked over at them and grinned. "Moira, I brought you some halibut. And look, here's our mysterious visitor again."

Moira kissed Nick on the cheek and hurried into the back room with the box of fish. Meredith stood still, annoyed but not knowing what to do. All she could think about was the way they had met. She could feel her face grow warm.

"Seen any bears lately?" He was still grinning.

Jerk.

She decided to take the high road and ignore the comment. "I'm just looking at this wonderful work," she said, gesturing back at the ceramic display.

"Yes, Cassandra does do beautiful stuff. Kind of

lost in here, don't you think?"

Before she could answer, Moira came back out, followed by a tall, slender woman in her mid-thirties, who was wearing a red flowing wool cape. Her wild, curly, black hair framed the perfect white oval of her face. Her huge dark-brown eyes flicked first at Nick, then at Meredith. A tiny wrinkle appeared in the middle of her forehead.

Moira smiled around at everyone. "Oh, Cassandra, this is Meredith. She's staying out at Rita's for a little bit."

Meredith smiled. "Nice to meet you. Your work is beautiful."

Cassandra continued to stare at her like she was a bug specimen pinned to a poster board. The wrinkle in her forehead deepened. "Hello," she said. She didn't return Meredith's smile.

"I've got to run now. Good-bye Nick, Moira, and...." Cassandra hesitated for a moment, "...Meredith." She swept out the front door in a whirl of red. Meredith looked after her, feeling confused. What had that been about? Had she somehow offended Cassandra by admiring her work? How could that be? She glanced at Nick and Moira, but they had launched into a discussion about somebody's boat and seemed to have forgotten her. She slipped out the front door, tossing back a quick "bye now" to Nick and Moira.

She stood on the boardwalk and took a few breaths of the fresh chill air, recognizing the faint bright tang of the ocean. She looked right and left. One way was as good as the other. She turned right and started to walk.

Nine

Two more days had come and gone. Three days, four, and then it had been another week. It was the second week of October. Rita kept to herself and didn't say much, and Meredith now understood that her repertoire of snarls and snipes seemed directed to the world in general and not particularly at Meredith. Rita certainly scowled a lot and thumped around the cabin, banging her cane loudly against the floor and anything that got in her way. She'd toss out curt directions to Meredith: "Need some more firewood in here," and, "That fridge bottom drawer could use a clean," but she didn't seem to be overtly hostile. But most importantly, she hadn't asked Meredith to leave. Neither of them had said a word about Meredith's staying longer, or her leaving. Most days, Rita rattled off in the truck to town for part of the day to work at the gallery, leaving Meredith alone in the cabin. Sometimes Meredith went along to town, and she wandered aimlessly up and down Pioneer Street or down to the rocky beach. If the sun was shining and she mustered the energy, she sometimes hiked through town and down the length of the long spit to the small boat harbor and the ferry terminal. Even on sunny days, the air had an edge that hinted winter was just around the corner.

Once she had seen a "Help Wanted" sign in the front window of The Twins restaurant, and it flashed across her mind that she could apply and maybe earn a little money for a while. But the next moment she remembered that she didn't really exist anymore. She didn't have a social security number or any references that she could use. It was one of those times when the stark reality of what she had done crashed down about her head, and she'd sat on a nearby bench and wept quietly. She had no idea what would come next for her.

One morning, Nick showed up at the cabin. He gave Meredith a hard, sharp look when he came inside to find her washing the breakfast dishes. After giving her a brief nod, he sat down at the table with Rita, opening the paper sack he'd brought to pull out some saran-wrapped halibut fillets. Rita's face pulled into a rare smile and she patted Nick's hand. Nick reminded Rita that she needed to make some doctor's appointment at the clinic, and Meredith watched as Rita waved his comments away. He left after giving her a quick kiss on the cheek, not bothering to say good-bye to Meredith. Rude man.

He came back two days later, finding Meredith and Rita at the kitchen table, sipping coffee and reading the newspapers from the day before. His brow furrowed as he looked at Meredith. He put a bag of bagels onto the table. A fragrant doughy smell wafted into the air.

"Well, Meredith, still here I see."

She leveled a not-too-friendly look at him. It didn't seem to faze him.

"It's a clear sunny day outside, and there won't be too many of those left. I'm betting on snow in the next two weeks. Rita, why don't you let me steal Meredith for a little while to show her the view from the point?"

Meredith was startled, but Rita shrugged and barely looked up from the paper.

"Sure, Meredith, go see the point. It should be pretty this morning."

Meredith pulled on her jacket and hurried after Nick, who had already crossed the meadow and was turning toward a narrow trail that seemed to run parallel to the beach. He strode ahead, not looking back, clapping his hands from time to time. He's doing that because that bear could be anywhere. She shivered and hurried after him. Although she guessed that he was in his fifties, he moved smoothly and efficiently, with the easy energy of a younger man. As they moved deeper into the trees, the path was barely visible. In spots, the exposed roots and overhanging branches of the alders and cottonwoods all but obliterated it. Her feet wobbled on the uneven ground, aching in her thin canvas shoes, and her ankles knocked against knotty tree roots and moss-covered rocks. The bottoms of her jeans were soaked through from the tall, wet grass that smacked against her legs. Her temper started to flare, but she refused to give Nick the satisfaction of hearing her ask him to go slower.

After about twenty minutes, they suddenly emerged into a clearing. A gray granite outcrop the size of a house protruded like an island out of the dense surrounding brush. Its edges were rounded but steep, and Nick leapt onto a low ledge, turning to offer Meredith a hand. She scowled but took it. She had no idea why he had dragged her here, but she suspected he had more motive than just showing her a pretty view. She followed him upward, and they scrambled to the top of the huge tumbled boulder looming above the treetops. Nick squatted down facing the bay, and she sat down beside him. She was panting, but she pressed her mouth closed and tried to steady her breath so he wouldn't notice.

They sat quietly for a few minutes, gazing out over the bay. She had to admit that he was right. The view was breathtaking. They looked over the trees to the choppy dark water, then farther to the sharp snowy peaks beyond. White seabirds coasted on the air streams above them, pealing out urgent cries. The restless rustling of the alder leaves whispered below as the breeze passed through. It wasn't blowing hard, but even the light touch of wind had a nasty, cold bite, especially now that the sheen of perspiration on her face had cooled. She crossed her arms and pulled her jacket closer around her. I'll need something warmer. Soon.

Nick cleared his throat. "Meredith, I've been around Rita for a long time. She talks a good talk, but she's not as spry as she used to be." He rubbed his hands together and pushed them into the pockets of his jacket. "She has a bit of a hard time taking care of herself lately, let alone taking care of someone else." He turned and looked into her eyes. Her face grew hot. So that was it. He thought she was taking advantage of Rita. Or that somehow she was going to be a burden to Rita if she stayed any longer. "Rita was kind enough to give me permission to stay." Her voice was halting, her tone icily formal. "I don't plan to add to her troubles. While I'm here, which you'll be relieved to know probably won't be for much longer, she won't have to worry about me or take care of me. In fact, we have an agreement, and I'm helping her."

If Nick noticed her red face or pursed mouth, he didn't show it.

"You're helping her out?" he said with a grin. "You're going to take care of Rita? Meredith, do you remember how we met?"

"Of course I do. But that's different. I don't expect to run into a bear every day. Besides, I know what to do now. I can take care of myself." Who was he to lecture to her? It was none of his business, anyway. Did he think she was some sort of crazed murderess come to do Rita in? Or more likely, some sort of weak, needy incompetent?

"Oh, you can take care of yourself. You've got it all figured out here, have you?" He shaded his eyes with his hand as he gazed up at an eagle drifting so high on the air currents that it was little more than a distant speck. "Well, then, why don't you lead when we go back?"

Meredith snorted. What was the big deal? She would just follow the trail. But as she glanced down to the forest edge, she realized she couldn't see the path. There were several spots where the underbrush was a little less thick, but after a few feet of clearing, the bushes dipped low and there was no obvious way through. Her face was flaming. She had just followed Nick in here, putting one foot in front of the other and trying not to trip, not paying any attention to where she was going.

Damn it, I'm going to look like a fool. She cast

around desperately for some plan of action, some method to find the way back, some tactic not to look stupid. Suddenly, she smiled. Of course.

She dug deep into the inside pocket of her jacket and fished out the tiny compass key ring that Ellen had given her at the airport as a funny going-away keepsake. "To help you find your way north, so you find your way back home," Ellen had said. It looked fragile and insubstantial, but the wobbly, black needle darted around the dial as she cradled it in her palm to show Nick. "I guess I'm not sure where the trail starts from here. But I'm not lost. You see, I do have a compass."

Nick gave a bark of a laugh. "Well, so you do." His mouth curved into a smug smile, but his eyes weren't unkind. "But, you see Merry, a compass won't do you much good if you don't know what direction you want to go, will it?"

She lowered her palm and rested it on her knee. He was right. She could find north, but she had no idea if north was the way home. They had made so many twists and turns on the way here that Rita's cabin could be in almost any direction, except straight into the bay. She felt like she should be mad at Nick for mocking her, but she wasn't. All of a sudden, the absurdity of her pulling out the compass seemed hilarious. She laughed, a deep, full-throated laugh that started Nick laughing too. She stopped and wiped her eyes.

"Okay, you're right again. I should have paid more attention to where we were going."

Nick grinned. "There's a trick. When you're walking out, turn around and look backward every few hundred yards, especially when the path isn't clear. The trail never looks the same going back as it does going out. If you keep looking back and pay attention, it's easier to find your way home."

He stood up and brushed his hands over his pants. He stretched his arms high over his head, leaning backward as if to loosen his back, and Meredith could see the muscles in his arms strain against his jacket. He was strong, she could see, but not the strong that comes from a workout at the gym. He works his body hard for a living, not for looks. He turned to look down at her. "Merry, you don't seem like a bad person, but people aren't always what they seem. I'm just looking out for Rita." He offered his hand and pulled her up to standing, then he ambled effortlessly down the rock face.

She didn't feel irritated with him anymore. The shared laugh had lifted her spirits. Nick was an annoying man, no doubt about that, but why shouldn't he be suspicious of her, just showing up the way she had, without any explanation? She shrugged and started to pick her way down.

And, she realized as she smiled to herself, he had given her a new name. No one had ever called her Merry before. It had usually been Meredith, and occasionally Mer but never Merry. Merry had such a fresh and festive ring. She liked it. She'd tell Rita and the others that it was her nickname. Merry. A new name for a new person.

Ten

Wind gusts slapped sodden cottonwood leaves against the windows, leaving a murky green-brown collage on the glass. A frigid mid-October rain was blowing in from the north, smelling like snow and spattering fat drops against the roof. When the wind paused, Merry could hear the raucous annoyed cawing of ravens taking shelter in the spruce trees outside. She drifted around the room, running her fingers over the back of the battered, old sofa, and straightening out the rug in front of the sink with her toe. Her fingers itched for a television remote, but the cabin only held Rita's massive console radio, its needle dial permanently stuck on Homer's NPR frequency. She had turned the radio on and off, and on and off again. She just couldn't muster any interest in the fuzzy voices discussing politics half a world away. There was nothing that needed to be done around the cabin, and she was bored, bored, bored.

She pulled the oversize sweatshirt close around her and shivered. The cabin was solid, but the autumn wind pushed a steady icy draft through the cracked window seals.

No TV, no DVD player, no computer, not even a phone...not that I'm planning to call anyone.

She heard the clatter and uneven roar of Rita's pickup on the road outside. As the truck clunked to an abrupt stop, Merry dashed out to help Rita with a couple of bags of groceries she was pulling from the passenger seat. Rita scowled at her, as usual, but she passed over the heavier of the two bags.

"Quick, girl, get inside before we're both soaked."

They stood in the middle of the kitchen and brushed

the water from their clothes with their hands. Rita struggled out of her dripping wet raincoat. Merry started to reach over to help her, but pulled back. She won't want my help. It didn't take long to put the few groceries away. Merry felt guilty, thinking about the food she was eating that she wasn't paying for. Sure, she was helping with the cleaning and caretaking, but that wasn't bringing in any cash. She needed to figure something out, even though she wouldn't be here much longer. She was sure Rita couldn't afford to support her, even for a short time.

Rita plunked herself down at the kitchen table and hunched over the local newspaper that Merry had already read, front to back. Her face hovered about six inches above the front page.

Merry sighed. "Rita, do you have any books?"

Rita pulled herself upright. "Books? What kind of books?" Her mouth was folded tight into its usual contentious frown.

"Well, any kind, really. I thought maybe I could borrow something to read. If that's okay..." Why does she always make that face?

Rita tapped her cane against the floorboards, which Merry now knew was a sure sign that she was thinking. "Go into my room. There're some books over there on that shelf by the door."

Rita's room was dusty and messy around an unmade bed, but Merry hadn't dared to go in to tidy up. She ran her hand across the spines of the well-worn books. Moby Dick, Jack London's short stories, collected books of Charles Dickens. She guessed she could bone-up on the classics.

She pulled out a copy of Gulliver's Travels. Peering closer now, she saw that the bookcase backed deeper into the cabin wall than it appeared. There was a second row of books, tucked far behind the first. She glanced at the door. Rita was still in the kitchen, making her evening cup of tea. Merry pulled out a few of the front-row books to see the hidden ones behind. She grinned. The first one she pulled from the back row had the picture of a tanned, bare-chested, longhaired pirate holding a sword in one hand, with a bosomy maiden in a torn, gauzy dress draped over his other arm. The maiden appeared to be swooning, her disheveled blonde curls tumbling down her back, stretching to the deck of a ship. Susannah at Sea.

Well, well.

She started to shove the book quickly back into place, but then she paused. She'd been tiptoeing around Rita since she got here. Just like she always did around Michael when he was in a bad mood. Rita's perpetual frown and her clipped, barked comments had made Merry wary of making much of an attempt to talk with her. But she did take me in. She let me stay here. I need to stop acting like a quivering rabbit. Or a little brown mouse. Michael had once called her that, his mouth twisted into a mean, thin smile when she hadn't wanted to get dressed up for yet another of his business dinners.

She stared straight ahead, her eyes distant, not seeing the books lined up in front of her. For a moment, she was back home. With Michael. Miserable and cowering, terrified of making a wrong move. I wasn't always that person. I'm not that person anymore. And I'm not a mouse.

She took a deep breath and grabbed the book. She walked into the living room.

Rita stood facing the counter, stirring milk into her tea.

"I see you're fond of the classics. Help keep you warm on cold Alaska nights?"

When Rita turned, Merry was holding Susannah in front of her, biting her lip to hold back a grin. Rita gasped and started to puff up like an inflating balloon. "What, what..." For once, her sharp tongue seemed to fail her. The sight of Rita's red face almost made Merry regret her tease. Almost.

Suddenly, one corner of Rita's mouth crept upward,

and she started to snicker, but the low snicker fast became a hearty bellow. The sound burst out of her and transformed her face. The rigid, stern mask disappeared. Merry felt an answering deep belly laugh rise up from her very core. She could feel something hard and tired open and give way inside her, as their laughter filled the dim, little kitchen. When they finally stopped, they both had to wipe the tears from their eyes. They sighed at the same time. Rita's mouth settled back into her frown lines, but her eyes were brighter.

"Well, Merry, I haven't read those in a while, but yes, you found out my secret. One of them, at least. I like them bodice-rippers. Started reading them when..." She shook her head and paused for a moment. A smile flitted across Rita's face, but then her mouth drooped even deeper into a frown. "I can't read much of anything anymore. These eyes are just giving out, even with them little cheaters." She pointed her chin at a pair of drug store eyeglasses, their lenses smudged with fingerprints, folded on the windowsill. She shrugged.

Merry stared at the wavy lines of water that were running down the window. Falling leaves pushed by the wind knocked against the glass. It's only October. What must it be like in deep winter here? Here all alone, like Rita lives? And she can't even sit down and read a novel?

Merry held up the book. "I tell you what. You just bring that cup of tea in here and sit down."

Two hours later, Merry's voice was giving out. They had made their way through the first fifty or so pages of Susannah, with Merry providing the dramatic reading, Rita interjecting some rather bawdy comments when the action got steamy, and both of them snorting at the "no, no" dialogue of the heroine, and the "oh, but yes" of her pirate lover. Now Rita dozed on the couch.

Merry touched Rita's shoulder. "Rita, time for bed."

Rita stirred and pushed herself slowly up off the sagging couch cushions. "Okay, Annie, I'm going...I'm going." Merry peered at her, startled by the unknown name, but Rita didn't say anything else. She seemed to stay half-asleep as she shuffled into her bedroom.

Merry rinsed Rita's teacup and put it in the drainer. She squinted at the wild night outside; the rain still slashed against the windowpane. She saw her face in the window's reflection, and it startled her. She hardly paid any attention to the small, tarnished mirror above the sink in the tiny bathroom. The face that looked back at her now was leaner and...peaceful. The eyes that for so long had stared back at her with such a hunted look were wide and steady. She smiled at herself and mouthed, "Hello, Merry."

She turned and made her way up the stairs to the attic.

But, she wondered, who is Annie?

Eleven

The mornings were dark, and the days were getting shorter. Sometimes the rain that fell was mixed with slushy snow. When a sunny day arrived, Merry stood outside the cabin, her face lifted to catch as much of the pale sunlight as possible. It was still cold, but in the shelter of the tiny porch, she could feel the last remnants of late summer. Not long, she thought. It was only mid-October, but soon this meadow would be covered with snow.

She could hear the rattle of a truck rumbling and bouncing down the potholed road. Nick. He hadn't been by in a couple of days. Sure enough, now she could see his red pickup through the bare trees. He wouldn't stay long today, though, once he found out that Rita had gone off early to the gallery.

It seemed that they had come to an uneasy truce. When he came to see Rita, Merry still had the feeling that he was watching her carefully, but he seemed more relaxed around her now. On his last visit, he had looked around the clean and tidy cabin with what she thought was approval. She had worked her way up and down every inch of the cabin, and the dust and debris she had found when she arrived was mostly gone. The Formica kitchen table still wobbled, and there were still threadbare spots on the corduroy couch where the stuffing poked through, but the windows were clean and the cracked white kitchen sink sparkled. A small pile of firewood was arranged on the hearth. Last week, when Nick had opened the refrigerator to drop in the fillets he had brought, she felt a little burst of pleasure to think that he must have noticed that the old sticky spots and stains had been scoured away.

Nick waved at her as he reached across to snatch a

paper bag from the far side of the front seat. He strode over to the porch. "Nice day, eh?" His lined face was smiling. "Probably not too many of these left. I'm guessing snow on the ground any day now."

Merry glanced up at him. His smile animated his face and made him look years younger. How old is he? Maybe fifty?

"I brought some bagels for you two for breakfast tomorrow. The bakery is having a special." He tossed the bag to Merry. "I saw Rita over at the gallery. I've got some halibut to clean. Some buddies of mine just brought it in, and Rita said she'd like some. So I thought I'd take you down to the dock and give you the fish, and you can come back with Rita when she's through."

Merry cocked her head to one side and looked at him. Couldn't he just have given the fish to Rita? She hesitated for a moment, but then she shrugged. Why not? "Sure. I'll just get my jacket."

They didn't talk much on the way to the small boat harbor. The breeze blew in fits and starts, knocking the last few yellow and brown leaves off the trees, dancing them down in whirling patterns across the background of the pale blue sky, slapping them to and fro before finally letting them patter to the ground. The sunlight streaming through the windshield warmed the truck cab, and Merry sighed and leaned back against the heat of the seat.

"Richie left the halibut in a cooler on the boat. I'll grab it and we'll take it over to the cleaning station." Nick maneuvered the truck into a vacant space at the top of the floating dock, and she strolled behind him down the boardwalk. The sun bounced off the lines of ripples in the water, and the air hung heavy with the salty reek of low tide in the harbor and the metallic tang of fish.

Nick stopped at a weathered but sturdy green-and-white boat tied to the dock with two thick ropes. "Dreamer" was written in large uneven black lettering on the bow. He glanced back at Merry. "It came with the name. It's supposed to be bad luck to change a boat's name. Not necessarily good luck to keep it though, I guess." He shrugged and smiled at her. She looked up at him curiously. Had he actually just made some sort of a joke? This day was becoming stranger and stranger.

He turned to face the boat, and she thought he was going to jump aboard. She sat down on a nearby wooden bench. But then he turned to her. "Merry, come on board. I need a few minutes to sharpen my knives." He held out his hand and bowed his head slightly, as if he were asking her to dance. "Come on. I'll make us some coffee."

Nick being polite? Offering her coffee? She took his hand and stepped on board, almost immediately tripping over a bucket. He gave an exasperated sigh. "Well, try not to fall overboard. Just sit down, okay?"

Well, that was more like the Nick she'd been around these past weeks. She eased herself down onto the floorboards and leaned back against the cabin wall, stretching her legs out in front of her, enjoying the heat of the sun. She was so often cold here. Alaska seemed to be pretty frugal with its warmth, but today was almost balmy. She tipped her face into the sun and closed her eyes, letting her back muscles sink against the warmed wood of the boat's cabin. The boat rocked ever so slightly in the gentle swells of the harbor. Seagulls called to each other, and occasionally the low growl of a boat motor cut through the quiet. She heard Nick moving below, some muted thumps and clunks, probably making some coffee. She sighed. The rest of the world and all her troubles seemed blessedly distant. Her mind drifted into a pleasantly blank space, and she dozed.

She dreamed she was back in Florida, sitting in the sunshine on Ellen's front screened-in porch, the way they used to in the early morning before the sun got too hot, their coffee cups nesting in their hands, their bare toes rubbing against the polished wood floor. It was so comfortable there. The tropical sun danced on her closed eyelids, and she thought she needed go home soon, to think about dinner for Michael. Yes, dinner.

But that was wrong, wasn't it? She might be going home, but Michael wouldn't be there. Michael was... She gave her head a little shake, trying to wake up, to clear her thoughts. Where was she? She opened her eyes.

Nick stood over her, looking at her, holding two cups of coffee. His expression was pensive. She shuddered a little, bringing herself back.

"Sorry, I just nodded off there. I'm so often cold here. It's just so lovely to sit in the sun. So comfortable, it just made me sleepy, I guess." She heard herself blathering, and she felt awkward, as if he'd caught her doing something she shouldn't be doing. The images from the dream lingered for a moment, and then they were gone. She took a deep breath.

"Well, you know what they say about Alaskan seasons," he said, handing her one of the cups and settling down next to her. "Here it's nine months of winter and three months of damn cold weather."

She put her hand to her mouth and grinned. That really had been a joke. Nick had made a joke!

She glanced sideways at him. He looked a little sheepish and embarrassed, and a little pleased with himself, all at once. And with those expressions moving across his face, he almost seemed a different person, younger, more vulnerable somehow. She felt her body relax.

While they drank their coffee, she asked him a few questions about Dreamer and about fishing, a little nervous that he would find her ignorance of even basic information to be offensive. But he seemed pleased with her questions and happy to answer them. Dreamer was a wooden schooner built in 1923, and at this time of year, it went out for trips of up to ten days, running the long lines for halibut.

Once he started talking, she didn't have to say much, and she just settled back to listen to him. As he spoke, she envisioned him working alongside the other fishermen setting the long lines, toiling on the icy unforgiving bay, laying the line for up to three miles along the ocean bottom with short lines and circle hooks spaced every ten feet or so. He told her about pulling the halibut in with the gurdy, gaffing them, stunning them and bleeding them, and taking out the guts, the gills, and the gonads, and how all the guts were just in one little pouch, high on the halibut's underside. These were huge fish, he said, some as heavy as 500 pounds, but most of the big ones weighed in at about 250 pounds or so. He described how the fishermen poked the ice into the fish's cavities, heads, and gills and packed the fish in ice at sea, so they would stay fresh up to ten days until they got back to the processors on the Homer Spit. And he told her what it was like to stay at sea for the trip of ten days or so, laying the lines, pulling the lines, icing the fish. It took no effort to lean back and listen to him, his voice animated, his hands gesturing. She realized how little she knew about life here. She had always loved those halibut steaks presented so delicately and garnished so artfully on a dinner plate, but she had been totally ignorant of the world that brought them to her.

"So what I usually bring to Rita is part of my home pack—that's the stuff besides halibut that gets caught on the long line. Sometimes it's yelloweye rockfish, ling cod, or thornyhead rockfish—they call that 'idiot fish'—and that makes great fish sandwiches." He suddenly stopped and grinned again. "Well, I guess you're probably sorry you ever asked. I suppose I've got a lot to say about fishing once I get started." He rubbed his hands along the smooth plank decking and gazed up into the clear sky.

She didn't think she'd known any man quite like him before. He was so comfortable in his own skin and seemingly contented with who he was. He didn't brag, but he exuded self-confidence. Michael had always seemed to be looking forward, strategizing about what he was going to do next. Nick seemed quite happy to be in the present.

They finished their coffee in companionable silence. She was curious about this man, but if she asked him any questions, surely he would ask questions of her in return: questions she couldn't answer. She sighed.

"So, Merry, how long are you planning to stick around?"

She froze. Well, she could at least answer that question without telling an outright lie. She tried to pitch her voice low and casual. "I don't know. I really don't. I'd planned to just pass through, see this place, you know, but I do feel that I'm able to help Rita and she doesn't seem to mind having me around...I don't know."

They sat in silence for a while longer. She slowly exhaled when it seemed that he wasn't going to ask any more questions.

He took her empty cup and pushed himself up. "Well, winter's a-coming. We could get some snow any time now. But then, Homer in winter is just as beautiful as Homer in summer. Just different." He disappeared down below deck.

She pressed her head into the cabin wall and closed her eyes. She really didn't know what to make of him. He was undoubtedly prickly some of the time, maybe most of the time, but he certainly was kind to Rita. And this afternoon had been nice. Quite unexpectedly nice.

Nick clambered back up to the deck. "Ready to go?" he asked, and she nodded. He jumped on the dock first, heaving the battered metal cooler of fish down next to him, then stretched his hand to help her off the boat.

And then, as she put her hand in his and took the long, precarious step off the boat, ever so briefly—did she imagine it?—she thought she felt his thumb stroke across her palm.

And when she felt it—had she imagined it?—a small warmth sparked deep inside her, just for an instant.

As her feet hit the dock, Merry stumbled off-balance, and Nick reached over to stabilize her arm. She took a long, unsteady breath and stared down at the dock, feeling confused. What was that? What just happened?

She heard a faint "hello," and they both turned at the same time, to see Rita waving, standing in front of her truck. Nick hefted the cooler up onto his shoulder and started toward the woman, while Merry trailed behind him, but more slowly and keeping a safe distance.

Twelve

Night came earlier and earlier as October waned, and the temperatures plummeted. Snow had fallen twice and then melted right away, but most mornings the meadow was silent and white with the weight of a heavy frost. Merry found a puffy vest in the attic bureau, and Rita brought out a tattered but warm wool pea jacket for her. She was thinner now, so she could layer her old Florida jacket on top as a windbreaker. When she caught view of herself in a shop-window mirror, she looked like the Pillsbury Doughboy, but she just shrugged. I'm warm, that's all that matters. Merry and Rita kept a basket by the door filled with fleece hats and gloves. Without them, when the wind blew, Merry's fingers throbbed from the cold, and her ears turned bright red and burned, even if she was just dashing to the woodpile.

She had too much time on her hands. She kept the cabin clean and picked up, but most days all the chores were finished in an hour or two. She liked to walk, but not when the wind whipped icy rain into her face and howled through the bare trees. She'd read books and newspapers until her eyes were sore.

When she sighed for the third time over the dinner dishes, Rita put down the bowl of stray buttons she was sorting through.

"What's wrong with you, girl?" her voice, as usual, held a scrape of irritation.

Merry turned and wiped her hands with the dishtowel. "I was just thinking how great it would be to have a project." She sat down next to Rita and pulled a handful of buttons out of the bowl. "What are you looking for, one for your brown coat?"

Rita nodded, still staring at her.

"What I mean is, I'm not complaining," She shot Rita a quick smile. "But take Cassandra Drake, for example. She makes that beautiful pottery. Just takes a lump of clay and works her magic. How amazing to be able to do something like that." She sifted the buttons in her palm, fishing out a large, flat, black one. "This might do."

Rita nodded again and took the button. "Yep. That one just might do it." She reached over for the old candy tin where she kept her needles and thread.

"Merry, you been looking at Cassandra's pottery since you got here. What are you waiting for? Go ask her if she'll show you how to do it. She just lives a half-mile from here."

Merry's eyes snapped wide open. What an idea—to learn to make the pots, the plates, the pitchers—that would be amazing. She had some artistic talents. She loved to sketch, and she knew she had a good eye for design and detail. It was a wonderful idea. But Cassandra was so aloof and unfriendly. She'd never say yes.

"Rita, I don't think she would do it. I don't think Cassandra likes me. She always glares at me and..."

"What's wrong with you, girl?" Rita was fumbling to thread a needle. Merry reached over to help her, but Rita slapped her hand away. "If she doesn't want to, she'll tell you. But how can it hurt to ask? Good Lord, girl, get some gumption. Go after what you want."

Rita jabbed the needle into the thick fabric of her coat. Merry sat looking at her.

Get some gumption. Well, I'm not really sure what gumption is, but I probably do need to get some. She shook her head. Merry, no more little, brown mouse.

~ * ~

Merry stood outside·Cassandra's cabin. It had been hard to find, even with the directions Rita had given her, because nothing out here seemed to have a street name or a house number. She just had instructions that seemed to come from an orienteering guide: "Go back up the road here for about half a mile. When you pass the Davises' place, it's a yellow doublewide with a big, old spruce tree in front, then take the second dirt road to your right. You'll find Cassandra Drake's place about a quarter-mile in. Can't miss it."

Can't miss it indeed, she had thought, as she pushed aside the sweeping cottonwood branches hanging low over the muddy-rutted road, their few remaining huge limp leaves still shiny with old aphid honeydew. How does she even get a car in here?

She had bitten at her bottom lip and almost turned back twice, but thoughts of Cassandra's pottery spurred her forward. Every time she stopped by the gallery, she was drawn to the display of Cassandra's work. She found herself stroking the bigger pieces, letting her fingers linger and drift across the cool, smooth surfaces of the brightly glazed pots. If only I could do this. It would be so wonderful.

The cabin sat high on a knoll by the road, snugged up to a meadow rolling with mounds of tussock grass. A complicated rope arrangement hung on the plank front door, intertwining dozens of ceramic beads in myriad shapes, sizes, and colors. The cabin face was modest and compact, with only two small windows, but Merry could see that the cabin extended into the meadow in a long rectangle. Cassandra's battered red jeep was parked just off the road in front. She hesitated, took a deep breath, and knocked on the door. There was no answer. She knocked again. Still no answer.

She climbed down off the porch and followed a gravel path that snaked along the side of the cabin. A row of tall windows faced the meadow, the trees, and the mountain range beyond. Through the windows, she saw Cassandra hunched over a turning wheel, her hands pushing against a shining mass of wet clay. Behind her the far wall of the studio was lined with shelves, all covered with pots and tea sets and bowls, all types of vessels, all sizes and shapes, glowing in the late afternoon light slanting in from the meadow. The dense rich fragrance of burning birch logs crackling in the fireplace escaped through an open screened window, along with a thread of music, the sharp rising and falling of a violin, full of longing and sweetness. As Merry watched, Cassandra bent deep over the wheel and pressed the spinning clay into a smooth bell-shaped hump. She plunged her fingers down into the center and, seemingly by magic, the clay parted and the curve of a bowl shape emerged. Cassandra stretched the bowl wall higher and thinner, stroking the clay upward with her fingers delicately positioned on the inside and outside of the piece, the newly created shape spinning around her steady, almost still, hands.

Merry realized she was holding her breath. It was so perfect, this scene. Cassandra's wild, black hair was gathered loosely away from her face, and a large red apron spattered with sprays of clay was tied over her jeans and work shirt. Her face was flushed and rosy from exertion, or perhaps from the heat in the room. Yet, with her face reflecting the fireplace glow, and her gaze of serene intensity, she was all of a magnificent and wise gypsy witch. Or Pele, the fire goddess, thought Merry. Something vibrant and brilliant and not quite of this world.

Then Cassandra looked up and saw her. Her eyes narrowed as she sat upright, and the wheel slowed and stopped. Cassandra wiped the backs of her muddy hands against her apron and frowned.

"You," she said.

Merry took a deep breath and pressed a screen door open. "Yes...maybe you remember? My name is Merry. We met at the gallery?" Merry could hear her words quaver, and she swallowed and inhaled again, trying to settle her voice. "I-I really like your work."

"Ah, yes, the mystery woman." Cassandra picked up a towel and rubbed her hands. There was no welcome in her face. She crossed her arms and glared at Merry. "And what are you doing here?"

Merry stared across the room. This was not starting well.

"Well, I really like your work, and I thought, perhaps, that you might show me...maybe not formal lessons, you know, but I could perhaps watch and learn, you know, and maybe in exchange I could help you with some stuff..."

This really was not going well. Cassandra's expression grew even colder and harder. A tiny frown line creased her smooth forehead.

"I don't give lessons," she spoke in a slow monotone. Merry waited, but Cassandra didn't say anything else. She continued to wipe her hands, the rest of her body absolutely still, her eyes unblinking and appraising, fixated on Merry's face.

"Well, okay, then..." Merry turned to go, but she hesitated and shook her head. She hadn't done anything wrong. She had walked all the way over here, just to ask. The old Meredith would have cowered and slunk away, but she didn't want to be the old Meredith. All she had done was to come to ask if she could learn. I don't deserve this kind of treatment.

She twisted around to face Cassandra.

"I don't know why you're acting like this. I haven't done anything to you. Your work is wonderful, it's so fluid and alive, and I just wanted to learn more about it. That's all." She turned away, but this time tall, this time with her head held high.

She marched through the door and along the gravel path, throwing a brief backward glance into the studio. Cassandra still sat over the wheel with her arms crossed, but the expression on her face might have softened just a bit, as though her gaze had gone inward, as though she was thinking about something else entirely.

Merry sighed and walked away.

Thirteen

By the time Merry trudged all the way back to the cabin, her head drooping low and heavy, Rita was in her bedroom. The next morning, Rita didn't ask about her visit to Cassandra, and Merry didn't offer any information. She was still mulling, rolling the evening around in her mind, imagining what she should have done differently, visualizing all the sharp and articulate rejoinders she could have thrown at Cassandra if she'd only been able to conjure them up at the time.

Rita disappeared right after breakfast. She'd been unusually silent that morning, even for Rita. While Merry finished the breakfast dishes, Rita wrestled on her jacket, grabbed her cane, and thumped out the front door. Through the kitchen window, Merry watched her make her way very slowly across the meadow. Merry didn't pay particular attention to Rita's abrupt departure right away. She might have warmed to her a bit over these past few weeks, but she kept her own counsel, and she certainly didn't bother to tell Merry where she was going, or what she was planning to do, most of the time. But when an hour and a half passed and Rita hadn't reappeared, Merry pulled on the heavy oversized sweatshirt that kept the cold wind at bay and went out to find her.

She found Rita down on the beach, huddled on a log bleached gray and brittle by the sea and sun. The ocean breeze was slapping tendrils of her thin hair into her face, but she didn't seem to notice. Her eyes focused on a far point somewhere out beyond the choppy water, as she tapped her cane against the rocks at her feet. She was ashen pale, her mouth shriveled into a tight knot.

Merry pushed her own hair back behind her ears

and sat down next to her.

"Rita, what's wrong? Are you sick? Can I help you?" Rita shook her head but didn't turn to look at her. Merry waited and wondered if she was going to speak at all.

"Merry, it's hard to get old. There is so much loss." Her voice was tired and sad, and its usual crusty edge had softened away.

Merry hesitated, then put her hand over Rita's. Rita didn't knock it away.

"I think I'm going to lose the cabin. I've lived there for thirty-four years, but I don't own it, you know. I've never had that kind of money. It's Moira's. We had a deal, a kind of trade."

Rita paused and dug into her pocket for a crumpled handkerchief. She clutched it so tightly in her clenched fingers that her knuckles turned a dead white. "I've worked at that gallery, helping out at the front, keeping the paperwork in order, picking up at the post office, even helped with the setups for some of the artists, too. But my leg is getting worse, girl, and it just takes me so long to do anything these days. And some days I'm just so tired and out of breath I can't hardly get around. I'm not really much help to her anymore."

Rita took a slow deep breath and shook her head. "I can see it coming. She's going to have to hire someone, pay someone, and she's going to need some rent money for the cabin to make it all work. I can see the writing on the wall. I got some money from a little pension to keep me going day to day, but I don't have no way to come up with more rent money. I pay next to nothing for rent now. The cabin's not much of a place, but Moira can get a lot more for it."

Rita rubbed her eyes with the back of her sleeve.

Merry squeezed her hand. "I can't believe she'd throw you out, Rita. You've known each other for so long."

Rita turned toward her then, her face crinkling with a wan crooked smile. "Oh, it would kill her to do it. She'd try anything to avoid it. But, Merry, I can see how things are. The gallery is a labor of love for her, but it don't make no money. I can't let her struggle because I can't do the work. She's got to get some real help, and she'll have to find a way to pay for it. I've got to figure this out. Problem is, I don't have a lot of options. I don't know where I'll go."

Rita's voice cracked and she shook her head slowly, gazing back over the water. The wind was picking up now, and whitecaps frosted the waves on the little bay. The waves hissed as they smacked against the pebbles on the shore.

An idea bloomed in Merry's mind, coming out of nowhere. It's crazy, but...why wouldn't it work? Why couldn't it work? At least for a while? She sat up and squared her shoulders. She knew she needed to choose her next words carefully.

"Rita, you've been so kind to me. You've let me stay and I haven't been able to contribute much, just a pair of extra hands around the cabin sometimes. I know how generous you've been. But what if, just for a little while, I helped Moira at the gallery?"

Her words tumbled out in a rush. "I'm not suggesting a permanent solution, but if you could let me stay, well...a little longer, I could help at the gallery. At least that gives you some thinking time, doesn't it? Time to figure things out, to plan ahead. And I would like to do it. I have a bit of design training."

Warning bells went off inside her head. No, she couldn't give any personal information about herself, anything that might jeopardize her new identity, anything that might link her to the past.

She hurried on to another subject. "Of course, I'd have to find some better clothes." She looked down at the old cargo pants and oversized sweatshirt, dug out of the attic bureau. "But I saw a thrift store in town. I bet I could get a couple of things really cheap."

A sharp crease divided Rita's forehead. "Merry, just because I'm old doesn't mean that I take charity. You don't have to take care of me. You hardly know me."

Merry bit her lip in frustration. Rita could be so damned prickly.

"Look, there isn't any charity involved. You're giving me a place to stay, and feeding me on top of that, and I don't want to be a charity case either. It will just be me earning my keep. For just a little while. And so it's good for you and it's good for me. It will give us both some breathing room. And if it doesn't work out, well, neither of us will be any worse off than we are now, right?"

Rita stared out over the water without saying a word.

"Oh, come on, Rita," Merry said. "You have nothing to lose. This doesn't mean we have to be best friends or anything. Think of it as a business deal."

Merry smiled at Rita then, and in return, Rita's mouth twisted into a hint of an upward curve. The awful pallor of her skin seemed to have lessened a shade or two. "Well, Merry," she said, "I'll just think about it." She paused. "And maybe I'll talk to Moira about it."

Merry felt a jab of happiness. It was a wonderful idea. She would be useful. She would be needed. She would do a good job and be appreciated. She could stay and help Rita and not be a burden. And it wasn't forever, of course, not a permanent commitment, but it could mean a little more time. More time to figure out what came next. Because at the moment, she still had no idea what was supposed to come next.

~ * ~

It was a surprisingly smooth negotiation, much easier than Merry had anticipated. Merry sat with Rita and Moira in one of the back rooms in the gallery, a cramped kitchen that Moira had converted to an office. The gallery's ancient heating system creaked and groaned like a fourth person in the conversation, spurting currents of dusty, warm air into the small space.

Rita didn't say much. She let Merry present the idea to Moira. Merry would take Rita's place, working temporarily in the gallery until, Merry said, Rita was feeling a little better. Just for a little while.

Moira's long, red fingernails tapped against the desktop as she looked first at Rita, then at Merry, then at Rita again. She frowned and opened her mouth to speak, then closed it without a word. She looked up at the ceiling.

Of course it was an obviously illegal arrangement, and Merry was sure all three of them knew it. Merry would work at the gallery instead of Rita, and Rita would continue to live in the cabin, rent-free. But Moira also had been paying Rita a small stipend. Rita was officially and legally a part-time employee, her tiny salary reported with regularity to the federal government.

However...

Moira didn't even blink as Merry put her proposal on the table, though her eyebrows shot toward the sky. Merry said she didn't really want a salary. But perhaps, if Moira thought it was appropriate, Moira could instead put a little money directly in Rita's account at the grocery store. That, Merry said, would certainly be helpful.

There was a minute of silence while Moira continued to stare at the two of them. Say yes, Merry thought. It will work. It will help Rita. I can stay.

Merry did feel a little guilty. She was putting Moira in a tough spot, she knew. It would have been so much simpler to put Merry on the payroll, even though the salary was a pittance, but then there was the little matter of the social security number. And she knew she was taking advantage of Moira's long relationship with Rita, because Moira desperately wanted a solution that didn't involve evicting Rita. And it was only for a little while.

Only for a little while. That was how they had talked about it, only until Rita got back on her feet. But when would that be? Even over the few weeks that Merry had been staying with Rita, Rita seemed more frail, more slow-moving, and more uncertain on her feet than she had been when Merry first arrived. She's starting to rely on me. I don't think she'd admit it, but it's true.

Moira continued to tap her fingernails on the desk. She probably thinks I'm an illegal alien. Maybe a criminal hiding out. Who knows what she thinks? Merry was casting around for something else to say when Moira said, "Okay. Let's try it. For a little while. Let's see how it goes."

Merry's face broke into a delighted smile, and Rita's shoulders dropped like she had been holding her breath and just allowed herself to exhale.

Merry had a job.

Fourteen

Merry inhaled the brisk morning air in deep, long gulps as she walked away from the cabin. Rita had offered her a ride to the gallery, but there was no reason not to walk up to the main road today. It was a long trek, but the day was fine and crisp and cold. Frost outlined all the fallen leaves in the frozen puddles. She could feel the air's bite in her lungs as she walked. Sounds seemed magnified in the early morning chill. A raven croaked lazily at her from a low overhanging branch, apparently undisturbed by her passing. The breeze rattled the frozen grasses on the roadside. She pulled her scarf close around her mouth and ears, and shoved her hands into her pockets. Even the hint of wind felt icy.

Her mind was calm, almost empty, but very alert. She was seeing everything so clearly now: the sharp outline of the scrub spruce against the pale blue sky, the ornate lacy patterns that the frost had drawn over the fern fronds growing from the nurse logs on the forest floor. She felt vital, so alive, as if the very cells of her body had realigned in just the right way to let her experience this time, this moment, without thinking about the past or the future.

It was as if she had come to the ends of the earth, as far away as she could have traveled. It had been well over a month, November now, and she was amazed to find that entire blocks of time passed without her thinking about the accident and her life before. When she did think back, it was like probing a sore tooth with her tongue. She couldn't quite leave it alone, but she didn't want to go there. When she first came here, the terrible memories and the dark realization of what she had done haunted her constantly. The images ran in a closed loop in her head. She could push them away, but they returned almost immediately, demanding her horrified attention. But the passage of time and the strangeness of this new world had slowly made their mark on her. Sometimes, even, she felt peace.

The day was warming a bit by the time she arrived at the gallery. She hummed under her breath as she went through the comfortable routine of opening up: unlocking the door, brewing the coffee, counting and readying the till.

Suddenly Cassandra burst through the gallery door, her red cape-coat swirling around her. She barely acknowledged Merry's greeting with a curt nod, then disappeared into the back room where Moira let her store her extra pieces.

Merry sighed. She had pretty much given up on Cassandra. It seemed there was nothing she could do that would make a difference with the woman. She shrugged and turned her attention back to the tasks at hand. There wouldn't be many customers this late in the year, but Moira had said that two tour buses would be stopping by, probably the last until next spring. In fact, even before the coffee had finished dripping, she glanced up to see a gigantic bus pull close to the door, and a gaggle of tourists began to drop from the tall bus steps and wander toward the gallery.

As always, she quaked a little when she saw the bus. It was impossible, with the bus right in front of her, to avoid thinking about them all: Paul and Brenda, who both talked too loudly in their New Jersey accents; or Marty, grouchy but ultimately kind, in his gruff way, as he herded them on and off the bus. All of them, not close friends, but people she had known, a little bit, for a little while. People who had been kind to her, who hadn't deserved to be blown to bits in such a senseless accident. Sometimes, as now, it took several deep breaths and a serious effort to push back the tears and the terrible memories that crowded back about that day. Her "Good morning!" as the first wandering couple strolled into the gallery sounded a little shaky, but she took another deep breath and stepped forward.

"Welcome to our gallery. May I offer you some coffee? Please, look around, and let me know if you have any questions." The visitors poured around the exhibit tables, picking up the beach-wood ornaments and sea glass jewelry, checking the prices on the ceramic ashtrays and the seagull-shaped salt-and-pepper shakers.

After a few minutes, Merry had sold a few souvenirs, and most of the tourists had moved down the street to the coffee shop. Only two thin, severely dressed older women remained, picking up pieces of Cassandra's pottery and talking in low voices.

One of them snickered at something the other said. Now that the others had left, Merry could hear their conversation.

"Thirty-five dollars! I could get this at Wal-Mart for three-fifty, I bet." The taller woman, bundled in a heavy black wool coat, plunked one of Cassandra's small pitchers back onto the table. Merry winced.

She sidled over to the table. "May I help you? These pieces are handmade by a very talented local artist, Cassandra Drake. You can see that they're quite unique and very beautiful."

The tall woman arched an eyebrow and stared down at Merry. "Yes, they're pretty enough, but really, these prices. You have to be kidding." They both laughed again.

Merry felt a slow seethe start to simmer inside of her. She worked hard to keep her voice calm and even. "Well, really, if you knew about the process, I don't think you would say that. Yes, you could buy a piece of pottery made by a machine in China for a fraction of the cost. And then you'd have a functional piece identical to, say, ten thousand other pieces? But this...this was made by an artist who worked and studied for many years to learn the skills to make this unique piece. Because of the time and effort she put into the craft, she was able to take a mere lump of clay and fashion it into this beautiful shape. She carved this lovely foot and attached the handle in a separate process. And then, after it was fired in a kiln once, she chose this particular combination of glazes to create the glowing finish you can see here before the piece was fired again. All in all, it took many hours to make this piece, and it is unique. There isn't another one in existence just like it. So really, comparing this piece of art with a factory-made mass-produced product is just...incorrect."

She said the last word distinctly and with great obvious restraint, and she was sure that the two women understood that she wanted to say something much stronger. They stared at her in silence. Her face felt hot, and she knew that it must be bright red. She gave them a weak smile and turned back to the counter. Fine, Merry, that certainly was great customer service. She ducked her head down low until she heard the front door bell jingle as they left, not saying another word.

Well, it wasn't like they were going to buy anything anyway, she thought. The bell jingled again, and she looked up just in time to see Cassandra's red cape flapping down the front walk.

"And good-bye to you, too," she muttered. There was every indication that it was going to be a long day.

Fifteen

Rita was standing near the sink, gazing out the kitchen window, when Merry arrived back at the cabin. Heavy snow was dropping silently into the meadow, transforming the landscape, covering all the sharp angles and distinct shapes with a soft, white blanket. Merry's jacket was soaked through from her walk. On the way to the cabin, snowflakes numbed her face as she tipped her head back and looked straight up into the sky, mesmerized, almost disoriented by the endless scattering, tumbling flakes. This time it will stick, she thought. Winter is here.

Rita glanced at her but turned her attention back to the scene outside. "Big snowfall tonight, I think. 'Bout time. Late this year."

Merry pulled off her jacket and rubbed her hands over her chilled face.

"Oh, and Cassandra stopped by. She said you could come by tonight and she'd give you a lesson."

Merry stood absolutely still. "She did what?"

Rita turned and frowned at her. "She said she'd give you a lesson tonight. Isn't that what you said you wanted, girl?"

Merry shoved the hair back from her face with both hands. "A lesson?"

Rita gave an exasperated snort and turned back to the window.

"Yes, girl, a lesson. Tonight. If you wanted to go by."

~ * ~

"Okay then." Cassandra leaned over the pottery wheel and snapped on a switch. "Sit down."

Merry tied on a clay-spattered apron and sat down

slowly in front of the humming, mud-splattered wheel. Her stomach fluttered and her breath quickened. She was going to do it. She was going to make beautiful things, just like Cassandra did. She had no idea why Cassandra had changed her mind, and Cassandra hadn't offered any explanation when she'd arrived. She'd just pointed to a hook in the arctic entry for her dripping jacket, and then she'd led the way back to the studio.

Cassandra walked to the far wall, her long loose skirt swirling around her, and twisted the knobs on an ancient-looking dusty tape player. The growl of Janis Joplin's voice filled the studio, blasting out of the speakers in the corners of the room. She tossed a log on the fire and stood swaying to the music, scrunching up her features and belting out the refrain of "Me and Bobby McGee." The firelight played across her face, and Merry thought she looked entrancing, magical, and a little frightening, like a wild woman from a world far away, an enchantress whose next action was completely unpredictable and unfathomable. By contrast, Merry felt infinitely dowdy. She was sure she would never in her life look as alive and vibrant as Cassandra did tonight. She would never have that confidence, that shimmering presence, that drop-dead flaming beauty. Jealousy stabbed in her chest. And on top of all that, Cassandra was so skilled and talented. The shapes and colors of her work were breathtaking. Suddenly, Merry was intimidated, and she wondered whether she should have come. But she wanted this badly. She took a deep breath and tried to pull her scattered thoughts together.

Cassandra poured two big glasses of red wine and handed one to Merry. Merry put hers carefully on the bench behind her.

"We start," Cassandra said. She made a grand flourish with her arm, waving her wineglass precariously in a wide arc. She smiled in Merry's general direction, but Merry could see it held little warmth and didn't reach her eyes. Cassandra certainly wasn't making any special effort to make her feel comfortable. Merry frowned. Is she mocking me? Is this some plan to make me look stupid? Well, I think it just might work. Cassandra dragged over a chair and straddled it backward, facing Merry and the wheel. She thumped a wet lump of clay onto the middle of the wheel. "First step, centering. Get right over that wheel, get it right between your legs." She laughed and took a big swig of wine. "Now step on the pedal and get the wheel turning fast. Always fast for centering. Put your hands like this…" she gestured to Merry, "and start putting pressure down and toward the center. You're going to make that little lump perfectly smooth and round. Go for it." She took another gulp from her wineglass.

Merry hesitated, then leaned forward and placed her hands on the slick rotating ball of clay and pushed. The lump resisted back, then suddenly whipped away, smashing into the plastic rim surrounding the wheel.

"Damn," she said. She rubbed the burning edge of her left hand where it had scraped against the spinning wheel head. Cassandra laughed again and swirled the wine around in her glass. "Again. Dribble some water over the top. This time, more pressure down with your right hand."

About half an hour later, the lump looked as weary as Merry was feeling, and it certainly didn't look smooth and round. Merry blew at the strands of hair that had fallen into her face and held up her hands, now covered in gooey, slick, gray clay.

"I can't do this. I just can't do it."

Cassandra looked at her from over the rim of her wineglass. "Just can't do it, eh?" She took another drink. "And you've been at it for all of what—twenty-five minutes or so?"

Merry felt her face flush. "Okay, so you've showed me that what you do is hard and that I'm hopeless. Is that what you wanted?" She wiped her mucky hands against the front of her apron and started to get up. "Well, good for you. I guess I'm done."

"You're an idiot." Cassandra's eyes were flashing now. "Do you think this stuff is going to happen just because you want it to? This is hard. You want to make beautiful things. Well, first you're going to have to work hard and make a lot of mistakes. A lot."

Merry sighed and sat back down on the stool. She felt deflated and defeated. "Look, I'm not an idiot. But I'm forty-two years old. I'm probably too old to learn new stuff like this." She realized that she was feeling sorry for herself. She could hear the whine in her voice, but she couldn't stop it. This had been a dumb idea.

"Well," Cassandra said, staring at the wall behind Merry. "Sorry, I don't have a gun, but maybe you could stick your head in the oven."

"What are you talking about?" Merry glared at Cassandra. Is she drunk? Or just plain mean-spirited? Merry started to get angry.

Cassandra rose from the chair and pointed her finger at Merry. "If you're 'too old to learn,'" she said, mimicking Merry's complaining voice, "why don't you just kill yourself now? You're done, right? You're everything you're ever going to be? Nothing new to learn, no changes to be made. Why not just kill yourself now and get it over with?"

Cassandra walked back to the counter and poured herself more wine. Merry stared at her back, not knowing what to say. "You're twisting my words. It's just hard to learn new stuff when you're...older." Cassandra's words hurt. She did want to learn, she did want to change, but it was so hard to fail, to look stupid. She was a mud-covered middle-aged woman who was struggling to best a lump of clay, and Cassandra was probably just toying with her. How dumb was that?

"Look, Merry, if you're perfectly happy with the way you are now, then fine. Don't learn anything new. But if that's not the case, just get over yourself and know that it's going to be hard. You're going to sit there at that wheel for hours and push that clay around. For a long time your pots are going to be ugly and lopsided and they'll collapse and..." Cassandra shook her head. She plunked her glass on the counter and crossed her arms.

"So I don't know if you're going to be able to do this. Not everyone can. It really depends on you. But if you act like a spoiled brat and don't even try, if you get discouraged just because you can't do something new perfectly the first time, then why should I even bother trying to teach you?"

Merry stood and ripped the apron up over her neck. "Spoiled brat? You stand there getting drunk and spouting nonsense. That's not what I call teaching. I'm done." She rushed to the door and grabbed her coat, wiping the muck from her hands on the legs of her jeans.

She could hear Joplin's raspy voice wail as she strode away from the cabin. It sounded so desperately sad.

Sixteen

It was the pink flamingos. There must have been twenty of them, scattered around the scruffy yard in front of Scary Bob and Miles's studio. The afternoon's flimsy sunshine reflected off their rosy plastic bodies, plump ovals topped with skinny stretched necks, perching on black stick legs planted into the three inches of heavy white snow that had fallen last night. She was walking by the studio on her way home from the gallery, her head tucked low against the wet wind. Then she looked up and there they were.

She had met Scary Bob at the library social hour, near the folding table with the coffee in paper cups and the store-bought shortbread cookies. He introduced himself ("Please just call me Scary") as one of the owners of the Whirlwind Studio and Gallery, about two blocks away. He nodded across the room to a well-groomed, middle-aged man in pressed brown slacks and a white shirt. His partner, Miles, he'd told Merry. Merry flicked her eyes back and forth, to Scary and to Miles, comparing the two. Scary was wearing bright red khaki pants, black high tops, and a flowing floral shirt. Scary told Merry that they were both painters who shared space in the studio. Scary worked in watercolor; Miles, in acrylics. And, as he explained, Scary also liked to do occasional temporary installation exhibits when the spirit moved him.

Apparently, Merry thought as she looked at the frozen flock, the spirit has been busy.

If it had been anything but flamingos—these absurd birds, with their long necks curved into question marks, the suggestion of black-webbed feet planted beneath the snow instead of in the warm wet marshes of Florida.

She had always loved flamingoes. The real ones,

that is. Their long, sinuous necks swiveling high to look away, snaking down to feed under the water. Their strange, delicate legs stepping so carefully in the wet grasses. And the glorious color, that improbable blush, the melding of hot pink and saffron.

But flamingos belonged in Florida, not here. Like she did. She trudged the rest of the way with a lump in her throat.

She leaned her head back against the faded cushions on the back of the sofa. Rita and the truck had been gone when she got back, her face and hair soaking wet from the sudden squall of sleet that had blown in when she was just a few yards from the cabin door. She had toweled off her head and made herself a cup of tea. It was quiet in the cabin. She looked around and noticed that a spider web had been reassembled in the kitchen window. She didn't have the energy to get up and deal with it.

She stared up at the planks in the ceiling. She felt pulled, suspended, between two worlds. This wasn't her home. This was a place she had landed and stuck when a freak accident had torn open the already weakened fabric of her life. But when she thought about Florida, she felt no inner tug, no urgency calling her back.

Memories flooded her brain, and she couldn't muster the energy to fight them off. Florida. Home. When she thought about home, she thought about Michael. She pressed the base of her palm against her forehead. When had it all gone bad? Was there some magic moment, some special point in time, when she could have done something differently, something that would have changed the course of her marriage? She shook her head in frustration. She could see the past clearer now that she had some distance, but she still couldn't pinpoint a turning point, a critical moment.

Because it had been wonderful, at first. She shook her head again. She couldn't be remembering that wrongly, could she? She and Michael seemed so good a fit in the joyous months before they were married, and in those first few years when they were working so hard to make a life together. Michael had always been ambitious and focused, but in those early years he seemed to come to her for refuge from the terrible pressures at work and his own unrelenting need to get ahead. He seemed to find peace in her presence, happiness in the quiet times that just the two of them shared.

Had she changed? Well, in these past few years she had tried to, because Michael became so impatient with her. She couldn't seem to do anything right. She pushed herself to be more outgoing, more polished, more a part of the slick high-stakes legal world that claimed him now. She understood that he felt he had an image to project, especially after he chose to join the firm's criminal defense section, specializing in high-profile offenses, organized crime activity, and criminal defense in the international arena. She understood it was a hugely competitive environment, and that lots of money changed hands, and that he believed he had to appear tough and competent. What she hadn't understood, she realized now, was how enticing that world could be. At some point, the façade he adopted had become his reality. And in that reality, she was no longer an asset.

She found it so painful to remember. Michael started staying late for drinks with people from work and with clients, and when he came home, he didn't want to sit down to dinner, and his eyes were hard and sometimes mean. He came into the townhouse and usually poured himself a whiskey. He'd toss his jacket over the back of a chair and loosen his tie, running his hand through his curly, blond hair. He'd lean at the edge of the front window, looking out into the manicured street, but she saw that his eyes were focused somewhere else entirely. His mouth would be pressed into a thin line. She learned not to talk to him then. If she tried to pull him out of the mood with questions or stories about her day, he turned on her. His eyes would rake over her face, and his mouth would curve into a lopsided smile that carried no humor. He'd question her, as if she were being cross-examined on a witness stand. How could she have let the Smyths walk away from the condo deal after she had invested so much time with them? Why didn't she make them feel guilty, make them realize that they had wasted her time, pressure them into the sale? Or worse yet, he would mock her. "You feel sorry for them because the bank wouldn't approve the loan. They should have told you right on the front end that they had credit problems. They took advantage of you, Meredith, and you just let them. They played you, took advantage of the way you always stick your head in the sand, thinking everybody is being upfront with you. You always want to fix everything. Maybe you should have been a social worker, not a real estate agent. Are we ever going to see some money from this real estate crap?" Then he'd twist away from her, dismissing her, and continue to stare out over the street.

She shuddered at the memories and rubbed her hands across the worn pillows. Tears of frustration pricked at the back of her eyes. She had tried so hard. But nothing she could do was right. She understood now, looking back, that maybe there wasn't a right. Maybe there was nothing she could have done to change Michael's trajectory.

It had been impossible to explain to anyone, especially since she didn't really understand it herself. Michael lost interest in seeing their old friends. For a while she had tried to keep in touch with them on her own, but that was awkward, and so many of them were starting families and had little free time. Michael's new friends were other lawyers and their wives. They were slick and smart and witty, and it was clear that she didn't fit in. He took her to parties where she knew no one, and he walked away from her without a backward glance as she stood alone. She was shy and tongue-tied, and often spent much of the evening sitting by herself. After a while, Michael attended most of the parties and celebrations on his own, not even bothering to ask her to go along.

Even Ellen—oh, how she missed Ellen—couldn't help. Merry pulled her knees up into her chest and sat huddled in a small, tight ball. She usually tried to keep all thoughts of Ellen away now, because the memories made her feel so lonely. She'd spent more time with Ellen than she did with anyone else. When Meredith needed a staging company to dress up the vacant properties for sale, she found Ellen. Ellen had just started her own company, and Meredith recognized her amazing ability to shop garage sales and consignment shops for cheap but unique household furnishings, and then to place them in properties to create the look of cared-for and personalized happy homes. She and Ellen were a good fit professionally, but their work relationship rapidly grew into a deep friendship. Ellen was brash and fun and a little gritty. She had been widowed a couple of years before Meredith met her, after her husband had fought and lost a battle with lung cancer. Sometimes when Ellen was pulled back into the abyss of her own grief, Meredith comforted her by just being with her, not talking about the past or worrying about the future, just being a quiet companion in the present.

Ellen wanted to help, of course. Meredith didn't like talking about her worries about Michael. She stumbled over her words and left sentences half-finished. "He's so unhappy...not unhappy entirely. He likes his job, I think. He spends so much time at the office. We don't... talk much anymore." Ellen didn't pry, but her sharp blue eyes under her spiky gray hair seemed to see beyond the words Meredith was willing to say.

Ellen had only asked her once why she didn't leave him. They'd met at Ellen's warehouse to look at some of her new finds, and they were drinking cups of green tea, perched on top of an antique Chinese chest that Ellen had just bought for a song at an estate sale.

"Leave?" Meredith could hear the tremor in her

voice.

"Well, you're not happy. Why not? Are you worried about money?"

Meredith had shaken her head. She didn't know any details about their household finances, because Michael always paid the bills and took care of that sort of thing, but in her mind, staying or leaving didn't have anything to do with money.

It wasn't just that she took her commitment to the marriage seriously, though she always had. No, it was just that now she couldn't imagine herself on her own. She didn't even really know who she was anymore, separate from Michael. She remembered her childhood and the past before Michael as a time of serenity, a time when she had been comfortable in her own skin. She'd always been a little shy and sometimes tongue-tied with groups of strangers, but that was just who she was. "Everybody's different," her mother had said when Merry felt uncertain about herself. "You're just a quiet one, that's all. Nothing wrong with that." But somehow, somewhere, the path of her life had veered, and her belief in her own abilities and inner strength had waned. She had become a moon, maybe just a small asteroid, circling the planet that was Michael, and without the planet, she would have no orbit, no purpose. He was so confident and so good at everything he did, and she was always messing up, making mistakes. She would just have to keep trying, trying harder, to make Michael happy.

And then, of course, there was the pain she never shared with anyone, the aching loss that she had tucked away, pushed deep into a dark, hollow place where she couldn't bear to look. Even now, with so much of her life changed, the memory of that time made her breath catch in her throat. She closed her eyes and forced herself to breath slowly and deeply. Don't think about it. Just don't think about it.

Merry opened her eyes and looked around the dim

room as the last shreds of the day's light faded. She had balled her hands into fists, and her fingernails had bitten red welts into her palms. She heard the rumble of Rita's truck as it pulled up outside, and she pushed herself upright and grabbed her coat. Rita probably had groceries in the back of the truck. She had work to do. She took a deep breath and opened the door.

Seventeen

The next day she was alone in the gallery, though it was almost noon. Merry had unlocked the door and brewed a pot of coffee, but no one had yet shown up to drink it. Moira explained that this was likely to happen. It was long past the end of the tourist season, early November, and most of the visitors had scurried for the warmer and more civilized locales back home.

Merry circled her shoulders up and back and felt her tense muscles give way, just a little. She loaded one of Moira's Bach CDs into the sound system and started to dust. The old gallery building seemed to shed dust nonstop from the rough plank ceiling boards. She turned first to the display of Cassandra's work, in her mind far different from the other tourist doodads and local souvenirs sold by the gallery. She paused to admire the pieces. The pitchers leaned enticingly and a little teasingly, as if inviting liquid to flow from them. The cups were whimsically tall and slightly asymmetrical, defined through long, graceful curves. Their lustrous colors seemed to glow in the midday sun slanting in low through the big windows. She liked to stroke the tips of her fingers over the satin glaze of the surfaces.

Now they made her feel a little sad, too, since her disastrous evening with Cassandra. She'd played it over and over in her mind. What had she done to make Cassandra so impatient and hostile? It was as if there was a missing puzzle piece somewhere. She shook her head and took the duster over to the postcard rack.

She liked being here at the gallery. The work was mostly unchallenging, but Moira had been welcoming and she settled in quickly. She felt useful, and she took pride in the fact that she was helping Rita. Merry sensed that her arrangement with Rita had evolved into a mutually advantageous and almost easy alliance. They had both said they knew that Merry working at the gallery was only a short-term solution, but neither of them had laid down a timeline. Merry understood that Rita would bridle against any suggestion that she was losing her ability to manage on her own, so Merry made sure her efforts were low-key. It was just logical that she stop by the grocery store on the way back from the gallery, saving Rita a trip. If Merry needed to go to the Laundromat and Rita was going to give her a ride, well, it was just easy to take Rita's clothes along too. Rita still snipped and snarled sometimes, but Merry felt that a lot of it was just for show now.

She turned as the entry bell jingled. Cassandra swept into the gallery like a sudden windstorm. Her long denim skirt skimmed the floor and a bright blue wool shawl cascaded down over one shoulder. She stopped and frowned when she saw Meredith.

"Where's Moira?" she asked, her eyes narrowing.

Why is she always like this to me? Meredith thought. I've never done anything to her, nothing at all.

"Moira's not here today. She had business in Anchorage. Can I help you with something, Cassandra?" She pitched her voice low and tried to sound soothing and cheerful.

Cassandra huffed out an impatient sigh. "I have the pieces she asked for in the truck outside. I'll get them and put them in the office." She wheeled around and left.

Merry's eyes followed her to the door. There seemed to be nothing she could do. It was clear that Cassandra just didn't like her, and she never seemed hesitant to show it. After the door closed, she started to straighten a row of salmon-shaped refrigerator magnets. The entry bell jingled again. A customer? She looked up. No, Nick was walking toward her, looking like the proverbial bull in the china shop. He must have felt that way, too, because Merry could see the tentative way he picked his way through the crowded aisles. "I saw Moira on her way out of town and I figured you'd be alone today. Do you want to close down for just a bit and grab some quick lunch? I've got to stick around town until the mail comes in."

Merry nodded. Nick still did more scowling than smiling, and his tone was brusque and businesslike, but she was pleasantly surprised and pleased by the invitation. She realized that she was feeling very glad to see him, and that surprised her too. In the days since their conversations on the boat, thoughts of him kept popping into her mind. Now when she heard the rumble of an engine outside the cabin, she sometimes found herself glancing out the kitchen window to see if it was Nick. She still didn't know if she had really felt his thumb sweep across her palm in a subtle caress, but even thinking about it made her face flush. This man was definitely more intriguing than she had first thought.

She knew he must realize that she was being purposefully evasive about her past. When he had asked where she hailed from, she had turned away and answered, "Oh, here and there. I've been traveling for a while." He had looked at her sharply, but he let the subject drop. She learned that it wasn't that hard to keep her secrets. She mastered the art of responding to questions with a word or two that revealed nothing, followed by a quick change of subject. If her questioner persisted, she made a quick exit. She was able to deflect the curiosity of most people she met, and she avoided the others as best she could.

She smiled up at him. "Thanks, Nick, that sounds great. I'm certainly not going to be overwhelmed by business today." She swept her arm around to show the empty gallery. "I just have to wait a minute for Cassandra to bring in some new pieces, and then I'll close up and meet you outside."

She hummed to herself as she dug in the cash

drawer for the door key. As she passed by the window, she saw Cassandra walk up the gravel path carrying a large box. She stopped and watched, when Nick met Cassandra and took the box from her arms. Nick's back was turned, but she could see Cassandra clearly. While they talked, Cassandra was transformed. Her smile glinted warm and bright, her eyes crinkled, and her head tipped back as she laughed at something Nick had said. He must have offered to carry her box, because he turned with it and strode toward the door. But before Meredith backed away from the window, she had a clear view of Cassandra's expression. Her face was full of want, and need, and yearning.

All at once, she understood. She knew why Cassandra's eyes were so cold and suspicious when they swept over her.

She loves him, Merry thought, feeling a deep ache in her stomach.

She loves him. And she is amazing. How could he not love her back?

Eighteen

The first few days of November ushered in a new kind of cold. Temperatures hovered just above and below freezing, turning dirt paths into slippery half-frozen mud tracks. Grimy gray clouds loomed low, making the scant hours of daylight into a prolonged twilight.

Today it was raining, a bitter splattering rain that battered the last of the snow into stiff, icy muck. A gloom seemed to have settled over the town. It had been a long, quiet afternoon in the gallery, and it had given Merry too much time to brood. She'd only seen one bored and disinterested tourist, and she suspected he had just come in to get out of the bone-chilling weather. She stood at the window for long periods of time, listening to the drips and plops of the water running off the roof and down the windowpanes. When the Mozart CD finished playing mid-afternoon, she didn't bother to put on anything else.

At closing time, she fumbled with the key, jiggling the door to line up the lock as Moira had showed her. This place is falling apart. She shook her head. She had been letting her thoughts come and go all afternoon, and they seemed more muddled now than ever. She had no plan for the future, though she kept telling herself she needed to make one. Whenever she thought about her next step, her thoughts veered away from the paths she felt were most logical—going back, dealing with Michael, picking up the pieces, and making some sense of the mess at home. Instead, her brain found any excuse to think about something else, or even nothing at all. But this charade couldn't go on forever.

The lock finally rattled closed, but when she looked up, she realized that she'd forgotten to turn the window sign from "open" to "closed." She leaned her head against the door and shut her eyes. A raindrop from the top of the doorframe found its way down her back and she shivered violently. Tears stung her eyes as she struggled to reopen the lock. What am I doing here? Once inside, she slammed the sign around. At least the second time, the lock fell into place more easily.

She hurried down the street, snugging her jacket close around her, and slogging toward the diner where Rita would be waiting. Thoughts continued to whirl in her head. When her mind wandered, she often found herself thinking of Nick. She didn't know what to make of her feelings for him. At first, after the bear encounter, she'd dreaded seeing him, which seemed to happen all too frequently. He was irritable and annoying and rude. But now, she saw a different side of him. A side that watched out for Rita without making a big fuss about it. A side that had a sense of humor. He was a man who worked hard at what he did, and did it well. And, although she felt her face redden when she admitted it to herself, she was starting to feel drawn to him. Nothing could come of that, she knew, since she was only here until she figured out her next step. She had to keep her guard up, but it was an undeniably pleasant sensation. You're just feeling lonely. Pull yourself together. But it had been so very long since she'd felt the beginning threads of desire, that little lurch of pleasure deep and low in her belly. But what about Nick and Cassandra? What was going on there?

She mused about Cassandra and her pottery as she plodded down the sidewalk, her head bent low against the driving rain. I did give up too quickly. She was right. Merry wanted to go back to try again, but she couldn't imagine that Cassandra would welcome her. Quite the contrary.

She dashed into a nearby covered doorway as a particularly determined rush of wind drove icy raindrops into her face. She had enough time to wait for a few minutes, to see if the rain might let up a bit. The low, gray clouds leached all the color from the landscape on Pioneer Street. Even the storefronts, with brightly painted façades, seemed dreary and rundown. It was probably sunny in Florida. It was always sunny at home. She shrugged and then smiled to herself. This is cold and miserable and nasty, but I'd still rather be here.

She was about to give up on waiting for the rain to lessen when she saw Cassandra across the street, striding in the opposite direction. Her red cloak-coat was streaming behind her, and her wild, black hair was plastered wet to her head. She was moving as if the weather was of no concern to her, not even worth her attention. As Merry watched, Cassandra opened the door to the bank and went it.

Merry took a deep breath. I've got to stop acting like a coward. Whatever is or isn't going on between Nick and Cassandra doesn't have anything to do with me. What's the worst that could happen? I've made a fool of myself before, and I've never died from it.

Cassandra emerged from the bank a few minutes later. "Cassandra, wait up," Merry yelled, as she dashed across the street. Cassandra halted and turned, and Merry could see that stern wrinkle line appear, bisecting Cassandra's forehead. I'm about as welcome as this rain, she thought.

"Can we talk?" She was breathless when she reached Cassandra, as much from anxiety as from her dash across the street. She grasped the woman's elbow and pulled her under the covered entrance of the knitting store next door. Cassandra's face was stony.

"Look, I'm sorry." She hadn't had time to choose her words carefully in advance, which she usually tried to do. "You were right. I gave up too quickly. I want to come to try again." She took a deep breath. "Cassandra, your work is amazing. I know you've been at it for years, and I'm just fumbling around. But I love the clay. I really love it. Please, will you let me try again?"

The words tumbled out in gasps and fragments, and now she stopped talking and gazed at Cassandra. Her face didn't change, but there was something about her eyes that seemed a shade softer, perhaps a trifle less guarded. She stared away from Merry, down the soggy street. There was no sound except for the forlorn splashes from passing cars and the insistent low strum of raindrops hitting the pavement.

"Come at seven o'clock tomorrow." Cassandra tossed out the words, then she swept away down the street, leaving Merry gaping at her back. "And bring some wine."

She said yes. Merry did a little hop.

She jogged down the street toward the diner, ignoring the rain now bombarding the ground with even greater force. She was drenched in less than a minute, but she didn't care. She had spoken up for herself and she was going to get a second chance. She could try again.

Rita was nursing a cup of tea and hunched over a newspaper when Merry arrived. She acknowledged Merry with a curt nod and stood up to leave without saying a word. Merry followed her out to the truck. Well, I guess I can't expect two miracles in one day. She ducked her head and grinned into the collar of her jacket as she pulled herself up into the passenger seat.

~ * ~

Merry rubbed her sweaty palms against her jeans. She had been so sure that she would never be in this cabin again, here with Cassandra, sitting before the humming wheel. Yet here she was, and Cassandra was going to let her try again. Her hands shook. She wanted to do this, she wanted to learn this, but it had all turned out so badly last time.

Cassandra carried over two steaming mugs of coffee. Merry sipped from the heavy cup and closed her eyes. The coffee was strong, fresh, and very dark. I can do this. If I try hard enough, I can do this. She opened her eyes and saw Cassandra hovering close by, looking down at her.

Her lips curled into a line of wry amusement, but at least this time her smile wasn't malicious and cold. Cassandra for once wasn't examining her as if she were something rather loathsome.

"Okay," Cassandra said, straddling a chair across from her. "You'll remember from our last not-so-great lesson," Cassandra rolled her eyes, but she was still smiling, "that the first step is centering. So simple, but not so easy. Hands like so." Cassandra helped Merry position her hands around the wet ball of clay. "Push in and down. The wheel needs to turn fast. This time, close your eyes and just feel the clay as you push it. As it starts to center, you'll feel the even smoothness just emerge."

It was just as bad as the first time. The clay spun and lumped and formed ridges instead of becoming smooth. The more she pushed, the bumpier it became. A clutch of despair sunk into her stomach, and a film of sweat covered her forehead. It was going to be just the same. She couldn't do this. It was a waste of time. She lifted her foot off the pedal and let the wheel glide to a stop. She waited for Cassandra's sarcastic comment.

"It's hard at first," Cassandra's voice was soft. "But you'll get it. You just have to keep at it. If you really want to do this and you keep at it, you can do it."

Cassandra moved her chair around to sit beside Merry. The heavy musk of Cassandra's perfume layered over the sharp, clean scent of the wet clay. Cassandra placed her hands over Merry's. "Start the wheel."

She guided Merry's hands against the clay, at first gently, then with more force. Merry felt the clay give way, the bumps softening and flattening, as if the clay were surrendering in her hands. Slowly, Cassandra moved her hands away. "Keep going. You've got it now. Keep it wet. Drop more water on it when it starts to get dry."

A few moments later, Merry beamed as she lifted her hands away from a shiny, symmetrical clay dome. I did it. I really did it.

Cassandra nodded her head. "Now, opening..."

An hour later, Merry's back and hands were aching, but sitting on the wheel before her was a small, crooked cylinder, roughly resembling a sticky thick-walled volcano. She had labored hard at opening the dome and pulling up the walls, and several times the little pot had simply collapsed under her hands, a slippery mangled mess, and she had to begin again. But Cassandra had urged her forward, told her to keep working, and now she had really done it. She had made a pot. She started to chuckle.

"I think I'll name it Mount Vesuvius. Maybe when it's done I'll put red flowers in the top to complete the picture."

Cassandra laughed too, and Merry looked up in surprise. She had never heard Cassandra laugh before, and it was a deep, rich sound.

"It's not a bad first effort. Really. We'll cover it with some plastic and wait for it to get leather-hard, and in a couple of days you can come and trim it. Now let's have some wine."

Merry grinned and stood up from the wheel, her legs wobbling and almost giving out from sitting so long in one position. She plopped onto the couch and leaned her head back against the pillows. The little pot that sat drying on the shelf was thick and crooked, to be sure, but it was a pot and she had created it. She had done it. She felt absurdly proud. She looked over at Cassandra, who was staring into her goblet and swirling her red wine.

"Thank you," Merry said. "Really, thank you. This was amazing."

Cassandra glanced over at her. "Well, you know you have a long way to go, but you're welcome." Cassandra turned to face her, a small frown wrinkling her forehead. "It sure was touch-and-go there for a while. Why do you give up so easily?"

Merry sighed and looked up at the cabin rafters. "I don't know. I guess I don't have a lot of self-confidence right now. Things haven't exactly gone my way lately—"

She stopped abruptly. There was only danger in talking about herself. She needed to change the subject. "Cassandra, you said you didn't give lessons, but then you let me come here after all. Why?"

Cassandra grimaced and stared up at the ceiling. She took a big gulp of the second glass of wine she had just poured for herself. "You can see the beauty in the work. Not everyone can." She looked at Merry. "Like those two old cows in the gallery."

Merry's eyes widened. Of course. She'd been there, in the back. "So...you heard my great sales pitch? My outstanding customer service?" Merry grimaced. "I'm glad you heard it instead of Moira."

Cassandra shrugged. They sat for a few minutes, sipping the wine. Outside, a lone raven repeatedly gurgled a resonant bell-like kloo-klak. Merry closed her eyes and cycled through the evening in her mind, step by step, trying to remember all that her hands had learned.

She opened her eyes and looked around the studio. "Cassandra, you do the most beautiful work." She swept her arm wide toward the wooden shelves stacked with vases, bowls, and pitchers, some finished and shining, others only partially constructed awaiting trimming, glazing, or firing. "It's as unusual and lovely as any pottery I've ever seen anywhere. There has to be a big market for this. Have you ever tried to sell outside of Alaska? You are so talented. You could work almost anywhere."

Merry watched with alarm as Cassandra's expression hardened. It was the old Cassandra now, her face rigid, her dark eyes flashing and cold. What have I done to upset her now?

Cassandra stood and walked toward the door. "I think we're done for today," she said, opening the door. "I have some work to do."

Merry pushed herself up from the couch, confused and hurt. She paused on the threshold and turned to

Cassandra. "Thank you, really. It was an amazing evening for me."

Cassandra's shoulders drooped slightly. Her voice was quiet when she spoke. "You're welcome. We can work again in a couple of days. You'll see, it will start to come easier."

She looked straight at Merry, and her face was calm, no longer hostile, just sad. Her mouth twisted into a small, crooked smile. "You aren't the only one around here who doesn't want to talk about the past." She gently pressed the door shut.

Merry stood for a moment, looking back at the closed door. Cassandra, brash and brilliant and beautiful. It seemed that Cassandra had a secret too.

~ * ~

Her eyes closed as she settled her head against the pillow. Memories of the day cascaded into her head, reappearing in snippets like a fast-forwarded movie. It had always been this way for her. She needed the quiet time, a plateau after the experiences of the day, to tumble events gently in her head, not really thinking about them, but observing them, sorting them, making them a part of her.

She thought of her own hands in the clay, pushing, molding, seeing the vessel's shape appear from the shiny lump in front of her. She remembered the awe she felt when a form emerged from the strength of her fingers. It was the stuff of magic. She saw Cassandra, mouth curled into an imperious smile, holding a wineglass, staring at her with cold eyes. And Cassandra again, this time her face gentle, closing the door as Merry left.

She remembered Nick, who had come by that morning, bringing some more halibut fillets for their dinner. She pushed her face into her pillow and grinned. She had never in her life eaten so much fish. Once again, she replayed the sensation of the slide of his finger against her hand on the dock. She was almost sure, almost positive, that he had stroked her palm. Such a little thing, but it could mean so much. Or maybe it meant nothing. Maybe he'd done it absently, not even realizing it. In the days that had followed, he didn't say or do anything differently than he had before. Well, maybe he smiled at her a little longer. But maybe he didn't. And he seemed to like to talk with her now. Maybe this was all in her head. And what about Nick and Cassandra? What was going on there? She flipped onto her side and hugged her pillow to her chest. I've got to stop this. It's like I'm sixteen again and I'm wondering if he'll ask me to the prom.

As she did almost every night, she promised herself that she would make a plan, figure out what she should do next. Every day she continued to stay here made any thought of going home and facing the music all the harder to imagine. She tried to be logical, she really did, and forced herself to march in her mind the path she needed to travel. She envisioned making arrangements to go home, then confessing and saying good-bye to everyone here. How would she explain it? Well, she had gone a little crazy after the accident. Maybe she was even delusional. But then the events of today crept back into her thoughts, and instead of thinking about going home, she was remembering that Rita was humming some old tune under her breath at the breakfast table, and that Nick had been wearing a bright blue shirt that made his eyes glow.

But when she finally slept, she didn't dream about the day. She dreamt of Michael.

It was years and years ago. Michael had rushed into their cramped first apartment, banging open the door as he always did, grabbing her around the waist, and twirling her around the room. He was laughing—something exciting had happened at work—and he stood in the kitchen with her and poured them both long-stemmed glasses of icy white wine while she tossed a salad. But then he took the wineglass from her hand and pulled her away to the bedroom, and they stood together, naked, as Michael ran his hands gently down her back and dropped his head to tease her nipples with his tongue. Desire snaked through her, heat rising from deep inside her as she reached for him, and her shuddering climax shook her awake, her breath coming in shallow gasps.

She lay still, hearing her breath slowly return to normal, relieved as she realized that the attic door and Rita's closed bedroom door were surely sufficient to block any moans or cries she might have been making in her sleep. She cupped her hand over the wetness between her legs and sighed. The unexpected pleasure, the release, made her body rest heavy and soft under the blankets she had piled over the bed against the cold air. As she stared up at the darkened ceiling, the fog in her mind lifted, and she remembered. In the dream it had been Michael sucking hungrily on her breast, but as she came, as all the tension inside her burst into a great exploding, it had been Nick who was kissing her, it had been Nick who was inside of her, as their bodies arched, joined, and shuddered together. In the end, it was Nick.

She turned on her side and curled her body into a fetal position around the bunched blankets. In moments, she was asleep again.

Nineteen

She stared at the blank computer screen. The gray plastic frame was cracked and grimy with fingerprints, and the squat body of the computer hummed wearily in front of her. A faint smell of hot electrical wiring hung in the air. "Yes, they're old," the librarian had said, pointing to the three public computers lined up at the back of the reading room. "We'll be getting some new ones very soon. But these work just fine, at least most of the time. That one on the far end is the most reliable. Let me know if you need any help getting started." And then she'd marched back to the front desk where she was now shuffling through some papers, glancing back at Merry from time to time.

Merry had been sitting there, in front of the old machine, for almost fifteen minutes. A peeling laminated page of instructions hung on the wall behind the computer. The thick, bold printing told her exactly what to do to get to the Internet.

She rested her fingers ever so lightly on the keys.

There was probably an obituary. She shivered, and her hands retreated into her lap. The idea of looking up her own obituary was terrifying, bad luck somehow, as if it would mean that she was really dead.

There might have been a story about the accident in the paper back home. Probably just a mention that a local woman had died.

Her hands stayed in her lap. Her palms were sweating, and she rubbed them against the legs of her jeans.

She could look up the law firm website to see what Michael's profile said now. Would it say that he was still married?

"Are you having trouble?" Merry jumped, startled.

The librarian hovered over her. Merry hadn't heard her coming.

"No, no, thank you. I'm just thinking." She gave the librarian a weak smile. "I'm doing just fine, thank you."

She turned back to the computer screen and put her fingers on the keyboard. Do something. She punched in the address for the National Public Radio website and the day's news popped up. The librarian nodded and smiled. Her heels clicked on the wood floor as she moved back to the front desk.

Merry saw words on the screen, but her brain only scanned them as meaningless patterns. She had no interest in the day's news. The world outside seemed so distant. She had forced herself to come into the library, reasoning that she might make some electronic connection to her old life that would help her to move forward. She had to make a plan. She needed to decide what she was going to do next. But as pictures of world events flashed at her from the screen, she sat mesmerized, but not by the images on the screen. Her eyes refused to focus, and her fingers didn't tap the keys to lead her toward home.

Home. What did she miss, she wondered. If she didn't think about the people, just "stuff," it was hard to put much on that list. They had their townhouse, neat and orderly. A little too flashy for her taste, but very stylish, and it worked well when they entertained Michael's clients or partners. She had loved to walk alone on the short path that led her down from the townhouse to the white-sand beach in the early morning, when she could hear the shorebirds crying out and diving for their breakfast. But by midmorning, the sand was usually littered with visitors on oversized beach towels and collapsible chaises.

She had personally chosen all the furnishings for the townhouse, and they fit the spaces well, but she thought of them with little attachment. She was fonder of the crooked Vesuvius pot she had made with Cassandra than the expensive museum replicas scattered around their living room. Everything about her home was comfortable, because it was familiar, but nothing about it called her back. And now that she had found an extra pillow and moved the attic bed a little further from the sloping ceiling, her little room at Rita's was cozy and warm. Sure, she'd had to run down a few spiders from the rafters, and she had a suspicion that the little pile of sludge she'd found by the door might be vole droppings, but she was snug there.

Her clothes? She smiled as she looked down at the cheap pink cotton shirt she was wearing over the faded jeans. As she shifted her weight in the chair, the scratchy wool of her thick socks made her ankles itch. Nowadays she wore the too-big clothes from Rita's attic dresser, and for the work at the gallery, some slightly nicer and much better-fitting pieces that she and Rita had picked out from the Salvation Army store. She had felt guilty about having Rita pay for them, though they didn't cost much, but she had to have them, and she wore them for the job that kept a roof over both their heads. In the narrow attic closet, her "good" clothes hung from five bent metal hangers. At home, her walk-in closet showcased more dresses and coats and pants than she could keep track of, all hanging in proper order on polished wood hangers. Yet, there wasn't a single piece she missed. It was actually a relief, in the morning now, to have such a limited choice. It was the black sweater or the blue tunic or the white blouse, the gray pants or the black pants.

Access to the health club gym near midtown? She'd been religious in her attendance, hefting her barbells and rolling through her Pilates routine several times a week. When she caught her reflection in a mirror or shop window now, she didn't think she looked any the worse for wear. Her legs were cut into muscled planes from the long treks to and from town, sometimes toting bags of groceries and supplies if she couldn't get a ride back, sometimes battling the wind and biting rain. Her back stood strong and straight. Her face was a little more weathered, she thought, but lean and brown with a healthy glow. She'd always thought she looked a little too delicate, with her very slim profile and long, narrow bones, but now she felt different, more solid.

So what did she miss? As the computer continued to hum and refresh the screen with updated photographs of international news, she leaned back in her chair and thought about that question. She regretted that she had run out of the small cache of expensive face cream that had been in her travel bag. The cheap drugstore replacement she found didn't smell half as nice. It would be pleasant, she thought, to have some new panties, because the five pairs that had come in a pack from the Pic-N-Save were already looking pretty gray and threadbare. But, after all, no one was seeing them but her. She had to reach, she realized, to find things she really missed, and none of them seemed very important now. She had enjoyed the elaborate trappings of her life in Florida—the expensive clothes, the tasteful art objects, and the luxury products. But none of them tugged her back.

She heard the faint tap of the librarian's shoes across the floor, so this time she didn't jump when the woman crept up next to her and cleared her throat to get her attention. "I'm so sorry, but I have to close up for lunch. I'll only be gone for about forty-five minutes if you want to come back later."

"Maybe. Thanks." Merry switched off the computer and stood up slowly, stretching her arms. She'd been sitting very still for a long time and her body was stiff. Then she grabbed her jacket and headed out the door. She thought she'd stop for coffee and then decide. She wasn't sure, but she didn't think she was coming back.

~ * ~

Merry took her cup of steaming black coffee from the waitress in the tie-dyed apron at The Twins and found a seat in the far corner of the main room. The restaurant was buzzing with the morning rush. Most of the mismatched chairs at the scarred oak tables were filled, and loud conversations rose and fell, competing with the clatter of pans and the loud swoosh of the espresso machine from the open kitchen. Scents of sweet and savory pastries hung in the air. It was below freezing outside, but it was hot and humid inside. Merry wrestled out of her jacket and dropped her gloves onto the table.

She was comfortable in the corner, almost completely hidden behind a tall and leggy split-leaf philodendron that drooped over her table. She settled back into her chair, sipping the dark bitter coffee, content to watch the bustling crowd before her. At the next table, a mother in denim overalls was trying to talk her toddler into eating some tiny orange carrots, while she spooned a white gruel into the mouth of a pink-cheeked baby perched on the tabletop in a carrier. The baby looked in Merry's direction and grinned, baring toothless gums and a mouthful of white mush. Merry felt a pull deep in her heart as she smiled back. A lump started to rise in her throat, and she quickly turned her attention away from their table to the center of the restaurant. It's been a long time, she thought. I thought it wouldn't hurt so much after a while.

She was gazing across the room at nothing in particular, thinking about the hours ahead, when Nick and Cassandra strolled through the door. Cassandra was looking over her shoulder at Nick and laughing, and Nick was guiding her forward with his hand resting lightly on the small of her back. Merry watched as they stood at the counter staring up at the menu scrawled on the whiteboard, placed their orders, then sat down at a table that had just opened up.

She had a fleeting thought that she shouldn't be watching them, that it seemed vaguely like spying, but she couldn't turn her eyes away. She hunched even deeper into her covered alcove and saw Cassandra lean forward over the table, staring into Nick's eyes. She said something, and they both laughed again. Nick stood to pick up their cups and pastries from the counter, and Cassandra's eyes tracked him.

Merry studied them carefully. She felt confident that every move Cassandra made showed that she was in love with Nick. It was there in the way she smiled up at him, crinkling her eyes, letting her face be open and happy with an expression that Merry had never seen her show to anyone else. The abrupt and aloof Cassandra simply disappeared when Nick was around. But what about Nick? He seemed to care about Cassandra, and it always looked like he enjoyed being with her, but Merry didn't quite see that he felt the same single-focused devotion. She shook her head. Maybe that was just wishful thinking on her part. She had to admit to herself that her feelings for Nick had gone from an active dislike of him to something much warmer. I'm just lonely and he's been around. That's all that's going on.

She watched Cassandra make large, graceful, sweeping gestures with her hands as she talked, her eyes always staring right into Nick's. I bet she's talking about her work, Merry thought. She always does that when she's excited about her work.

Merry knew a lot more about Cassandra and her habits now. She and Cassandra had fallen into a sort of pattern, though Merry wouldn't have called it a routine, because Cassandra was too unpredictable. Two or three times a week after dinner, and sometimes during the day if she wasn't needed at the gallery, Merry walked up to Cassandra's cabin. She practiced on the wheel, or worked with slabs or coils at the canvas-covered table where they constructed handles for the pitchers and hand-built some of the larger pieces. Merry's bowls and cylinders were still thick-walled and often crooked, but she could see improvement in her work. As she struggled, she felt even more admiration for Cassandra's talent. Cassandra's hands flew over the clay with both strength and delicacy, as the walls of her vessels rose tall and straight. And when Cassandra worked on altering the thrown forms, Merry watched in awe. She bent, cut, and reattached the hardening clay into amazing asymmetrical shapes. Her taller forms often seemed to be stretching up, reaching for the sky.

Merry helped around the studio, hauling bags of clay and mixing pails of glazes. She learned how to load the unfired pots and to keep watch over the kiln in the attached shed out back. A lot of it was tedious hard labor, but it was all worth the privilege of plunging her hands into a ball of soft clay and willing a form to emerge.

Yet there were times when Cassandra's mood turned black for no reason that Merry understood. One evening Cassandra simply stopped her at the front door and told her to go away, closing the door firmly in her face. On another day, Merry watched as Cassandra sat quietly at the wheel, staring at a hump of clay, and then she started to tremble. A hint of a whimper escaped her lips, and she quickly rose and poured herself a big glass of red wine, although it was barely past noon. She stood, taking deep breaths, then a big gulp of the wine, holding the stem of the glass so tightly that her knuckles had turned white. At first, Merry asked her if she was all right, but Merry soon discovered that Cassandra rejected any attempt to help or comfort her, and she wouldn't answer any questions. Merry learned to just wait. Cassandra would either make it clear that Merry should leave, or she would suddenly pull herself back from the brink of whatever emotional cliff she was teetering on.

When Cassandra wasn't in her dark mood, Merry could tell that she had softened toward her. They'd laughed together over some of Merry's unsuccessful attempts on the wheel. Cassandra even teased her now and then, especially when Merry started to get frustrated. And they often shared a glass of wine at the end of the evening, after they'd cleaned up the wheel and put the clay away, though Merry noticed that Cassandra usually seemed to have started drinking before Merry arrived. A half-filled bottle of red wine and a smudged long-stemmed glass were common fixtures on the table behind the wheel.

Though their relationship had definitely changed, Merry understood that they both had set limits. They spoke a lot about the craft and art of the pottery, and maybe a little about the gallery and life in Homer. But they didn't fall into familiar banter, dropping little bits and pieces of information about their lives, the way that Merry knew two women usually did when their friendship started to grow. At first, Merry had been on guard for questions about where she had come from, why she was in Homer, and what her plans were, but Cassandra never asked. And though she wondered about Cassandra, she kept her curiosity in check. To ask about Cassandra's life would be to invite questions about her own: questions she couldn't answer.

Merry glanced down at her empty coffee cup and thought about getting up for a refill. But then she'd have to pass their table, and she'd have to stop and smile and greet them. She didn't want the small orbits she had with each of them to converge. She didn't want her fragile relationship with Cassandra to shatter as she thought it might, as she imagined Cassandra's eyes flicking back and forth to Nick, then back to her. And she didn't want to stand side by side with her new friend in front of Nick, to have him look from the fiery flame of Cassandra to her, standing smaller and simpler in her drab hand-me-downs. No, she'd stay put in her corner.

Cassandra was pushing her loose, black curls behind her ears. Nick was leaning back in his chair, brushing crumbs from his shirt. She and Cassandra never spoke about Nick. Merry, gently probing, had thrown Nick's name into their conversations a few times, but Cassandra always changed the subject or ignored Merry's comments entirely. Since the first time that Merry had watched Cassandra and Nick outside the gallery, she had seen them together on half a dozen other occasions, at the gallery or on the street. She had never again seen that haunted look of love and desperation on Cassandra's face, but she didn't doubt that she had recognized it.

And, she had to admit, there was some relief in the fact that Cassandra didn't talk about Nick. Merry wasn't sure of her own feelings about him, but she found him in her thoughts a lot these days. If Cassandra spoke up and staked a claim to Nick, Merry realized it was going to be hard to push those thoughts away.

She continued to watch them now. After a few minutes, Nick looked at his watch, and they both stood up to leave. Merry sat still, cradling her mug in her hands. The morning crowd had started to thin and it was much quieter now. Even the young mother and her two kids had left. She looked over at their now empty tabletop, seeing blotches of white goo and the partially chewed remnants of carrots, and then she stood up. It was time to move on.

Twenty

Scary and Miles's opening reception for their show at The Twins had been scheduled at the very last minute. Merry hesitated at the door, looking into the crowded restaurant. She had told them she would come. She had to at least drop in and make an appearance. She wove her way through the group standing and laughing in the small entry, nudging past protruding arms and legs, and edging around the rack of heavy coats. Inside, the space was packed full of locals standing elbow-to-elbow, clear plastic glasses of wine in their hands.

When Scary and Miles had dropped by to see Rita the day before, they asked both Rita and Merry to come by for the opening. Miles told Merry that they were nervous about the reception, afraid that no one would show up. Rita grumbled that she was just too tired and begged off, saying she wanted to rest. Merry was starting to get worried about her. She moved even more slowly these days, taking her time as if to muster her strength before rising from a chair, huffing and puffing after climbing up the three steps to the cabin. She'd snapped, "Leave me alone, girl. I'm just old, that's all," when Merry had asked if she was feeling all right. Maybe I should talk to Nick about her. Merry knew how much Rita would hate that. She couldn't stand anyone fussing over her, but Merry felt protective of her these days. Neither of them had said the words, but she knew that she was much more than just a casual temporary boarder now. Rita depended on her, as much as she might not want to.

What will she do when I leave?

Scary's frantic waving caught her attention and scrambled her thoughts. He pointed from across the room to a corner where a large table was covered with stacked columns of plastic glasses, open bottles of wine, and a messy platter of cheeses and mostly broken crackers. She smiled back at him and threaded her way through the crowd toward the table. Today, Scary was clad in leaf green from head to toe, including a shiny tight-fitting shirt that looked to be made of satin, a pair of bright green sneakers, and a jaunty gondolier hat. Merry grinned, remembering Rita had told her that the wilder the outfit, the happier Scary was. He must be pretty darn happy tonight, she thought. Miles, by contrast, had come in pressed dress slacks, a white shirt, and a buttoned vest. In the midst of the raucous Homer crowd, Merry thought Miles looked much more out of place than Scary.

She was thinking about Rita, wondering if she should wrap up a piece of the reception cake for her, when Scary appeared at her side and put his arm around her. "Merry, thank goodness you've come. It's so wonderful you're here." His other arm swept to the side in a broad arc that whacked against Millie, the owner of the local bookstore, and knocked her wine glass from her hand. A little fuss ensued, as Scary apologized profusely, and Millie frowned at him and swiped at her dress with a paper napkin. Scary reached over to the table and quickly downed an available glass of wine. Not his first tonight, Merry thought.

"We're so excited everyone is here," Scary said, pouring a glass of wine and pressing it into Merry's hand. He had filled it all the way to the brim, and she almost spilled it as she took it from him. "You just drink up and join the party." He waved at Miles across the room and headed in his direction. Merry sipped her wine, surveying the room, and was surprised at how many people she recognized. Millie was still mopping at the front of her dress and talking to Gerry from the auto shop. Miles was deep in a discussion with Johnnie from the Pick-N-Save, gesturing at one of the paintings. Merry ducked a little farther back into the crowd, finding a spot against the far wall. She suspected that Johnnie had a crush on her. He always went out of his way to prolong conversation with her when he was bagging her groceries, and sometimes he followed her out the door. She didn't relish getting trapped in conversation with him here, without a graceful getaway plan. She shifted her gaze and watched as Anastasia, the part-time librarian, carved herself a generous piece of the cake on the counter.

How long had she been here? Eight or nine weeks? And she knew more people at this party than she did at most of Michael's events, even after all these years. She shook her head and continued to scan the room.

A hand cradled her elbow and she found Nick next to her. As she turned to face him, she was pressed up against him by the crowd, and she could feel her face warm. He smiled down at her. "Merry, glad to see you made it. Here, let me get you another glass of wine."

She looked down at her glass in surprise. Somehow, she had finished the glass she had been holding without noticing. "Nick, I'm not much of a drinker. I'd better slow down." But he had already filled up a new glass for her, and she took it from him. The cold white wine did taste good, tart and dry and a little fruity. She took another sip. She was enjoying the ebb and flow of the crowd, the animated voices rising and falling, and she was pleased, very pleased, that Nick had found her. He made no move to leave. They both leaned against the wall, looking out over the room.

"What do you think of their work?" he asked.

She hadn't yet made it around the room to see all the paintings, but she studied the ones closest to her. Scary painted scenes of Homer in a very traditional style, realistic and serene. In the painting right beside her, soft fog floated over the tops of dreamy firs, while an open orange boat tied up at the shoreline seemed to bob quietly on steely blue calm water. Miles's paintings, on the other hand, were more abstract, with bolder colors and stronger strokes, suggesting rather than showing the rugged mountains, an impenetrable forest, restless waters. Rita had told her that Scary and Miles had shared a studio for years. Although their styles were dramatically different, Merry thought they complemented each other—Scary depicting the beauty of the landscape quietly at rest; Miles showing the wild and sometimes violent spirit of the place.

She struggled to put her thoughts into words. "I don't know a lot about painting." She hesitated. "But there is some synergy here I think, with their paintings together creating an impression of the landscape that you wouldn't get if you only looked at their work individually."

She wondered if she sounded foolish, and she tilted her head up to look into Nick's face. There was something about the way he was staring down at her, as though she were the only person in the room, that made her stomach drop. She quickly looked away from his eyes, down to the floor, but then she turned back, held his gaze, and smiled.

He took her glass and put it on the table. It was empty again. Perhaps, she thought, that was why she felt a little breathless as he took her hand, steered her toward the door, and out into the parking lot.

"It's too hot and crowded in here. Let's go up to my cabin," he said, opening the truck door for her. His voice had a low, rough edge. She climbed into the cab, not saying anything. She had never been to his cabin before, but Rita had pointed it out once on their drive into town. It stood alone in an old oat field on a high bench of land above the highway, looking out over the spreading expanse of the bay. The truck engine growled and protested on the short steep ride up the hill. They didn't talk, but after a minute Nick reached over and covered her hand with his while he drove. She exhaled in a quiet hushed gasp, but didn't move her hand away. She kept her eyes looking straight ahead, but inside she was quaking. She opened her mouth to say something, to say that the wine had gone to her head and that maybe she should just go home, but then she took a deep breath and closed her eyes. She wasn't sure what she was feeling, but she wasn't ready to have it stop quite yet.

~ * ~

As soon as Merry walked through the cabin door, she started to shiver. The air was freezing inside, maybe even colder than outside, so cold that she could see her warm breath tumble in small, white clouds. Nick grabbed a thick blanket from the chair near the door and wrapped it around her shoulders. His fingers pressed against her arms before he moved to the fireplace, and his light touch made her shiver even more. Her breath caught in her throat.

She glanced around her. An open door led into a small bathroom and a partially separated kitchen nook, but most of the small cabin seemed to be this one room. A sofa and two chairs were pulled close to the hearth nestled near the far wall. Everything was spare and simple. A huge high bed covered with a puffy, white comforter was tucked against the far wall, next to a wooden table overflowing with books and papers. She found herself staring at the bed. She turned away and looked down at the floor, feeling herself blush.

Nick hovered over the hearth, piling some twigs into the fireplace. She pulled the blanket close around her and watched him break apart small branches and pile wood, her eyes drifting to the long, straight line of his back and legs. Why had she ever thought him unattractive? There was such strength in him, strength in the power of his body, but strength, too, in his clear way of seeing things, and his kindness and care for Rita. These past few weeks, she realized, her impression of him had completely changed. She no longer thought of him as abrupt and overbearing. She could see now that what she took for rudeness was just his manner of forthright honesty and directness. He seemed to have no use for pretense.

She gave her head a quick shake. What was happening here? She buried her face in the blanket, letting her breath warm the fabric against her skin. When she looked up, she saw him standing still, his eyes on her. The fledgling fire crackled behind him.

"You're cold. Come closer." His voice was low, soft. "Come and get warm."

She stood staring at him. She felt a pull, a gathering, right from her center. A pull toward him. She took an unsteady half-step forward.

"I'm...better. I'm feeling warmer."

He continued to look at her. He didn't move, but extended his hand and she walked to him slowly, almost without any conscious volition. She took his hand. It was warm and rough and absolutely steady. He pulled her in, pulled her to him, until they were standing very close to one another next to the hearth.

His wind-burned face tipped down toward her. "Merry," he said. His voice was husky now, and in his voice her name was a caress.

She trembled, feeling her hand in his, feeling his breath on her cheeks. Slowly, lightly, he began to stroke her arm with his other hand. She couldn't look up. She was a wild animal in a trap, and he was there to rescue her, gentling her, making her warm and safe, making her want to press against him, making her want to lift her face, even knowing if she did he was going to kiss her. And more.

And it would be so easy. She pictured them together in that down-covered bed, their bodies side by side, discovering each other, careless in their passion and delighted by the joy of it. She imagined savoring the weathered salty taste of his skin, the warm, musky scent of his chest where her head would rest, the ready surrender she would feel when he pulled himself over her. She could see it all, and she could have it—she could have him, right now. And she wanted him, so very badly.

But...she had never lied to him. She hadn't answered all his questions, and she had been evasive, but she hadn't lied to him. But this would be different. If she let this happen, if she made this happen, she owed him the truth. The truth about who she was, the truth about what she had done, the truth about what a coward and a liar she was. And after that, how could he care about her? How could he be anything but be repelled by her?

She shook her head slightly. It took all her will, but she pushed back from him.

"No," she said.

She felt his body tense. She didn't look up, but she could easily imagine the look of confusion and hurt on his face. She pulled her hand out of his and turned away.

"I'm so sorry. I can't explain. I just can't. I'm so sorry."

She almost ran to the door, throwing the blanket on the chair as she passed it. He moved to follow, but she turned around, holding her hand out palm forward, warding him away. "It's not far. I want to walk. Please. The wine...I need to clear my head."

"Merry..."

"Please, Nick. Please."

She closed the door behind her and ran down the road toward the highway, the full moon above lighting her way, the cold wind biting at her flushed face.

Twenty One

Merry crouched in the shelter of a cluster of driftwood thrown high above the tideline. The stiff breeze knocked scatters of sand against the cracked and weathered logs. Patches of gritty crystalline snow, flattened and hardened by the wind, stretched across the beach to the water. She barely noticed the sunlight playing on her face, or the sharp, salty, tangy smell from the ruffled blue water, or the calls of the squawking gulls riding air currents right in front of her.

All week she had been obsessing over Nick, wondering what would have happened if she'd made the other choice, the choice to stay with him. When she was feeling strong, she told herself that she'd done the right thing. She hadn't gone down a path that would only lead to heartbreak for both of them. She hadn't lied to him. But more often she ached at the thought of what that night might have been, how it would have felt to lie in his arms, to feel the power of him against her.

If Rita wondered why Nick hadn't been by all week, she didn't say so. Rita had suddenly decided to clean out the jumbled closet in her bedroom, and she'd spent most of the last few days laying out old outfits on the bed, hemming and hawing at great length about whether to keep them or not. She'd take a wrinkled dress out, drape it over the bed, frown at it as if it had done something wrong, then put it back in the closet. Then she'd sigh, and pull it out again. She'd often be working on the closet when Merry left for the gallery, and she'd still be fussing over some jacket or a pair of shoes when Merry came home.

Today was Monday and the gallery was closed. Merry had lingered with a cup of coffee at the kitchen table, and Rita was pulling on her old rubber boots, getting ready to go to town. They had both looked up, surprised, as an old blue mini-van careened up to the cabin, squealing and spraying ice chunks and rocks as it spun to a stop by the front door.

"It's Rachel." Rita frowned as a disheveled young woman lurched from the driver's seat. "Something's wrong."

Merry had only met Rachel once before at The Twins. She had bounced over to where Merry was sitting with Rita and given Rita a hearty hug and kiss. She'd introduced herself to Merry and explained that they were neighbors, that she lived just about a half-mile away, closer to the main road. Merry had been a little surprised Rachel greeted Rita so warmly, because Rita really wasn't a hugging type of person. But then she could see, as Rachel circulated through the crowded room, that she had a hug and a kiss for almost everyone. She was a tall buxom blonde, her cleavage pressing over the top of her low-cut T-shirt, her streaked hair flying in every direction.

Today Rachel hardly looked like the same woman. Her hair was flattened under a brown wool cap, her face was swollen, and her skin was red and blotchy. Her eyes brimmed over with tears as she stumbled to the front door. She looked at least ten years older than the happy, exuberant woman Merry had met in The Twins. She threw herself into Rita's arms, almost knocking the woman over, and sobbed. Her story came out in a quick flood of words. Adam was gone; he had fallen in love with someone else; her marriage was over.

Merry walked to the beach as soon as Rachel left. She leaned her head against a bleached log and closed her eyes, pushing her hands into the cool grainy sand. Rachel's tearstained face was so clear in her mind's eye. The image of Rachel slumped over Rita's table, crying over Adam's betrayal, shaking with hurt and loss, was raw and painful. Rachel, you're going down a hard road.

She shook her head, but the memories wouldn't go away. Remembering sent her slipping inside Rachel's skin and she felt Rachel's searing pain, and her own pain too, cutting fresh even after all this time.

It had been a beautiful Florida morning, soft-edged and warm, and Meredith had been interrupted by the sound of knocking. A froth of fuzzy blonde hair bobbed in the high window in the back door. She frowned. Betty Ann? It had to be Betty Ann, but what was she doing here? She hadn't called, and Betty Ann never stopped by uninvited.

When Meredith had opened the door, it was indeed Betty Ann. She tottered into the kitchen on the five-inch heels that made her tiny frame seem even smaller. "Oh, hello, Meredith," she had chirped, flashing a grin that somehow looked more determined than genuine. "I'm so glad I caught you. Are you busy?"

"Well, no, Michael had to run down to the office to pick up some work he forgot to bring home for the weekend. I'm just having some coffee..."

She cocked her head and looked at Betty Ann, who was rearranging the sugar and creamer set on the kitchen counter. "Betty Ann, is something wrong?"

"Oh, no, Mer," she had said a little too quickly. "I was just passing by and I thought I'd say hello. I just haven't seen you in a while. I just wondered...how are you doing?"

"Just fine, Betty Ann. It has been a while. Let me pour you some coffee."

Meredith had glanced at her guest as she filled another cup. Betty Ann was notoriously jumpy and birdlike, but that day she seemed unable to stay in one place, even for a few seconds. She moved around the kitchen, absently tidying a stack of papers by the phone, tapping her hot-pink fingernails rhythmically on the countertop, and brushing imaginary crumbs from her bright blue sweater.

Meredith had sipped her coffee and waited. She had

known the woman for years, well enough to know that her ditzy exterior covered a big and loyal heart. Two years before, when Betty Ann's son Casey had been injured in a nearly fatal car accident, they'd sat together in the hospital through a long, desperate night, Meredith holding Betty Ann's hand while Betty Ann cried, Meredith urging hope and optimism and patience. But she really hadn't seen much of Betty Ann lately. Suddenly, she had felt a stab of fear. "Betty Ann, is Casey okay?"

Betty Ann looked startled. "Casey? Oh, Casey's fine. He's off at basketball camp this week. He called last night and it sounds like he's having a great time." She smiled weakly and clutched her cup. "Oh, Casey's fine."

Betty Ann held the coffee cup in both hands, close to her chest. "I was just wondering, Mer, does Michael have family visiting in town right now?" Her lips curled into a small smile, but she wasn't meeting Meredith's eyes. Meredith had stared at her, puzzled. Something just wasn't right.

"Well, I don't think so. But his sister Sandy comes through here pretty often, and he doesn't always mention it to me if he just sees her during the workday. Why do you ask?"

Betty Ann turned away to pour some more coffee in her cup. The pot trembled ever so slightly in her hand. Meredith could tell by the smell that the coffee was getting stale. She started to offer to make a fresh pot, but Betty Ann's voice cut in.

"Well, that's probably just who I happened to see him with, yesterday afternoon, down at Murdoch Park, over by the lake. I was walking Missy down through the woods. It was such a beautiful day, and I didn't want to walk over and interrupt them, because they seemed to be so deep in conversation, you know. So involved, you know. And how nice that you'll be an aunt again soon. Sandy looked like she was pretty far along."

Betty Ann's voice fell away. Meredith stood

absolutely still. Sandy wasn't pregnant. Suddenly she understood. She understood what Betty Ann was trying to tell her, and how hard it must have been for her to come here. But still, she'd felt a flash of anger—anger at Betty Ann who had walked in the door and toppled her world. Her hands shook. She needed to be alone. The blood pounded in her ears. She didn't know if she could speak. Suddenly, the cup had slipped from her hands and smashed into shattered pieces on the kitchen floor.

Betty Ann gasped, her face a mask of worry. "Oh dear, goodness, let me help you." She grabbed a roll of paper towels from the counter.

Meredith's whole body was shaking. "No, it's all right, I'll do it..." She was stuttering, her throat was closing. Her stomach rose, and she was going to be sick. "Look, Betty Ann, I was just going out. Do you mind...could I talk to you later? I'll...I'll do this. Just later, okay?"

Betty Ann's face was full of sadness and understanding. "Okay. I have to get going anyway. I'll call you later, Mer. I'll call you this afternoon. Call me if you need me."

And she was gone. Meredith had leaned against the closed door, pressing her forehead to the smooth wood. Could it mean anything else? Could there be an innocent explanation? Did it really mean what it seemed to mean? Somehow, little pieces clicked into place in a larger puzzle frame. Michael working late, night after night. Michael hanging up the phone quickly when she came into the room. Michael... There was a deep pain in her chest, a deep ache.

Now, worlds away, the breeze ruffled her hair and cooled her face, drying the tears that had slipped down her cheeks. She could still feel the wound, even now, the deep, aching throb in her heart. It had been the beginning of the end. No, that wasn't right. The end had started long before, she knew that, but that morning with Betty Ann had been the beginning of the wrenching horrifying crash that had robbed her of the life she knew, or at least the life she thought she knew.

She stood up unsteadily, stiff from curling her body into the little shelter. She wiped her face with the back of her hand, but the bitter bay wind had long since dried her tears. She took a deep breath, and the clean salty air filled her lungs. That life belonged to someone else. She wasn't that person anymore. She started back down the beach.

Twenty Two

There was no sign, nothing to warn her that anything was wrong when Merry arrived back at the cabin, lugging the sack of groceries she'd picked up on her way home from the gallery. The wind was blowing steady and fierce, knocking the few remaining brown leaves off the trees, and rattling the frozen grasses along the roadside and in the meadow. The trace of snow that had fallen last week was rain-washed and hardened to a brittle crust that crunched under her feet. She'd been lucky to hitch a ride almost all the way back with Johnnie, the cashier who always flirted with her. She didn't have to shove the pile of groceries into Rita's shredding backpack and hike back along the side of the road like an overloaded Sherpa, which was what usually happened if Rita didn't show up to give her a ride.

The fact that Rita hadn't appeared wasn't troubling, either. Rita still treasured her independence, and Merry knew that she didn't want to be tied down to anyone's schedule. Sometimes Rita showed up, and sometimes she didn't. It wasn't that much of a walk, a mile or so, and even when the wind blustered and blew icy cold, as it did now so often, and the rain against her face stung like frozen needles, Merry could make it back just fine. Often, when the wind howled and whistled through the trees, and she walked huddled under the protection of her jacket, it was even strangely comforting. She was in her own world, then, completely self-contained, the bitterness of the weather offering a hostile but insulating barrier between her and a world of complicated entanglements and confusions. Her only task was to brave the elements and to make it back to the cabin without getting drenched and cold to the bone, and with enough luck to avoid any bear encounters. Simple.

She'd been thinking about the bear as she walked down the final stretch of road to the cabin. Don't run from a grizzly. Drop and play dead. Put your hands over your head. She'd memorized the mantra, but she questioned whether she could really do it if she had to face another bear. She had a strong suspicion that instinct would take over, and that she'd just run in the opposite direction as fast as she could, all lessons to the contrary. But they hibernate, don't they? Maybe it's asleep by now.

It was odd that the cabin door was slightly ajar, creaking back and forth as the wind gusted. Rita often left it open on warmer days, letting the fresh air carry the scent of the wet, earthy meadow into the kitchen, but not since winter had arrived in earnest, and not on a day like today. Perhaps it had blown open? The wind had picked up considerably in the last few minutes, and little twigs ripped from the battered trees knocked the side of the cabin like staccato birdshot.

Merry nudged the door open with her hip, dropped the bag onto the counter, and leaned hard to close the door against the gusting wind. She stood for a moment, savoring the silence of the room after the noise and turmoil outside.

A prickle of anxiety ran down her spine. She froze. Something was wrong.

The cabin was quiet. The thick log walls muffled the sounds of the storm outside. But something was amiss. Then she heard it. The slightest sound, a hint of a moan, from Rita's room.

Wary, she crept to the door. She gasped when she saw Rita sprawled on the floor, her eyes closed and her face slack, a pool of red under her head.

"Rita!" she shrieked, running into the room and crouching by her side. "Rita!"

Rita's lips trembled, but no sound came out.

Merry fluttered her hands around Rita, not touching her, trying to decide what to do. Her breath huffed in shallow gasps, and her brain didn't seem to be working right. She couldn't think clearly. She forced down a wave of panic and took a deep, shuddering intake of air. Pull yourself together. You're needed here.

She put her hand lightly on Rita's chest. She shouldn't move her, not until someone came. The blood. Yes, there, a cut behind her ear. Did she fall and hit her head on the side of the table? Maybe knocked herself out. What to do? No phone! Damn, no phone! She had to get help, but could she leave her here? It was dangerous to move her, but she couldn't leave her here. She had to take her to the hospital. But how?

Merry sprang to her feet and ran into the kitchen to grab a clean dishtowel. She pressed it against Rita's cut as gently as she could with her shaking hands. Rita didn't move.

But she was still breathing. Merry had to do something. Now.

Oh God, there's a lot of blood.

She wanted to yell for help, to scream, but there was no chance that anyone would hear.

"Rita, stay with me. I'll take care of you. I'm going to get you to the hospital. It's going to be all right."

It was a bad plan, but the only one possible. Merry had never driven Rita's battered, old truck. Rita had never offered it up, and anyway, it was a stick shift and Merry didn't know how. She knew where Rita kept the keys, on a nail above the sink.

Merry snatched the keys and ran for the truck. The wind hurtled down rain mixed with wet snow, big heavy drops that smacked her jacket and soaked her back. Her hands shook so badly that she dropped the keys on the truck floor, and she scrambled to find them among the debris of twisted old wires and flattened cans under the driver's seat. A razor-sharp can lid sliced into her left palm, but she hardly registered the bite of the cut. She jabbed at the ignition, missing the slot several times before the key found it. She twisted the key, and the engine jumped alive. She tried to take a deep breath, but her chest felt like it was pressed under a block of concrete. I can do this. I have to do this. There isn't any other choice.

She had seen her father drive a stick shift, and she was pretty sure that she remembered how it was supposed to work. But all she managed to do was produce a grinding shriek and stall the engine, time after time, when she tried to shift the gears. She pounded her fists on the steering wheel, her wet hair slapping into her face.

Wait, the other pedal...the clutch...

Shouting curses, she turned the key again and wrangled her feet against the clutch and the gas pedal. The car gave a lurch and popped forward, and stalled again. But this time she had it.

I can do this.

She lurched the truck, yard by yard, as close to the front porch as she could bring it, almost driving it up onto the first step. She left the engine running and ran back into the house. The towel she had placed under Rita's head was dripping and soggy with blood. Cursing again, she ran upstairs and grabbed a bath towel.

Rita was smaller and lighter than Merry, but not by much. She wound the bath towel as tightly as she could around Rita's head, then put her arms behind Rita's neck and knees and lifted. She felt her spine shift and pop as she stood, and a searing pain spun across her lower back and down her leg. She ignored it. Cradling Rita, she staggered through the kitchen and out into the storm.

The steps were the hardest. She tried to inch down them, taking each one slowly, pressing her back against the flimsy handrail for support. On the last step, her foot slipped on a slimy, slick leaf and her ankle bent almost to a right angle. She screamed in pain and almost dropped Rita. Rita's head dropped backward, and the rain hammered against her chalk-white face. Hobbling now, unable to put any real weight on her foot, she pushed Rita into the passenger seat and fumbled with the towel, trying to rewrap it tighter around Rita's head. Already the fringes were deep red with blood. Rita didn't stir.

She sobbed and cursed as she pulled herself around to the driver's seat, leaning onto the hood to keep weight off her left ankle, which throbbed rhythmically in time with her pounding heart. The storm threw rain against the windshield. Above her, the bare trees strained, knocked, and creaked, and a large branch broke loose, clattering against the side window, making her jump and cry out. She peered through the pattern of fallen leaves plastered onto the windshield to the muddy road ahead. Now do this. She stepped on the clutch with one foot and the gas pedal with the other, wincing in agony as she pressed her left foot down and inched the truck forward.

~ * ~

She huddled deep into the cold, white plastic chair in the waiting room, resting her head on her crossed arms, hoping that the pain medication would take effect soon. Her ankle throbbed and the slice in the palm of her hand was on fire. The shot Dr. James had given her before he stitched up her palm was wearing off, because now she could feel a deep, raging ache through her entire hand. Behind her eyes, a cruel insistent fist coiled and struck when she moved her head. She concentrated on breathing and keeping as still as possible.

Dr. James had patted her shoulder as he walked her out of the treatment room and back into the lobby. "You should feel better in a few minutes. Just sit here quietly." She'd heard him ask the nurse to bring her a bottle of water as he left, dropping his clipboard on the nurses' station on his way back into the emergency room. His footsteps echoed on the shiny, white linoleum floor. Her mind was foggy, dazed. It was better not to think about anything, just to breathe, just to keep still.

After a few minutes, Merry took a deep, shuddering breath and tried to sit up straight. Her head swam and she felt dizzy, but the staggering pain in her temples had receded just a little. She moved her bandaged ankle tentatively. Even the slight movement sent a searing line of pain through her foot. She tipped her head, bracing herself for the stab of the headache that was definitely less brutal than it had been, and eyed the crutches the nurse had left propped against the wall next to her. She wrapped her arms around her body. Breathe, she said to herself. Breathe. It's okay. It's over now.

She hadn't seen Rita yet, but Dr. James had assured her that Rita was going to be fine. Merry sobbed when he had sat down with her after leaving Rita's room. All the terror she had been holding at bay had broken loose, but then she could push the fear away. She's going to be all right.

Her lower back was stiff and burned when she twisted, but the doctor had said that it would settle down in a few days. The cut in her palm was angry and had started to swell. Dr. James said it should heal up quickly too. The ankle sprain might be bad, though. She might be hobbling for a while. She sighed. It didn't matter. All that mattered was that she had gotten Rita here in time, and that Rita was going to be okay.

She could feel a blanket of fatigue settling over her. Her body felt so heavy. She closed her eyes and leaned back against the hard chair. Rita is going to be all right.

"Merry? Merry, are you okay?"

She opened her eyes, and Nick loomed over her, concern and fear evident in his lined face.

"Merry, you look terrible. You look like you've been beaten up. Are you all right?"

She gave him a weak smile and tried to speak, but no words came out. He sat down in the chair next to her and took her hands, carefully cradling the bandage over her left palm. She felt a wave of relief wash over her. She wasn't alone now. Nick was here.

He squeezed her uninjured hand. "It's okay. Bill—

Dr. James—told me all about it. We're old friends. He said Rita will be fine. She'll be fine because of you, Merry. Because of what you did."

Tears leaked from her eyes and ran down her face. Yes, Rita was going to be okay. And Nick was here, the warmth of his hands so comforting. She didn't want him to ever let go.

Her words tumbled out now, though her voice was raspy and hoarse. "She has a heart condition. I...I didn't know. She never told me. And the doctor said she must have passed out and hit her head on the corner of the table when she fell. There was so much blood, Nick. I was so scared." Merry knew she was babbling, but she didn't care. Nick was here. She was safe.

"I know, I know. Rita's a tough, old bird, but sometimes not a very smart one. I've tried and tried to get her to put a phone back in, but she'll have none of it. Ever since..." He paused and shook his head, looking up to the ceiling and frowning. "But she's going to be okay, Merry. You got her here in time. She's going to have one hell of a headache I'll bet, and I know Bill is going to read her the riot act about taking care of herself when she's well enough, but she'll be fine."

She rested her hands in his. The past hours already felt like a foggy bad memory. *How did I ever get her here?* She was spent, and she doubted she even had the strength to stand now.

Nick reached over and put his arm around her, and she leaned into his chest, burrowing her face into his jacket, smelling the musty scent of his body and the wood smoke from his stove. They sat quietly for a few minutes. She felt like she could stay here forever.

Nick sighed. "She was lucky to have you there, Merry. I don't know what would have happened if you hadn't been there." He pulled away from her slightly and looked down at her face. "Bill said you were quite the sight coming in here, soaking wet, hopping on one foot, and screaming for help."

She smiled at his description. "I was a mess, I'm sure. I'm not much good at any of this sort of thing. I really didn't know what to do. Just dumb luck got us here, I think."

He frowned. "Merry, you are so much stronger than you give yourself credit for. I don't understand it. You didn't panic. You made this huge effort to get Rita in here. You fought for her. You probably saved her life." He paused and took a deep breath as he looked out over the brightly lit lobby, empty but for the two of them, sitting close in one corner.

"Not to mention that she's actually let you stay out there and help her. Rita doesn't take to everyone. Well, practically no one. But there's something peaceful about you, Merry. You're easy to be around. You let people be. You didn't expect her to change or be someone else for you. You don't push or probe. A person can be quiet with you."

She sat very still. Was all that true? Was that what she was really like? She frowned. Her mother, yes, her mother used to say that. Her mother said she had the gift of quiet strength. How could she have forgotten? With Michael she always felt like a drab brown sparrow, forgettable and inconsequential, next to the loud parrot-bright wives of his friends, and Michael was always impatient with her when she was lost in her own thoughts. She was sure that Michael had never thought she was strong.

She swallowed and cast around for the right words.

"Nick, about that night in your cabin. I never explained..."

He cut off her sentence with a shake of his head. "You don't have to explain anything. I got a bit carried away." He grinned at her, a little shyly. "Maybe we just need a little more time to get to know each other. Maybe it was all just happening a little too fast. Let's just get you and Rita taken care of and not worry about anything else right now."

She leaned back against his chest and he rubbed her arm, holding her close. She closed her eyes and felt some of the tension in her body release and relax. In this moment, she felt safe and warm and happy—yes, happy— even after all that had happened today. It had to be the pain medication. The ache in her back was more distant now, and the throb in her ankle less raw.

Nick's voice seemed to be coming from farther away now. "Let's just get you home. I told Bill you'd come back in a day or so to fill out the paperwork. It's not by the book, but he's a good guy and I just want to get you home now."

Paperwork. She frowned a little, trying to pull her fuzzy thoughts together. Paperwork. Medical forms...hospital. Of course the nurse had mentioned forms, medical cards, but there had been no time and so much chaos when she brought Rita in. She really couldn't focus. She would have to think about it later. Right now, though, it was enough to know that Rita would be okay, and that she would be okay, and that Nick had his arm around her. She didn't want to be anywhere else. She was content right here.

Twenty Three

Rita scowled when Merry and Nick arrived to drive her home from the hospital, muttering at them about too much fussing, but she leaned heavily on Merry's arm as she struggled upright from the deep armchair in the waiting room. She only had to stand, turn, and sit in the nearby wheelchair, but her face was pale when the nurse tucked a blanket over her knees.

"Are you sure she's okay?" Merry spoke quietly to Dr. James in the hallway.

"Well, you know Rita." Dr. James shrugged. "She won't stay here any longer, though I think at least one more night would do her good. But she tells me that she'll do fine, that you'll take care of her, so I think she'll be as well off at home as here. Just remember to get her to take her pills and call us if you have any problems."

Merry frowned. That would be a good trick, since we don't have a phone. But she and Nick had worked out a plan. He would take Rita's truck and leave his—an automatic transmission, thank heavens—so that she could get help if there was any problem. Rita had told Dr. James that Merry would take care of her. She felt a little flicker of happiness. I need to be here to help her.

Nick drove slowly over the bumpy road. Rita sat between them on the slippery bench seat. Merry didn't dare put her arm around Rita, so she pressed up close to steady her. Merry could feel Rita's weight leaning back into her arm. She looked over at Rita's pinched face. She couldn't tell if she was in pain or was just exhausted, but her eyes were closed and her head had fallen forward and was bobbing slightly with the rocking of the truck.

They hustled her into bed as soon as they reached

the cabin. Rita was barely awake, and she didn't protest as they fluffed her pillows and tucked her blankets. She closed her eyes almost immediately.

"If you need anything, just call me." Merry leaned close and ran her fingers gently down Rita's arm.

"Okay, Annie, okay..." Rita's words trailed off, and Merry could tell she was already asleep.

Annie again.

She hobbled outside, awkward with her sprained ankle in a tight compression bandage. Nick was sitting on the porch step with his legs pushed straight out in front of him, staring up into the sky above the meadow. "How is she?" he asked.

"Asleep." She sat down close to him and grabbed the tattered blanket Rita always kept on the porch, wrapping it around her shoulders. There was no wind today, but the temperature was well below freezing.

She hesitated for a moment. "Nick, who is Annie?"

Nick didn't answer right away. He kept staring at the meadow, at a bald eagle circling far above. "That's not my story to tell. Ask Rita." He glanced over at Merry, smiled, then got up and fished his keys out of his pocket, tossing them to her. "I'll check back here tomorrow morning." He walked down the steps and out toward the road.

"But," he said, turning and walking backward for a few steps, "you're wearing her clothes." He grinned and waved.

She looked down at the blue denim work shirt and worn jeans. Annie's clothes?

~ * ~

She stood in front of the dresser in the attic. She had been all through the top two drawers. Most of the clothes in the drawers were too big for her, but she didn't mind cinching in the jeans and flapping around in the big shirts. No one here minded much about clothes, and no one in town gave her a second look. But once or twice, when she'd come down the stairs in another sweatshirt or sweater, she thought Rita had gaped at her, just for a moment. Annie's clothes.

She'd stayed out of the bottom drawer. When she opened it on that first day, she saw that it didn't contain clothes, just some books and small boxes. She'd closed it then and hadn't opened it again since. But if Annie's clothes were in the top two drawers, what was in the bottom one?

She pulled out the drawer, wincing as the old wood squeaked. She ran her hands over the top of the boxes and books and hesitated. She suspected that she was invading Rita's privacy, but she found the mystery irresistible. The first books she pulled out were high school textbooks, battered and yellowed. In the front cover of one, she found "Annabelle Alagnagick" written in a round childish hand.

There was a box of pictures, faded and curling. A grinning round-faced, dark-haired teenager in a plaid shirt held up a shiny salmon. There were pictures of older women, sitting around a kitchen table, smiling widely right into the camera. All had some teeth missing. They were wearing brightly colored loose garments like heavy long-sleeved tunics, with hoods fringed in fur. Merry had seen some clothing like that displayed in the gallery. Kuspuks, she thought. From where? She frowned as she tried to remember. Somewhere in the middle of Alaska? There were some landscape photographs too, of small wooden houses heaped with snow crowding along the sides of a narrow street of ice, leading toward a flat, white horizon. No trees.

There were other books and boxes in the drawer, but she stopped. She nestled the box back into place and pressed the drawer closed. This isn't the way to find out about Annie. She would wait and ask Rita when the time was right.

~ * ~

She sat at Rita's bedside. The mid-morning sun

streamed through the window, making the dust motes dance. Merry could see diamonds in the snow outside. Over the past week, the sun had offered light but little warmth as the air temperature plummeted, and she knew the spread of snow in the meadow would be crisp and crunchy underfoot after the subzero night. When she went outside, she needed thick gloves now and something to cover her ears. Rita had brought her a good pair of bunny boots from the Goodwill store, and she wore them everywhere. Her thin canvas shoes sat at the foot of her bed, abandoned.

Rita had been getting up early every day. Dr. James had told her to move around, but he'd also said that she needed to rest for a little while, every morning and every afternoon. Rita refused to acknowledge any wisdom in that advice, and Merry had to nag her to lie down on the couch or in bed. They fell into a little ritual. Merry made Rita a cup of tea, then she picked up their current torchy novel and read aloud for a half-hour or so. Sometimes, when Merry glanced up, she saw Rita napping ever so lightly. But if she stopped reading, Rita snapped awake and glared at her. Being bed-bound had not improved Rita's disposition. She was clearly bristling and impatient with her own frailties.

When they took Rita to the hospital to have the stitches in her scalp removed, Dr. James talked quietly to Merry and Nick outside the treatment room.

"She really shouldn't be living on her own. It's all right now that you're around, Merry, but if you weren't, I don't know if she could get by. The medication will help, but only if she remembers to take it regularly, and she's so frail now that she could lose her balance and fall anytime. It's really crazy that there's no phone out there."

Nick shook his head, clearly frustrated. "No cell reception out there, and she won't let me have a landline put in. She had one years ago, but she had it taken out." He sighed. "I know it's crazy. I'm not sure what to do, but right now we'll just carry on. Merry's here now, and I'll go by every day."

Merry's heart had given a little flip of happiness. Every day.

He had been coming by at least once every day, usually in the afternoon, rolling up in his big, noisy truck, bringing some fresh bread, fruit, or fish for their dinner. She found herself glancing out to the road every few minutes after lunch, wondering when he was going to show up. And when she did see him coming, she always rushed into the tiny bathroom to run a comb through her hair. She smiled self-consciously into the dim mirror, a little embarrassed at herself, but enjoying the zing of anticipation and excitement she felt deep inside when she saw him. And she didn't think she was imagining that he was happy to see her too. He grinned and waved from the truck, hopping down from the high bench seat with his bag of whatever goodies he was bringing that day. He strode down the path to the cabin where she waited, opening the door for him.

He always went right to Rita first, asking her how she was feeling, and usually getting a glare and a shrug in answer. But Merry could tell from the sparkle in Rita's eyes that she looked forward to Nick's visits too. Merry made them coffee or tea, and they sat together at the kitchen table while Nick told them about what was going on in town, how the winter fishing season was shaking out, and whatever other news and gossip he had collected since the day before. The days had a quiet, timeless feel to them. It was easy not to dwell on the past or worry about the future, and instead just live the days as they came, watching over Rita, doing little chores, visiting with Nick and the few others who stopped by to see how Rita was doing.

~ * ~

A cold front settled over the peninsula, and the temperature plummeted to fifteen degrees below zero. The cabin stayed warm and snug for the most part, although icy air invaded around the window sashes where the seals leaked and took sneaky paths across the floorboards. Merry and Rita both wore their heaviest sweaters, and Merry kept a watchful eye on the fire crackling behind the grate. They had everything they needed to be safe, but the massive power of the world lurked outside and encircled the cabin. The heavy frigid atmosphere and prickling sting of the weightless drifting ice crystals were a palpable looming presences. It wasn't threatening exactly, but more of a reminder: Don't make a mistake. Make a mistake here and you can die.

They sat by the fire, ruffling through the newspaper. Rita sipped a cup of tea. Merry scanned the grocery ads for bargains. They both jumped at a loud knock on the door. Nick let himself in, huffing and stamping, bringing an eddy of cold inside with him. He grinned as they looked at him in surprise. "Don't worry. Everything's fine." He pulled off his thick wool gloves and tossed them onto the table. "I was driving home, and I decided there was something Merry should see tonight." He strode across the room and whispered in Rita's ear. She nodded.

Rita pointed her finger at Merry. "Merry, get your jacket on. And your hat and gloves, too. And wrap that fleece scarf over your face."

"What...why?" Merry peered at the dark window, edged with a rim of hard frost. The thought of going outside wasn't appealing.

"Just come and see. Don't you like surprises?" Nick's tone was unusually light and playful, and Merry smiled. Nick hardly ever teased.

"Now don't stay out long. You'll get frostbite in no time." Rita shifted in her armchair like an old hen settling on her nest. "And you might bring a few more pieces of wood when you come back in."

Merry bundled herself into her coat and pulled on her heavy boots. She wobbled as she straightened up. When she dressed for the weather, she felt like the Pillsbury Doughboy, clumsy and overstuffed in her bulky layers. Nick led her outside. "Close your eyes." He took her arm as they stepped off the porch.

Her eyes had watered from the first sharp splash of cold. As she squeezed them shut, she worried for a moment that her eyelids might freeze together. The insides of her nostrils stung as the subzero air slapped against her face, and her breath caught tight in her throat. Nick seemed to be leading her right into the meadow, away from the house. A hint of a breeze carried the sweet smell of dense wood smoke. The brittle ice crust over the snow crackled under her feet. After a few steps, they stopped.

"Now look up."

She opened her eyes to the cloudless night. Stars dotted the sky like white diamonds on black velvet. But then a shimmer, and another, as transparent waves of blue, green, and purple dropped and curtained the sky, appearing and disappearing, wavering, folding on themselves, washing across the sky. She realized she was holding her breath. Beautiful.

"We don't get Northern Lights that often here. They show up much more often up north. But a few times a year, especially when it gets really cold, we might see them. These are good ones, tonight, lots of color. What do you think?"

She gaped at the sky and shook her head. She had heard of the Northern Lights, the aurora borealis, but she never imagined the display of light playing across the sky existed in this world. A photograph wouldn't capture it. A photograph wouldn't show how the whole sky glowed afire with this eerie light, how the lights pulsed and twisted and ebbed and flowed, appearing from nowhere and then fading, gone, until more colors spun onto the black canvas of the night.

She felt Nick's arm around her, solid, and she leaned against him. Cold was already climbing up her legs and creeping down from the tops of her boots. They couldn't stay out here, still and quiet, much longer. But she lingered. This moment stamped itself into the fabric of her soul. The cold made her shiver, yes, but now it was only a distraction. The world above opened up to her, took her in, said to her, Look at all this, look at what you are a part of. Nick's gloved hand rubbed her arm. He was an integral part of this moment, too, this man who stood next to her, who had brought her outside to show her the universe.

She couldn't find the right words. "Wonderful," she whispered. And then, "I never knew."

His voice pitched low. "We should go in." He paused. "I just wanted you to see."

They stumbled back inside, their bodies stiff and awkward from standing in the frigid night. Nick hesitated just inside the door. Rita was nowhere to be seen, and her bedroom door was shut. Nick shuffled his feet. "I've got to go. It's late."

She nodded. "Thank you." They shared a look straight on, a look that lasted just a little longer than it had to.

In an instant he was in front of her, pulling her close, hugging her so tightly that she felt the power of his arms even through the heavy layers of clothing between them. Her face rose to meet his as he kissed her, gentle and long. He tasted of lip balm and coffee and wood smoke. He tasted exactly how she had imagined he would taste. She realized that she had been waiting for this moment, this moment when everything would change between them. When they broke away from the kiss slowly, they stood together, their foreheads touching. Her breath came fast and shallow, and she felt Nick's chest rising and falling, his breath mirroring hers.

Rita called through her closed bedroom door, "Merry, don't forget to check the fire before you go to bed."

Merry and Nick grinned at each other. Merry's voice rasped as she answered, "Sure, Rita. I won't forget."

He ran his arm up and down hers. "I'd better go. I'll see you tomorrow." He pressed his cheek against hers as he stepped away. They shared a smile before he shut the door quietly behind him.

She turned off the lights and moved to the window. She craned her head over the sink to look upward, but only a flat blackness pushed against the glass.

The fire had burned low, and she stirred the embers and snugged the grate in tight before turning toward the staircase. Her stomach was still fluttering, and her hands shook as she reached for the light switch.

Light shimmering and streaming across the night sky.

Nick.

I never knew.

~ * ~

She surprised herself by falling asleep right away, but she awoke, fully alert, very early in the morning. All was quiet downstairs. It was too early even for Rita, and she often thumped around long before six o'clock.

She curled into a fetal position, swaddled in her sheets, replaying last night over and over in her mind. Each time she felt the same flush of excitement, the same thrilling buzz sliding through her core. She remembered the weight of Nick's lips on hers and the way her body settled against him when he pulled her close. She brushed her fingers over her lips, and her breath quickened again.

But she puzzled about what it meant. When she was younger, sometimes kisses meant something and sometimes they meant almost nothing. This hadn't been a playful kiss. When Nick kissed her, a part of her had loosened and given way. She had crossed a threshold. She frowned at the rough ceiling boards overhead. But how could she know what it meant to Nick? She supposed he might have been carried away by the moment, nothing more, but that didn't ring true.

She pulled her pillow close to her chest. It had been so many years since she'd kissed anyone but Michael.

Michael.

Thinking of Michael took her breath away. I'm married. Those two words in her head rang hollow and false. She realized she didn't feel married anymore. Michael had betrayed her. Michael had abandoned her. And were they even still married since she was...dead? By now, some court might have declared her dead. Michael wouldn't have waited long to make sure that step was taken. He'd clear the decks as soon as possible.

She realized she was feeling guilty, but not about Michael. She hadn't been honest with Nick. He had no idea that the woman he kissed last night was, or had been, married. He knew nothing of the outrageous complications of her life. He hadn't asked, but what would he assume when she came to Homer alone with no ring on her finger? She squeezed her eyes shut and pressed the palm of her hand to her forehead.

"Merry, you up?" Rita's cane banged its way across the downstairs floorboards.

"Yes, coming."

Merry untangled herself from the sheets and reached for her jeans. "Down in a minute." She shook her head. So he kissed me. It was just a kiss.

But as she hustled down the stairs, she knew she was only trying to fool herself. Nick's kiss was a question asked, and when she kissed him back, she had answered the question. Last night she had taken a few steps down a new path. She just didn't know where the path was leading.

~ * ~

That morning Rita was unusually talkative. When Merry had put down The Lost Countess for a few moments to rest her voice, Rita wondered aloud about whether they had enough firewood for the winter. "And maybe we should ask Nick to look at that spot on the wall over by the kitchen sink. It sure looks kind of wet to me. Had trouble with that spot before. I'll ask him when he stops by today. Might ask him too if he has time to take me to the gallery tomorrow, since that damn doctor don't want me driving.

Or maybe you could drive me, Merry. I'm sure Moira's been missing you helping out, since you been here with me all this time. Though the gallery don't do much this time of year. Yes, I'd sure like to have a nice sit-down with Moira."

Merry was pleased to see Rita so animated and lively. It did seem that she was making steady progress.

Rita paused and stared up at the ceiling, seemingly deep in thought. She sighed and looked at Merry. "Look, girl, you got more than you bargained for when you moved in here, didn't you? You didn't know you'd end up a nursemaid to an old bag like me." She gave a little snort of laughter. "Well, I have to thank you. That damn Dr. James probably wouldn't have let me come back if you weren't here to help me out. Damn doctors," she muttered, and started picking at threads in the comforter she'd pulled across her lap. "Anyway, I guess it was a good thing I let you stay that first night."

Merry cocked her head to one side as she looked at Rita. "Why did you, Rita? You didn't have to just because Jan asked you."

Rita frowned and didn't say anything for a few moments. Then she sighed again, smoothing out the comforter with the palms of her hands.

"You took me by surprise, girl. You look a little bit like someone I used to know."

"Annie." Merry said the name flatly, almost without thinking. Rita's eyes widened, and her mouth settled into a hard, sad line.

"Yes," she said, "Annie."

The name hung in the silent air between them. Rita's hands were shaking.

"Rita," Merry said softly, "you don't have to tell me anything you don't want to."

Rita's teeth worried at her bottom lip. "Pour us some more tea, girl, and let's sit down at the table." She refused Merry's arm, letting out exasperated puffs of air as she pushed herself upright from the couch and reached for her cane. She walked slowly to the kitchen table and sat down. The cups of tea sat cooling in front of them.

"When I first saw you there, girl, I'm not even sure what made me think of Annie. You're smaller than she was, as you know..." Rita waved her hand at Merry's shirt, rolled up to the elbows. The shoulder seams dropped halfway down her upper arms. "You maybe look a trifle like her, in the eyes." She peered at Merry closely.

"It was something about the way you stood there. Kind of lost, quiet, like you didn't know what was going to come next. Annie used to be like that sometimes, especially at first. Like the world was a place she couldn't possibly understand." Rita rubbed her eyes, and Merry wondered if she was on the brink of crying.

"Annie was a Yupik Eskimo from the Delta. That's the Bethel area, way in interior Alaska. I first met her when she was about twelve. Her mother sent her out here to her auntie a couple of times of year, when things got too bad at home. And things could get very bad at home." Rita paused and her eyes seemed focused very far away.

"You don't come from round here." Rita looked at her straight on, as if it were very important she pay attention, and tapped her index finger against the tabletop. Merry sat very still, her eyes on Rita's face, her two hands cradling the tea mug.

"You don't know how it is in some parts of the state. The Alaska Native people...their culture don't mesh so well with ours. When we came here, we didn't put value on their art or their beliefs or how they lived. We introduced them to television and sugar-loaded junk food...and alcohol."

Rita stopped and pursed her lips, staring down into her teacup.

"Now so much of their culture is lost. They're in a no-man's-land, trying hard to hang on to what's left, and trying to live in our world too." Rita shook her head, looking down at the table. It was very quiet, and Merry could hear the kitchen clock ticking and a raven croaking outside: a lonely solitary sound.

"Annie's family was broken. Her mother was a good woman, I met her once. But she drank too much. Everyone in that family drank too much. Alcohol is the curse of the Delta."

Merry nodded her head slowly. Rita's voice wavered with sorrow and shades of a deep regret. Merry wanted to reach across the table to her, but she sensed that she should just sit and listen.

"Annie was a bright and loving child. Alice, her auntie, had really bad arthritis, and after a while had to go into care. She couldn't take Annie anymore. And Annie had to get away from her family when they were drinking, it was her only chance, and no one wanted her to go into foster care. So Alice asked me if Annie could live here, just for a little while, you know."

Merry took the box of tissues from the kitchen counter and put it in front of Rita. Rita's hand shook as she dabbed her eyes. She had shrunk into herself and seemed tiny and shriveled.

"Rita, if this is too hard for you to talk about—"

"No, it's all right." Rita managed a weak smile. "There's not too much more to tell." She dabbed at her eyes again.

"Annie stayed with me from when she was fourteen until she was nineteen. She went to high school here, did pretty well too. We got along great. I'd been on my own for a long time then. I was married when I was young." A fleeting smile passed across her face. "But it didn't last long. Well, that's another story. But Annie was easy, even though she was a teenager. Pretty quiet. A lot like you, really. After she graduated she had no interest in college, at least not right away. Got herself a job at the front counter of the Oceans and Islands Center, talking to visitors. Did real well. And she seemed happy to just stay here with me.

I got real fond of that girl." Rita's voice caught in her throat. "I thought, well, when the time was right we'd talk about college. I figured we'd manage it somehow. She was bright enough."

Rita put her elbows on the table and pressed a hand against her mouth. She was silent for a long time. Merry just waited.

When Rita spoke again, Merry could tell she was trying to keep her voice steady, but it cracked on the first sentence. "You see, Merry, she died. In a stupid, pointless accident. She was out with some kids she'd known at school and they weren't very careful. They were walking right alongside the highway at dusk, coming back from a lake. And this driver..." Rita paused again and took a deep breath. "This woman didn't see them or couldn't control her car or whatever, and she plowed right into them. Annie's friend Kathy died at the scene. Annie died about a week later."

Rita was crying openly now, but quietly. Merry put her hand over Rita's. For once, Rita didn't scowl and pull away.

"That driver, she had a blood alcohol reading twice the legal limit. It was all so pointless. Had that damn phone pulled out after the trooper called to tell me about Annie. Told myself I don't ever need another call like that." She paused again and shook her head slowly. "We got Annie out of Bethel, away from her family because they drank too much, and she comes here and gets killed by a drunk driver."

Rita sighed and gazed up toward the ceiling, shaking her head.

"Life just don't make no sense, Merry."

Twenty Four

She stood at the woodpile, her gloves soaked and her hands half-frozen, glowering into the dull, gray sky. Once again, the temperatures had crept above freezing, and now a miserable light rain drifted down. The snow that had fallen the week before was reduced to a sloppy slush. She shook her head and bent down to pick up more pieces of birch. She had never really liked winter weather, but now she wished it would just get really cold and stay cold. Anything would be better than this drippy, bone-chilling dampness.

Rita was taking a morning nap. She had been subdued after their conversation yesterday, as though talking about Annie had stunned her, bringing back memories that still resonated deeply with the power of love, grief, and loss. Merry watched her all that evening and saw Rita pause several times to stare into space. But she ate her dinner, and she even patted Merry's hand before heading into the bedroom last night. And this morning, although she was perhaps even more taciturn than usual, she was focused on getting ready to go to town to visit Moira.

Merry's gloves squished out water as she grabbed the wood and stacked the wet pieces in her arms. Annie's gloves. These were Annie's gloves. She had become accustomed to putting on some stranger's clothes each morning, cinching tight the belt on the too-big pants, rolling up the sleeves of the oversized sweaters. But now it was different. These clothes belonged to someone real, someone who had mattered, someone who had died. Last night, she found herself stroking the sleeve of the pajama tops she wore every night, thinking about Annie living here, sleeping in this bed, dreaming of her future.

She balanced the wood and tried not to drop it as she wrestled with the doorknob. She stopped inside the door to listen. No sounds came from Rita's room. Good. She's still asleep. She needs the rest. As she stacked the wood and rubbed her aching fingers, she thought ahead to the day to come. They would drive to Moira's after Rita got up. Maybe they'd have lunch first. Nick would probably come soon.

Nick. She smiled as she draped her gloves over the sink faucet to dry. She smiled a lot now when she thought of Nick. She looked around the little cabin and her smile faded.

What was Rita going to do when she left?

Now she saw herself as a different person from the lost and grieving woman who had stumbled into this world. She thought less and less often about home, and when those thoughts seeped into her mind, she usually nudged them away. But she hadn't anticipated that her presence here would change lives other than her own. She cared about Rita, and Rita depended on her now. She doubted the woman could manage on her own in her present condition, and no one had suggested that her condition was going to change for the better any time soon. Merry's feelings for Nick had grown, and although she didn't know where they were headed, she sensed that he was opening up a part of his life to her. Even Cassandra was, though she seemed so independent and self-contained. Sometimes Merry saw her face light up when Merry arrived at her front door. She frowned. Thinking this way made her uneasy. It was one thing to career into this new life haphazardly, without a plan, not knowing what would happen next, when she had only herself to consider. She had been impulsive and reckless, propelled into this life by her need to avoid the heartbreaking pain that awaited her at home. But it was another thing entirely when she thought about the effects she was having on other people's lives, people she now knew and cared for. She stared into the room, her eyes unfocused. People I care about, and people I've lied to. Oh, maybe she hadn't told them outright lies, but she hadn't told them the truth, had she?

She began the refrain that she marched through her mind whenever she was forced to think about the future. She needed to make a plan. She needed to figure out what to do. She couldn't stay here forever.

Why not? For the first time, the unbidden thought dropped into her mind. It was crazy, but she had heard stories, mostly about criminals, people who ran away and built a new life and weren't discovered for decades, sometimes not until after they died. They had families and careers and friends and...

She heard the rattle of gravel knocked aside by tires. Nick. She pulled her mind back, composing herself. Nick's arrival must have woken Rita too, because she could hear the creak of Rita's bedsprings.

She greeted him at the door with a smile. He looked a little harried, but he grinned back at her.

"Hi, Nick. I think Rita's just getting up. Come in and have some coffee."

"Thanks." He shrugged off his jacket and draped it over a chair. "I've just been down at the dock. Damn boat engine. I think I need a new carburetor." He took a cup from Merry and sat down. "Hey, I ran into Bill this morning. He asked me to remind you to come by the hospital and fill out that paperwork when you get a chance."

She turned quickly to the sink. She'd been avoiding Dr. James and she felt guilty about it. He'd taken care of her, stitched up her palm and wrapped her ankle. She hadn't filled out any of the admissions forms that night, just given the nurse a quick history about not having allergies, and they trusted her to go back to fill out the forms, probably because they knew Rita and Nick so well. The main focus that night had been on taking care of Rita. Merry went back to have her stitches removed, and she'd darted away before the nurse had any opportunity to bring up the missing forms. When she thought back to the muddle of that night, she realized that Nick had most likely paid the emergency room charge for her care, because no one had asked her about it.

She turned back toward Nick and flexed her foot. "Hey, look at this. My ankle is almost completely better. Much faster than they said. I'm not even wrapping it anymore."

Nick opened his mouth to say something, but the tap of Rita's cane caught his attention. He got up and gave her a quick kiss on the cheek as she hobbled over to the table.

"Ready to go see Moira?"

Rita nodded. He turned to Merry. "Merry, you come too. You and I can go by Scully's and have a beer after we drop off this old bird to have her coffee klatch." He grinned at Rita and she scowled back, but with a smile underneath. "Moira can bring Rita home, and I'll drop you back."

She felt her face flush with pleasure. "Sure. Just let me find some dry gloves."

She hurried up the stairs to the attic. Yes, she had some prickly loose ends. But right now she was going out with Nick. Why, it almost seemed like a date.

~ * ~

Daylight pushed against the blue cotton curtains covering the few small windows in Scully's Cabin Bar, but little of it made it through. Merry paused in the doorway. Coming from the thin sunlight into the bar was like entering a cave.

It was only mid-afternoon, but the one-room cabin was packed. Fishermen still in their folded-down rubber waders and crushed woolen caps stood elbow to elbow with some locals Merry recognized from around town. A couple of out-of-season tourists nursed their beers, perching on barstools by the door in their clean shirts and pressed jeans. Laughter, voices talking over one another, and the clink of glassware all came together in a dull convivial roar.

Nick's hand pressed lightly against her back as he threaded her through the crowd to a tiny wooden table tucked close to the wall at the far end of the bar. She wrinkled her nose at the reek of old beer and grubby sawdust strewn across the uneven board floor, melding together with the smell of warm, wet wool and the tang of ocean. It wasn't unpleasant, only a bit overwhelming after the crisp, clean air outside.

Nick grinned and waved at two red-faced fishermen, who roared out his name from across the room. As they sat down, he leaned over to her. "Scully's is always busy on Sundays," he said, bringing his mouth close to her ear, "but I'm guessing by the size of this crowd that it was too rough to go out on the water this morning."

She felt almost giddy to be away from the cabin and here with Nick. Merry felt less of a need to stay by Rita's side as much as possible now. Rita was doing so much better, and Moira would take good care of her and get her home. Though she walked ever so slowly, Rita had more stamina and seemed more lively. Before her nap this morning, Rita had been sitting at the kitchen table sorting through some mail order publications. Merry wasn't sure, but she thought Rita was perusing a page of a Victoria's Secret catalog that was advertising bustiers. Well, it could be an interesting winter if she decides to order some of those.

She smiled and let her back muscles relax against her chair. Nick's warm breath against her ear made her shiver. She pulled off her jacket. Voices rumbled around her, too many and too loud for her to hear anything but bits of conversation and laughter. It was easy just to be here, sitting next to Nick, letting the tide of the crowd ebb and flow around them. Nick pressed his way to the bar and came back with a small pitcher of dark beer and two glasses.

She couldn't really talk to him over the din, but that

didn't seem to matter. Nick seemed content to sip his beer, occasionally leaning over to point someone out or to offer her a refill. She held her glass in front of her with both hands, enjoying the yeasty smell and the strong, bitter taste. She had never really liked beer before, but in this rowdy warm room, it tasted bitingly cold and fresh. Another change, she thought. Another way I'm different now. The thought stuck with her and blossomed, as she leaned back in the old wooden chair. Am I really different? I'm in a new place, but am I any different, really?

At least now her breath didn't break into sharp, shallow gasps when she thought about Michael and the life she'd left behind. She didn't bend over, a deep angry throb gnawing at the pit of her stomach, when she thought about what she'd done, how she had run away. Now when she thought back it all seemed like another person's life, far away and long ago. Now when she woke in the morning she thought about the day ahead, if she needed to walk to town for groceries, if it was going to snow again, if she needed to go to the Laundromat. Little things.

But who was she now if she wasn't that Meredith anymore?

She pulled her mind back, looked over at Nick, and frowned. Something had caught his attention. He sat very still and stared steadily across the room. His face now was hard, wooden. She turned, and as the crowd shifted, she could see Cassandra sitting with Kathy, one of the waitresses from The Twins, at the very back of the bar. They were laughing, and their tiny table was littered with five or six empty beer bottles and a pile of peanut shells that Cassandra was pushing around on the tabletop with her fingertip. Both of their faces were flushed, and they had the soft, ripe look that came after hours of steady drinking. Even drunk, Cassandra was lovely, lithe, and fiery. She leaned farther over the table and pushed her thick, black hair away from her face, revealing long drop earrings that danced and sparkled with a deep green fire. Three men lounging at the next table were scanning her with obvious interest. Merry looked back at Nick.

She leaned over and touched his arm. "Are you okay?" He glanced back at her, startled, almost as if he had forgotten she was there. But then he shook his head and gave her a little grin. "Sorry," he said, "I was somewhere else for the moment." He scraped his chair closer and turned to her, raising his voice a bit so she could hear him. "This place is too crowded, I know, but the beer is good and cheap and it's convenient. I hope you're okay with it." She smiled back at him and nodded. When she looked at him now, she felt a soft flutter of pleasure and a need to touch him. She placed her fingers gently on his arm. She hadn't drunk that much beer, but breakfast had been a long time ago, and she felt the beginning of a pleasant mellow buzz. She had to lean close to him to make herself heard, and she could smell the clean musky scent of him. "I'm great. But some peanuts would be nice."

He patted her arm and got up to make his way toward the bar. Suddenly, the noise of chair legs scraping and the clatter of a wooden chair hitting the floorboards rose above the general roar. Merry turned to see Cassandra standing, her back against the wall. Kathy was nowhere to be seen. One of the men from the next table was standing close to her, hovering over her, and Cassandra was holding one hand out in front of her chest, as if to push him away. He was grinning at her and talking, and as Merry watched he moved to drape his arm casually against the wall above her. Cassandra shrieked then, and the shrill screech of her voice silenced all the other voices in the bar. The beer bottle fell from her hand, and beer gushed over the floor in front of her.

In an instant, Nick was at Cassandra's side, pulling her away. He shoved the other man aside, almost indifferently, and pulled Cassandra toward the door, cradling her under his arm. Merry saw that Cassandra was shaking. What just happened? The three men stood together, looking confused and defiant. She could see one of them mouth "bitch" before they sank back down into their chairs. Slowly the threads of conversations in the room began to swell again.

Nick was moving Cassandra toward the door. Is she sick? Does she need help? Merry pushed her way toward them. "Nick...wait...let me help..."

She was startled as she looked up into his face. It was angry and grim. Nick scowled at her. "Go back to the table, Merry. This has nothing to do with you." His words slapped against her, and she stopped still, confused. Nick shouldered the door open and pressed Cassandra through it, following close behind her. The door swung shut, hard, right in Merry's face. Stunned, she looked around. No one was paying any attention to her. The general rumble in the room continued as before. She picked her way back to the table, pushing hard to get through the standing crowd near the bar who didn't seem to notice her. She dropped into her chair and stared at the tabletop.

The bartender wove his way through the crowd over to her table and pointed toward the back door. "Nick poked his head in and asked me to tell you he's sorry, but could you please find your own way home? He says he'll talk to you later." He hurried back to the bar, where someone was banging an empty stein and demanding more beer. She sat very still. All the warmth and contentment she had been feeling just moments before had evaporated. No one was paying her any attention, but suddenly she was the old Meredith. The old Meredith who always came in second, or third, but never first. Nick had just discarded her, just like Michael had. Nick had chosen Cassandra over her and left her alone, sitting in a bar. Cassandra had gotten drunk and someone had made a pass at her, and just like that, Nick had left to take care of her.

I should have seen it coming. All the signs were there. He loves her. I've just been convenient.

She fought back tears as she made her way out into

the fresh air. The skies had cleared, and it was a perfect afternoon turning toward evening, the air still and the thin sunlight drawing long shadows at the bases of the leafless birches. She began the walk home, pulling her jacket close around her and crossing her arms to keep herself warm.

Poor me.

The words bubbled into her mind from nowhere, in her own voice, whining, and she could hear them as clearly as if someone were whispering right into her ear.

Poor me. The same words again, but this time the words mocked her.

She stopped, dead still. Damn it, she thought, I'm doing it again. I'm being the old Meredith. The victim. I might as well be wearing a "kick me" sign.

She scowled up at the bare birch branches above her, rubbing and knocking ever so slightly against each other in a wisp of breeze.

So he's a jerk after all. So he left me sitting in a bar without so much as a backward glance to take care of Cassandra. That's about them, not about me.

She rubbed the toe of her scuffed boot into an ice patch at the edge of the dirt road. It hurt, it hurt a lot, to know that Nick had left without a word other than to send her a quick message to go home alone. If Cassandra really needed help, I could have helped too. He wouldn't have left like that, without even talking to me, unless he doesn't really care about me.

She took a deep breath and squared her shoulders. Okay, so it wasn't the way she had thought—and hoped—with Nick. That was too bad and it hurt. She knew that her feelings for him had been growing. But she would just pick herself up now and go on. She was building something new here, and she wasn't going to let Nick ruin it. It was hers.

She stared down the road and started walking, quickly now, her feet skidding on the frozen mud.

Twenty Five

Nick drove in two days later. She was alone. Moira had come by to take Rita to The Twins for lunch. Merry had just lifted the burners off the stove, and she was scrubbing at the chipped white surface with an old sponge that was falling apart. She recognized the sound of his truck pulling up in front and her throat closed. I won't cry. I'm not going to cry.

She had tried to rehearse the scene in her mind, to compose and prepare herself for his reappearance. She imagined herself wearing a mantle of indifference, not letting him see how much he had hurt her. She'd offer a casual and distant initial greeting, keeping her eyes level and neutral as she looked at him, and a shrug if he offered up an apology. She reasoned with herself, cautioned herself to be sensible. After all, we didn't make any promises to one another. I hardly know him. But the moment the engine rumbled and stopped in front of the cabin, her breath came short and fast, and her hands trembled. Despite her intentions, she couldn't push away her feelings.

He knocked and let himself in, as he often did. She heard his footsteps stop just inside the door, but she didn't look up from the stove. "Hello, Nick." She tried to keep her voice steady, but she could hear the flat empty tone of her words.

He didn't say anything at first. She was afraid to look up, afraid that seeing him would reopen wounds, that all those feelings that had been churning through her these last two days would be raw again. Hurt, anger, humiliation. Betrayal. Loss. She was afraid to look at him, but she couldn't help it. Her hand stilled on the stovetop. She slowly turned toward him.

He was standing in the doorway, his arms crossed, his eyes focused on the floor. He was frowning, and his mouth worked silently, as if he were chewing the words he was trying to get out.

Finally, he looked up, his eyes sweeping over her. "Merry, we have to talk. Let's get some fresh air. Walk with me over to the bluff."

He waited on the porch while she put on her jacket and gloves. They walked side by side, but certainly not together, across the coarse frozen grass in the meadow. They stood side by side, but not together, on the edge of the bluff facing the bay.

Nick's face was rigid, the lines of age and weather sunk deep and hard. He faced the choppy, gray ocean. Neither of them said anything for several seconds. Her stomach felt achingly raw and sore, as if she'd taken a sucker punch.

"You don't understand," he said. His voice was gravelly and flat. He paused. "You don't understand, but how could you?"

He turned to her then, his eyes searching her face. She couldn't bear to look at him, so she stared at the ground, her arms crossed tightly in front of her.

He took a deep breath. "Look, I don't like talking about other people, especially people I care about." He paused again. "And I do care about Cassandra. Very much. But it's not the way you must think."

What way is it then? You left me sitting alone in a bar. You walked away from me without a second glance. Merry gave her head a little shake.

"Look, Merry, it's not like I even know very much about you. You show up one day, living with Rita, almost getting yourself killed right off..." He flashed her a quick, rueful smile, but it didn't last long. He sighed. "People end up here for a lot of different reasons, and they like to keep their pasts to themselves."

He looked down and shuffled his feet, tapping his

toe against a rock. "Cassandra isn't who she seems." He blurted the words out. "Or, she isn't what she seems."

Merry waited. Nick took a deep breath.

"Merry, Cassandra came here as a child. Her parents—well, that's another story, but Cassandra ended up here living with an aunt and uncle who took care of her just like she was their own. Everyone around here knew she was incredibly talented from early on. You know. You've seen her work. There's nothing else quite like it."

He hesitated and gazed out over the bay. Merry didn't move. She had no idea what he was trying to tell her, but she could see that the words weren't coming easily. This was a story he didn't want to tell.

"She was always a bit of a wild young woman. Her plan was to leave as soon as she could, to make it big in the art world. She got a full scholarship at an art college, a really well-known one in Chicago." He rubbed the back of his hand against his forehead.

"She wouldn't let anyone pave the way, wouldn't let anyone help her. She packed her bags and went off, 'to leave this backwoods place forever,' as she put it."

Nick's voice had gotten rougher now. Merry was almost holding her breath, listening carefully. She stood very still, afraid he might stop talking.

Nick turned toward her. His face was full of pain, as if it hurt him just to have to say the words. "She wasn't prepared. She'd been kind of a big fish here. But she didn't know anything about being in the big city. The first week she was there, she got drunk with some guy she'd met in a park, and then they met up with his friends. They offered her a ride home, and..."

Nick's voice faded away, but Merry's mind had already filled in the gap. She closed her eyes and put her hand over her mouth.

"She was in really bad shape. After they...raped her..." His words were coming out in choked syllables, "they beat her up for good measure and left her in an alley.

I got a call from her aunt, because I was down in California, trying to straighten out some pieces of my own life."

Merry felt a sob rising in her chest. Cassandra, lovely and talented and bold, left beaten in an alley.

"Well, I got to the hospital and stayed with her. I told Shirley, her aunt, that I'd take care of Cass and get her home. Cass wouldn't even talk to me at first. She wouldn't talk to anyone."

Nick rubbed his hands along the front of his pants. Merry could hear his breathing between the words, harsh and rasping. "I spent every day with her while she was in the hospital, for about two weeks. When she was well enough, I brought her back."

They stood in silence for some time. He reached out toward Merry, but then dropped his hand back to his side.

"She's never been the same. She puts on a good front, but that's what it is. She wants to be the way she was, but she's broken inside. I think the only thing that really keeps her together is her work." His mouth twisted in a dark grimace, and Merry wondered if he was thinking about those men and what they'd done, and what he'd like to do to them.

His voice was gentle now. "Merry, I'm one of the few people she really trusts. Shirley is gone now, just last year. And yes, I know Cass thinks she loves me."

Merry's body stiffened, and she stared at the ground. The ocean breeze ruffled the dead, brown grass at her feet, and a tiny black spider hurried by, moving in fits and starts.

"She thinks she loves me, but I think it's because she knows I'll be there for her. And I will. But Merry, I don't feel that way about her. I love her, but not that way. But when she needs me, I can't say no."

They stood together, side by side, not talking. A wave of exhaustion washed over her. She had so many feelings. Horror for what Cassandra had gone through, relief at understanding what had gone on at the bar, and—yes—even envy, because Nick might not love Cassandra that way, but he was going to take care of her.

She thought of Cassandra, alone in her cabin, fashioning her vessels with the soaring fluid walls and graceful curves. Cassandra, alone on icy black Alaskan nights, sitting at her wheel, the infinitely sad cry of violins filling the air around her. Cassandra before, the world beckoning to her, and Cassandra later, betrayed and damaged.

Merry turned to Nick. "I'm sorry." It was such a simple statement, and it covered so much ground. She was sorry, so sorry, for Cassandra. She was sorry she had misunderstood what Nick was feeling. And she was sorry, so very sorry, that such terrible things could happen in the world. She was sorry for herself too. What was she doing in this strange place? She really didn't belong here. Other people were rooted here. They had lives and histories and they took care of one another. She was an impostor and a liar and an interloper. What right did she have to stake a claim for Nick's attention? He was honest and honorable, and she was just someone who had run away. What did she have to offer him? How could she explain to him why this pain cut so deeply in her, how the soft inside of her was already so bruised that his walking away had torn her open? How could she make him understand when everything that made her this way was a secret?

He was real. She was a fake.

Her muddled thoughts roared in her head.

She brushed her hand lightly down his arm and turned to walk toward the cabin, leaving him looking out over the water. She ached inside, she was empty, and she had nothing else to say.

~ * ~

Cassandra's door was open. Wildly fanciful classical music crashed and boomed inside. Merry thought she recognized the music from the old Fantasia movie, the part with the demon on the mountain. The music poured out as if a full orchestra was laboring in Cassandra's studio. Merry took a deep breath and stepped inside.

She hadn't been back here in a week. She kept to herself, working at the gallery some days but then going straight to Rita's. Her thoughts roiled and she couldn't make sense of them. Rita looked at her strangely once or twice, but she didn't ask any questions. Nick stayed away, as she thought he would. She was sure they both knew that the next move was hers. But what should that move be? Her answer to the question changed hour to hour.

Cassandra walked through the open back door carrying a bucket in one hand and a large handful of dripping trimming tools in the other. She waved the tools at Merry and dropped them in a heap on the counter near the window. She yelled over the crescendo of the music, "Just cleaning up. Come on in. I've been trying to wash down some of this stuff. There's too much dust in here. Do you want to throw today?"

But then Cassandra stopped abruptly, and the delicate wrinkle creased her forehead as she peered into Merry's face. She moved to flick a switch to turn off the music. After the pounding chords, the silence was startling. Merry could hear the distant caw of a raven and the squeal of a gull seemingly answering.

"What's wrong?"

Merry stared at her. She didn't intend to say anything about the bar and Nick and what she now knew, but she realized it was probably plain to see. She had never been able to hide her feelings. They always danced across her face.

"N-nothing," she stammered. She looked at Cassandra and saw her injured and broken, lying in a hospital bed with Nick by her side, not speaking, just enduring, not yet able to look into her own life, which overnight had been scarred forever. Her life brutalized by the unspeakable violence of strangers. Something in

Merry's heart broke open again, and the knowledge of the pain this woman had suffered rushed in.

And somehow Cassandra knew. Merry could see it. As Cassandra looked at her, her face became wooden, her eyes hard. Her easy grace as she carried in the bucket and tools was gone. She stood rigid, staring at Merry as she had stared at her on that first day, with intense distaste and dislike.

"You know." Her voice was flat and lifeless. "So someone told you all about me, did they?"

Merry opened her mouth to deny it, but she couldn't. "I'm so sorry," she whispered.

In one swift movement, Cassandra picked up a bisque-fired teapot from the shelf and smashed it against the floor. It shattered into tiny pieces that explored outward. Merry winced as a fragment stabbed into her ankle. Cassandra was panting. "Damn it," she said. "Damn it, damn it, damn it."

"Cassandra, stop, please." Merry saw that a shard had broken the skin on the back of Cassandra's hand. Blood dripped down her fingers and onto the floor. Merry grabbed a towel and moved toward her. Cassandra backed away from her, hissing, "It's my business. Mine. You have no right to be talking about me. I just want to be left alone. Just leave me alone." Tears streamed down her angry face.

Merry walked across the room and put her arms around her. Cassandra struggled to push her away but Merry held on, tight, until Cassandra's shoulders drooped and her body went limp.

"Damn it." Cassandra was whispering now.

Merry pushed her onto a stool. Cassandra didn't look up. She shook as she grabbed behind her to find the half-full glass of red wine on the counter.

She took a deep swig of the wine, and when she looked up at Merry, her eyes were hard and dry.

"Well, mystery girl, you never told us one single thing about yourself, but you like to pry into other people's business, don't you?"

Her words landed like a hard slap. Merry turned to face the door of the cabin, taking a deep breath. Through the window, she could see the tops of the spruce trees rocking wildly in the rising wind, and she could hear the restless banging of their swaying branches. It was almost fully dark now. The raven cawed again.

She turned back. Cassandra gave her a look of pure malice, as if the days they'd shared had never happened.

Merry was so tired. The secret she carried day and night, the secret she hid from everyone here, pressed dense and heavy against her chest. She was so very, very tired.

"I'm going to get some of that wine," Merry said, "and then I'm going to tell you a story."

She grabbed a wine goblet from the dish cabinet and poured in red wine, almost to the brim. She took a deep gulp. The wine burned her dry throat as she swallowed. She took another gulp, then after a pause, another.

"Remember that bus accident back in September, at the Fairbanks airport?"

Twenty Six

Merry woke on the couch, lying tangled in Cassandra's patchwork throw. She pushed herself slowly into a sitting position, then dropped her head into her hands and groaned. Her brain pounded and her mouth must be filled with sand. She surely hadn't had a hangover this bad since college. She pressed the base of her hand hard against the middle of her forehead as the memory of last night rushed back in a painful flood. Oh God. Cassandra knew now.

Her impulse to tell Cassandra last night, to confess, had been too strong to resist. Once she started, the wine made her bold and the story tumbled out. Her marriage was falling apart, she was so unhappy, and so, when the chance came, she let it all happen. She hadn't planned it, but she'd been pulled along on the tide of events. She was dead on the bus, but she wasn't. Even as she slurred the words, finding it hard to focus as the wine sank in, she knew it sounded crazy. It made no sense.

Cassandra had sat absolutely still. Her face was blank and unreadable, and she hadn't said a word. Merry couldn't even remember how the evening had ended. She must have passed out.

But now, in the light of day, she was filled with regret.

Merry shivered as the cabin door opened, ushering in a hurried rush of cold air. The eerie hollow chortle of a raven echoed from the spruce trees. Cassandra walked inside and put a paper bag and a loaf of bread on the table. The warm comforting yeasty scent of fresh baking floated over to her, but the thought of eating made her stomach lurch.

"I went to town to pick up some food for breakfast. I thought you might be hungry." The words were friendly enough, but Cassandra's voice was coolly neutral. She leaned against the sink, staring at her guest.

"Look...last night..."

Cassandra turned and started to pull groceries out of small bag. Some cheese, a stick of butter, a couple of apples. Merry watched her deliberate movements. She didn't know what reaction she had expected, but this dark fog of apparent disapproval unnerved her.

"You don't understand," Merry said. "I know it was crazy, but I had reasons. It was bad back there."

"It was bad." Cassandra took a deep breath, and when she spoke, her words were flat and measured. "You're right, I don't understand. I get bad. I know bad. So what? He didn't beat you, or steal from you, or threaten you. You were unhappy and your marriage was in a rotten place. I get that. Marriages break up all the time. But Merry, you walked away. You threw away your friends and your job and...everything. You just let the chips fall where they may. You just left. Everyone thinks you died. I just don't get how you could hurt everyone like that."

"I was so unhappy." The tears started to slide down her cheeks.

She looked up, but Cassandra's face stayed stony and closed.

Damn you, Merry thought. Damn you.

She took a deep shuddering breath. Last night, she'd told Cassandra about running away after the accident, running because her marriage was disintegrating around her, but she hadn't told her everything. Somehow, even after all that wine, she'd kept some of her secret. But only half the story didn't make sense, she knew. She wasn't really sure that the whole story made sense.

She felt a sudden surge of rage. Cassandra had suffered a terrible wrong, and had been cracked open and broken like no one should ever be. But in the end, she had

Nick to bring her back to the place she belonged and to help put her back together again. Nick didn't let her drift away. Cassandra couldn't make herself back into the person she had been before the monstrous attack, but she could put herself back into this life. She could come back to Homer and start again. She could take her damaged self and put it into a place where she was welcome and wanted. But Merry didn't have that kind of anchor. She didn't belong anywhere that way. Cassandra couldn't understand that kind of alone.

When Merry spoke again, her voice sounded thin and bruised.

"It wasn't just how things changed between Michael and me. I haven't really been right since...I lost a baby. It was so bad, Cass." She shook her head and squeezed her eyes shut. She never talked about this. It hurt too much. Even mouthing these words was agony. "We were young. We'd only been married about five years. And we both didn't think the time was right. Even then, I think I knew that Michael and I were in trouble, that the marriage wasn't what it should have been. But I thought it wasn't the time we would have chosen to have a baby, but we'd make it work. But Michael was so sure that it would have been a mistake. So sure."

She stopped. She didn't want to go on. Her head throbbed from all the wine last night, but also from the words she was forcing out. These past few weeks she'd been able to move all these thoughts and feelings away, like dropping them in a box and pressing the lid closed. But now they were rushing back, and it was worse than ever, as if they had gathered malevolence and despair about them, even more hurtful for having been put away. Merry didn't want to say the words. But Cassandra just waited, silently, her arms crossed.

"Damn it, he pushed and pushed. He said I had to get rid of it, he wouldn't leave me alone..."

She was almost shouting now, all the sentences

running together. Her headache went nuclear, the pounding in her head rhythmic and ruthless. Tears streamed down her face.

"And I was going to do it. I was going to do it even though I didn't want to. All the arrangements had been made, I wasn't eating or sleeping...

"And then I lost it. I lost her. I'm sure it was a girl. One night I started cramping and bleeding and then she was just gone. And I didn't get to the doctor fast enough, or maybe it wouldn't have made a difference anyway, but I got really sick. The doctor said there would most likely be no more pregnancies because of all the scarring..."

She began to sob, remembering. She couldn't make Cassandra understand. Years had passed, but she had never forgotten. She lived the loss every day. She had shoved it all into some deep, dark compartment in her mind, but the pain surged again as the memory bloomed anew.

"It's done now. It's over." Michael's voice had been firm.

She'd sat crumpled on the couch. The tissue she was holding was shredded and pressed into a soggy mat. She wasn't crying now, but her eyes ached from all the hours of weeping. All the hours when she felt that her soul was seeping out of her body. She wasn't sure how she was even remembering to breathe.

"It's for the best. You have to know that."

Meredith had looked up so sharply that she could see his eyes widen momentarily.

"How can you say that? That was our child."

"You're being ridiculous." His voice was harder now, with a nasty impatient edge. "That wasn't a child and you know it. And we agreed anyhow. You agreed, Meredith."

I agreed, she'd thought. Her thoughts were foggy, confused. She shook her head, trying to clear it. That was true, wasn't it? Michael had made all the arrangements. How was it possible that she had agreed? She was drowning, she was going under, the weight of this loss and sorrow was more than she could possibly bear.

"And what about the future, Michael? What about what the doctor said? No more babies?"

He had moved to stand behind her and she felt his hand rest on her shoulder. "I'm sorry, but we have to face it. It's better things went this way. You didn't even have to go through the procedure, and besides, it was never that clear that we were ever going to have children."

Had he really just said that? Where had that come from?

"Michael? What...?"

"Look, Meredith, I am sorry that you're feeling so bad, but this is over now—"

She had gotten to her feet unsteadily and brushed away his hand. She pressed her hand to her abdomen. It still throbbed when she moved. Nothing there but pain.

"You're right. It's done. I'm going to bed."

Her head swam as she rose, and she grabbed the side of the couch to steady herself. She walked slowly, and when she reached the door, she turned around. He was standing, motionless, his arms crossed, looking out the window. There was no particular expression on this face. It was blank, impassive, his dry eyes staring into the darkness outside.

"It's done," she had said softly. She moved through the door.

Cassandra's arm encircled her shoulders. Merry was crying again, cool sad tears of a deep chasm of grief and regret.

"I don't understand, but then it's your life, not mine. I don't know, Merry, don't you think he might be sorry? That he might be really missing you?"

Merry didn't answer. She couldn't talk anymore; she was too empty, and she couldn't put together the words to tell the rest, the last bit of the story, the final blow that had crushed the little that was left of her. Merry shook her head silently.

~ * ~

There was no way to avoid it now. She might try to put it all out of her mind, but now that Cassandra knew, it was real again. Someone here knew about what she had done.

Merry walked away from the cabin toward town. She couldn't go back to Rita's yet. She needed to think. It was early Sunday morning and only a battered, old pickup truck passed her, the man inside raising a languid hand as the truck wobbled over the rutted roadbed. The branches in the overhead trees were heavy with frost, and the sun hadn't yet penetrated deep, though the day looked to be fine. There was a clean, sharp smell to the air that she now recognized. Snow. Another snowfall was probably on its way. She took winter for granted now. Frost, snow, and icy air had become the customary backdrop to her life, though it was just November. She shivered and pulled her old jacket closer around her, shoving her hands into the pockets for warmth. She had forgotten her hat, and her ears burned in the cold breeze.

The problem wasn't that she thought Cassandra would tell anyone. Merry really didn't think she would. Cassandra was often unfriendly, moody, and aloof, but she certainly wasn't a gossip. But Cassandra would look at her differently now. Merry wasn't the mystery woman who came to town, who was becoming Cassandra's friend. In Cassandra's mind, Merry was now the person who had run away, who had let everyone believe that she was dead to escape from her own life, and who had left everyone else at home pick up the pieces.

She was no longer suspended in a bubble of a new life. No one but Cassandra knew, but now she felt the weight of her old existence settle down upon her. She didn't chase away the thoughts this time. She let them wash over her, the memories, the dread of her life back home, the agony she felt about what was going to come next there.

And she thought, too, of what must have happened since she'd run away. She suddenly realized that they had probably had some sort of memorial service for her. She and Michael had never discussed what they wanted in terms of funeral services. She imagined a large space, solemn faces, soft music. But then she rubbed her hands hard over her face. She had put a lot of people through a lot of pain.

When she thought about Michael, she was still bewildered, shocked, and angry. She even cracked a crooked, wry smile, thinking of him handling her memorial service. Had Michael given a eulogy? At the time she left, she thought he had told very few people about his defection, but could he stand up at a service and say nice things about her? About what a loving wife she had been? About how he missed her? Yes, she thought sadly, he could. Maybe it was all those years as a criminal lawyer, dealing day after day with drug dealers, murderers, and criminals who stole millions of dollars from innocent people. Was that why he seemed so cold now, so indifferent to any obligations of loyalty and the vows he had made to her? She could hardly remember the Michael she had married, the Michael who had laughed uncontrollably with her on their wedding night as they sat in bed with glasses of champagne, both of them giddy and a little embarrassed at having been the center of attention all day. The Michael who couldn't wait to come home to her, to tell her what nutty things had happened at work that day. Where had that Michael gone?

She mulled over her feelings for him, probing them, trying to see them clearly. She didn't love him anymore, and hadn't for a long time. Why hadn't she seen that sooner? She had just been existing, living day to day, assuming that this was the way the rest of her life was going to be. She thought that was what happened, more often than not, in a long marriage. People grew apart, but they were supposed to stick it out. They weren't supposed to betray their wives, and worse yet, they weren't supposed to find someone else. She felt tears prick her eyelids, and she shook her head, hard. No. No more crying. She pulled her left hand from her pocket and stared at her bare ring finger, remembering that she had twisted off her wedding ring, almost without thinking, on the car ride from Fairbanks with Jan and Evan. She frowned. What had she done with it? Had she put it in her travel bag? No, not her bag—she had put it in her jacket. Yes, she felt it there through the fabric, in the tiny zipped inside pocket of her now almost threadbare windbreaker. She worked her fingers inside and felt two lumps.

Merry left the ring nested in the pocket and pulled out the little compass key ring, remembering when Ellen had given it to her at the airport when she dropped Merry off for her flight. The same compass she had pulled out to help her find the trail back to Rita's cabin with Nick, seemingly so long ago. The tiny black needle waggled back and forth as Merry balanced it in her palm. "To help you find your way north," Ellen had said, hugging her. "And so you can find your way back home." She rubbed the key between her fingers. The key attached to the compass was to Ellen's house, not Merry's.

Ellen. What had she done to Ellen? That was the worse thought of all. Ellen would have been devastated by the news of her death. They had been there for each other for so long now, sharing their little victories and successes, commiserating and comforting each other. Ellen, whose cheery, "C'mon, let's just have a glass of wine," started many a long evening of laughter and companionship, especially those days more recently when Michael was so often gone. Merry sometimes felt that Ellen was the only one who still really saw her in sharp focus. For everyone else, Michael especially, she was just fading away, disappearing into the dull fabric of her life. Oh, how she missed Ellen.

Merry reached the outskirts of town. The Texaco

station was right across the street, and a pay phone was pasted to the wall in a covered booth attached to the glassed-in office. The longing in her chest was a physical burn, a painful, deep-pitted yearning so strong she crossed the street as if a cord attached to her core was pulling her over. Ellen. To hear Ellen's voice. Just to hear her voice.

She tried to think clearly. Ellen didn't have caller ID on her land line. It was one of her personal quirks. She used all the bells and whistles on the cell phone for her business, but she had only the most basic level of service on her home phone, a re-mastered old vintage model that even had a circular dial. If Ellen answered the phone and there was no one there, she wouldn't think a thing about it, just some kid playing a prank, nothing worth a second thought. But, Merry thought, I could hear her voice. Just know that she is still there.

Her hands shook when she exchanged dollar bills for change inside the office. The voice in her head screamed that this wasn't a good idea, to act on this impulse, to take this chance. Her brain shouted, Wait, wait, let's think about this. But right then what she wanted most in the world was to hear Ellen's voice, her funny little two-tone "Hell-o." She dialed Ellen's number and tumbled change into the slot.

The phone rang four times. She's not home, Merry thought, feeling frustrated and saddened but maybe a little relieved too.

But then Ellen answered. Her hello rose and fell as always before. Merry sucked in her breath. She'd heard Ellen's voice. She should hang up now. But she gripped the sticky black receiver hard and closed her eyes. Ellen was on the other end of this line.

"Hello? Hello? Anyone there?" Ellen sounded anxious now, and Merry expected her to hang up any minute. "Is anyone there?"

There was a long pause, but no disconnect click. Then Ellen said in a low voice, "Meredith, is it you?"

Merry started in shock. She didn't say anything, but her throat gasped for air with a quick, hard intake.

Ellen's voice was louder now and agitated.

"Meredith, is it you? I told Michael I just knew you were alive. Meredith, is it you?"

Merry slammed the receiver back onto the phone and doubled over, her stomach churning. She was going to throw up. Ellen didn't know. She couldn't know that Merry wasn't dead. Maybe she had just refused to believe it because she didn't want to. But what was going to happen now? What if Ellen really did believe that it was Merry on the phone?

Merry leaned against the phone, shaking. Her stomach hurt and her head pounded. The garage attendant squinted at her through the office window and she gave him a little wave, trying to smile. She needed to get back to Rita's, she needed to settle down and figure this out. What would Ellen do now?

Twenty Seven

It seemed as if she were holding her breath for the next two days. She forced herself to walk through her routine, but her nerves thrummed and sleep was next to impossible. A knock on the door of the cabin, the screech of tires on the road outside, everything seemed to be a harbinger of doom. She would be found out, exposed as the fraud she was. Everyone, both here and at home, would be shocked and disgusted by what she had done. And this fragile life that she had built here would collapse in an instant like a house made of snowflakes.

But then, a little at a time, she started to relax again. Nothing happened. No solemn-faced uniformed state trooper came to the door, looking for Meredith Cynthia Benton. She found she could walk through town without her fleece scarf swaddled close around her face. She didn't startle every time she heard someone's voice behind her.

After all, she hadn't said anything to Ellen. Ellen—dear Ellen—had just been making a guess. After she hung up, Ellen probably thought it was just a wrong number or a prank call.

But it did feel like there were the beginnings of loose ends now, a threatening of unraveling. She still avoided walking by the hospital, and she had hidden behind the potato chip display when she saw Dr. James at the grocery store. She'd thought long and hard, but she couldn't think of a way to avoid filling out the hospital forms. She could lie, of course. She could make up a phony social security number, list her address simply as "homeless" or "none," but wouldn't the hospital find out? Surely they'd try to verify the information. And besides, she hadn't lied before. She sidestepped questions, she obfuscated, she changed the subject as quickly and as subtly as she could manage, but she'd not yet had to out-and-out lie. Maybe what she was doing wasn't that different, but that was a line she was reluctant to cross.

And Nick. He was one hell of a loose end. Her thoughts were full of Nick. The next move was hers. What was she going to do about him?

She battled her worries all day, shoving troubled thoughts away, shaking anxieties out of her head like they were a swarm of annoying and persistent flies. But at night, when sleep finally crept in, she had no defense. Sleep took her back. Sleep made her remember.

Meredith had waited for him at the kitchen table. She sat with her hands pressed together in her lap. A tight pain rooted deep in her stomach, and an aching throb pulsed beneath her collarbone. She could feel her blood thrum in her ears. Outside, a sparrow twittered, and she heard it with disbelief—that there could be normal sounds, sounds of life continuing, comings and goings, when her whole world had just cracked apart.

Maybe I'm wrong. Maybe there is a totally innocent explanation. She shook her head. There wouldn't be. From the moment she had realized what Betty Ann was saying, she knew the truth of it.

The clock ticked over the stove. The minutes seemed endless, unbearable. She didn't know how much more waiting she could stand. She had looked at the clock for the hundredth time. He's late.

She had heard the door from the garage bang open, heard the thump as he dropped his briefcase on the chair next to the door. "Meredith?" That was his voice, his normal voice, the voice that talked to her every day. Her husband's voice.

He had walked into the kitchen. She saw his eyes find her. She watched his gaze sweep over her body hunched low in the chair, her clasped hands, her red-rimmed eyes, and her blotchy face. He stood still, exhaling in a sharp puff through his mouth. He had stared at her and didn't say anything, but his face rearranged itself into a pattern of hard lines.

"Michael." Her voice caught and rasped. "Michael, I know."

She hadn't had to say any more. He slapped his hand on the counter and turned toward the kitchen window.

She had heard his breathing, hard and strong. He turned back.

"I'm sorry, Meredith. I should have told you. I'm sorry you had to find out another way." She heard the words, but he didn't sound sorry. His voice was flat and firm, business-like.

He made no move toward her, and she sucked in her breath, hard, and wrapped her arms around herself so that she wouldn't reach for him.

"Another woman, Michael? A pregnant woman?"

Michael let out another huff of air. "Meredith, I am sorry that this is difficult for you, but yes, Belinda is pregnant. We intend to get married."

Meredith had looked at him, confused. What did he mean, get married? He was already married to her. Belinda? His partner from work?

She started to sob with great gasping breaths. This couldn't be happening. There had to be a mistake. She reached for him then, without thinking. She held her arm out, wanting him to come to her and explain this away, to comfort her somehow, but he didn't move. He just looked at her and sighed, then looked away. Outside, the sparrow twittered again. She saw its shadow dance on the windowsill. It was on a branch right over the window.

"Meredith, this marriage has been over for a long time. I've been waiting to get a few things in order before telling you, but it's time. Jake can take care of the legalities for us. We can probably fast-track this whole thing, so that we can both get on with our lives as quickly as possible."

She shook her head, her vision blurred with tears.

"But, Michael...I don't understand. When we lost the baby, you said... you didn't want children."

His voice scraped hard and flinty now. "That was a long time ago, Meredith. Things change. I've moved on. Belinda is due in a few months, and I'd like to have everything settled before our baby comes."

She had her head down, but she felt his stare boring into the top of her head.

A baby. Oh my God, a baby.

"You won't be able to afford to keep the townhouse, but I'll buy your interest in it. You should stay here now, and I'll be at Belinda's. We can work out the details later." His voice was crisp and brisk. "I really am sorry, Meredith, but in the end this will be best. I'll come back tomorrow and pack up some of my things."

The weight of the truth had thudded into her chest like a physical blow. How long had he been planning this? How many nights had he laid beside her in bed, thinking about his future with Belinda? And the nights he reached for her, although there hadn't been many of those for a while, did he close his eyes and imagine that he was with Belinda? She had been played for a fool. She had been humiliated.

And now, she was being put aside and he would have a new wife. A new wife and a baby.

He'd turned and left. She heard him slap the switch to open the garage door, then the engine of his car came alive. The garage door screeched and banged shut.

She had sat very still. The clock ticked. The sparrow twittered.

Twenty Eight

She stood at the kitchen window, clasping her coffee cup with both hands, and watching the soft, wet snowflakes drop silently from the sky. The big flakes were sticking and blanketing the ground with a thick, white mat. When she went outside to bring in three damp pieces of birch, her feet left slushy rounds in the white of the path to the woodpile. The air hung chilled and sodden, heavy with moisture. The snowfall brought an eerie silence to the meadow, shutting the little cabin away from the rest of the world.

She heard Rita stirring in her bedroom. Merry was always quiet in the early morning now, because Rita often had restless nights and needed to sleep a little longer. She glanced over at the coffeepot. Enough there for Rita's morning cup, when she was ready.

The gallery wouldn't open today. There were so few customers this time of year that Moira had started opening the gallery only on weekends, when some hardy souls from Kenai or Anchorage might brave the highway. Tourists didn't usually come this way when all the colors in the landscape turned to gray, brown, and black, and the roads were often covered with thin sheets of treacherous invisible ice. Merry sighed. It was the way of life, she thought, to slow down in the winter months. I suppose here it's a time for reflection, inside work, reading. Her thoughts meandered. What will I do here, every day, without the work at the gallery? The thought created a little quaking desperation in her chest. When she was busy, when chores and tasks demanded her time and attention, it was easier to keep her grim thoughts at bay. Her mood had been dark lately, mirroring the weather and the ever-shortening days.

Well, she knew she could make her way to Cassandra's and work on her pottery. They fell into an uneasy truce in the days following the night she had confessed. On the outside, it must have looked like they were just the way they had been before. Merry was relieved that Cassandra still opened her door to her, that she hadn't decided that what Merry had done was too despicable to allow their work to continue. And, as Merry had somehow known, Cassandra had kept Merry's secret. Maybe, Merry thought, it's because her own story causes her so much pain that she understands a need to hold sadness close, to build a shell around it so it can stay buried deep. On the first day she went back, they kept their distance from one another, talking little and only of their work, and not of the dark histories that they now knew each carried deep inside. But sometimes now, when they stood side by side at the end of the day looking at the new bowls and plates, the ever-present glasses of red wine in their hands, Merry felt that something had changed between them.

They were both bruised women, Merry knew now, two women who had lost their way. Their stories weren't the same. Cassandra had been scarred in a brutal attack that she might never overcome. But Merry realized now that she had been damaged too, that she had run away because she had just been fading away, and everything that she had hoped for and worked for and believed was ebbing away as if she didn't matter. Michael's savage belittling of her for so long, his constant erosion of her confidence and dreams, and then his betrayal, had chipped away at her to the point that she wasn't sure how much of her was still left. The bus accident had let the rest of her, the uneasy remnants of her, completely disappear, and from the horror and chaos a new Meredith, a new Merry, had begun to emerge. Yes, a Merry who was guilty and confused and a mess, but the heavy weight of a life gone so sour was slowly receding. And though they didn't talk about it, Merry knew there was some comfort for both of them in the hours that she and

Cassandra spent together. Last night, when they stood side by side at the window watching the first heavy snowflakes drift, Merry had leaned over, ever so slightly, and let her shoulder touch Cassandra's. And Cassandra had not pulled away.

Winter was Cassandra's big production time, so Merry thought she might spend more time there. But of course she had to keep a close eye on Rita. Rita might want to spend more evenings in town as the long, cold nights encased their little cabin. She sighed and poured the dregs of her now-cold coffee into the sink.

She pulled out a clean cup and mixed coffee with lots of whole milk, the way Rita liked it. First knocking gently, she opened Rita's door a crack. "You up?" An annoyed huff and the rap of Rita's cane against the floor was the only answer, but Merry had lost her fear of Rita's grunts and growls. She pushed open the door and found Rita sitting on the side of her bed, struggling to put on her shoes. Merry knew better than to offer to help. She put Rita's cup on her bedside table, and Rita scowled but sent a glimmer of a smile in her direction. Merry suppressed an urge to pat her on the shoulder. She left and closed the door behind her, making a mental note to squirrel out Rita's sheets before they went to town today. Rita's room smelled a little fusty and the bedclothes could probably use a good wash.

Daily life was a bit easier now. When everything settled down a bit after Rita's accident, Nick taught her how to work the stick shift, and now Rita wasn't so possessive about her old truck. Nick. She rubbed her temples. Chances were she'd run into him today, since Rita said last night that she wanted to go to lunch at The Twins. He was waiting, she knew. He was waiting for her to come around. She shook her head as she took the wet sponge to wipe off the already clean table. Her feelings were raw now, broken open and bleeding from the scene at Scully's and from the horror she felt when she'd told Cassandra what she had done. Now that Cassandra knew, nothing would be the same. Her old life and her new life had begun to converge.

Rita came out slowly from her bedroom, her cane in one hand, and the coffee cup tipping dangerously in the other. Merry quickly pulled out a chair for her and took the cup. She put down a glass of water and Rita's four pills on the table, and made a note on the calendar hanging by the door of the time and dosages. Rita snorted and pursed her lips together, but she swallowed the pills.

"Let's get going, girl. We'll be running out of daylight soon."

Merry smiled to herself, but she didn't comment that it was Rita's slow rising that had delayed their departure until mid-morning. She got ready to leave and waited while Rita pulled on her jacket, her hat, and her gloves.

"I'll drive today, Rita. I need the practice."

The truck cab was icy cold and the windows were etched with spider webs of frost. Merry started the ignition and jumped out to scrape the ice on the windows. Her breath came out in puffy white clouds and the freezing air slapped her cheeks. She needed to remember to start the truck before she let Rita out here. She was learning to deal with the challenges of ice and snow and the darkness that drew in sooner each day. It was mid-morning now, yet it was just past dawn. She climbed into the driver's seat, shivering. Rita sat huddled deep in her puffy black coat, looking like a giant raven with its feathers fluffed out against the weather.

They made it most of the way up the dirt road toward the main highway, and the ancient heater had just started to put out some tendrils of warmth, when Merry realized the truck was pulling relentlessly to the right. Oh no. But she knew what was wrong. She shoved the gearshift into park, opened the door, and slipped down from the cab. Yes, right there. Flat as a pancake.

Rita rolled down the passenger window. "What's wrong? Did you hit something?"

"It's a flat tire." Merry looked around. They could wait for someone to come by and help, but it could be a long, cold wait. She heard the creak of the passenger door opening and saw Rita's legs shoved sideways as she positioned herself to get out.

"Rita, stop, you don't need to get out."

"'Course I do. Spare's somewhere in the back. We just have to find the jack and get it changed."

Merry bit back a smile at the mental picture of Rita trying to jack up the truck. "Stay in the car. Let me think a minute. Maybe we can—"

She looked up at the sound of an engine right in front of her. A bright and shiny red SUV, clean of dirt and clear of ice unlike any vehicle she'd recently seen in Homer, barreled down the road toward her. She lifted her hand to wave.

She stiffened and stared at the Florida license plate, now just a few feet from them.

It couldn't be. It looked just like the Harris's car, the one they parked in their driveway because it was too wide for their garage. Ben Harris always smiled and waved across the street when he saw her. He'd retired a couple of years ago, and now he and Greta traveled all the time. Her heart pounded in her chest, and she had an almost uncontrollable urge to run. Oh my God—it's Ben and Greta Harris. What should I do? What am I going to say?

Rita was mumbling behind her, but the blood was pounding in her ears and she couldn't make out the words. Both doors to the SUV popped open, and she saw jeans-clad legs drop to the ground on both sides behind the open doors.

They'll know me. I'm sure they'll know me. What are they doing here? What will I say? Can I hide my face? She started shaking, and her breath seemed stuck in her throat, coming out in painful, short gasps. What should I do?

A tall, tanned, graying man in a blue North Face parka walked around the open door.

"Having some problems?" he called out.

Merry felt lightheaded, and she reached out for the support of the hood of the truck. It's not Ben Harris. It's not.

"Are you all right?" The man's face was worried now, and he walked toward her. "Are you okay?"

She nodded and continued to concentrate on breathing. "Just...a flat tire. We just have a flat tire."

He smiled at her. "Well, I guess I can help you with that." He turned toward the SUV. "Sarah, they've got a flat. Wait in the car and stay warm while I give them a hand." He waved at the well-coifed woman in a matching parka who seemed very happy to jump back inside.

He turned to Merry. "I'm Jacob, and that's Sarah back there. We're from Florida. Crazy time to come to Alaska, but Sarah's got a cousin who's getting married in Anchorage next week, so we decided, hell, we'd just take a month and drive up the Alcan and see the country in the winter." He shook his head in wonder. "Craziest thing we ever did. You ever drive the Alcan?"

Merry shook her head, still feeling faint. It's not Ben Harris. It's just some tourist. It's not anyone who knows me.

He moved behind her and introduced himself to Rita, and now she was telling him where she thought the jack was. Merry closed her eyes and concentrated on breathing, in and out.

It wasn't Ben. This time. But one day it would happen. Florida was far, far away, but one day someone was going to show up here that knew her. And even if that day was a long time away, even if it never came, she would always be looking over her shoulder.

She realized that she was so cold that her teeth had begun to chatter. Her stomach had congealed into a tight, painful ball. She forced herself to face Jacob, to move to help him find the jack. They both turned toward the grind and squeal of another vehicle pulling up behind the SUV.

Rita called out through the open cab door. "Oh, Jacob, it's our friend Nick. He knows all about fixing a flat."

Jacob and Nick were about the same height, but the resemblance ended there. As they shook hands, Merry watched them. Jacob was rake-thin and tanned, and he would have looked at home in a white-cotton shirt, sitting in a seaside bar, sipping a drink topped with a paper parasol. Nick was solid. His powerful shoulders and arms strained against the fabric of his old lined denim jacket. His face was weathered ruddy from the bite of the north wind, not the kiss of the warm southern sun. The city and the country. Or is it the tropics and the far north? She was still rattled from her scare, but her breathing had returned to normal. Her thoughts still weren't coming together very well.

Nick assured Jacob that he could fix the flat alone, and Jacob's SUV roared back up the little road toward the highway. Nick stuck his head through the cab window and said a few words to Rita, making sure she was all right, then he'd immediately turned to the task of finding the jack. He didn't say anything to Merry. She hugged her coat around her and stamped her feet, which were starting to go numb. She walked back to where he was struggling to shove the jack under the front tire.

"Hello, Nick."

He barely glanced up. "Merry, it's too cold for Rita to sit here. Take her to the cabin in my truck, and then come back here. I should be done by the time you get back." His voice was even and impersonal. She felt some need to protest about being ordered around, but she knew his words made sense. Rita shouldn't be sitting in a frigid truck cab.

It didn't take long to drive Rita back home and

return, but when she got back Nick had already changed the tire. The punctured tire was lying on the side of the road, and he was leaning against the truck, rubbing his hands together.

She turned off the engine and took a couple of deep breaths. I have to talk to him. He turned to face her when she opened the door and climbed out.

He stood looking at her, his arms crossed.

"Merry, I don't understand."

"I know." She didn't know what else to say.

"I know that your feelings got hurt. I didn't handle that whole situation well, and I'm sorry. Sometimes I know my manner is a bit rough, but what's all this about? I don't understand why you can't let this go. I explained the situation to you."

She could feel her eyes filling up with tears and she hung her head. His explanation was straightforward and made sense. Her feelings had been hurt, but she suspected that her reaction was way out of proportion. But she could still feel the hollow ache in her belly when she remembered him turning from her, cradling Cassandra, and brushing her aside like she didn't matter.

"Merry, Cassandra needed me that afternoon."

She shook her head. She couldn't say all the things she wanted to say. I thought you chose her. I thought you left me. I thought it was happening to me all over again. I don't want to be hurt anymore. I want to matter. It hurt so badly, so very badly. I don't want to disappear again.

How could she explain all the messy confused thoughts in her head when he had no idea who she was and where she had come from?

He walked over and put his hand very gently on her arm. "I'm not sure what's going on with you, Merry, but you are going to need to trust me. I want you to trust me."

Trust. That was the hardest thing of all. She looked up at him through her tears. A thought rushed into her mind, unbidden.

He's not Michael.

Nick was many things, strong and sometimes impatient and loyal and a little maddening and gentle, but...he was not Michael.

His voice was soft now. "We can still take it slow, Merry. But I care about you."

She crushed her face into his jacket as he wrapped his arms around her. She had no idea what to do with these feelings she was having for him. No idea at all. But she was glad he was here, holding her now.

They stood together for a little while, not saying anything. Then he pulled away and looked down into her face. They had both started to shiver. His voice was gravelly now.

"We'd better get back to Rita. I know she'll start worrying. I've got to give her a message from Bess about Thanksgiving dinner, and I have to get back to town soon."

Thanksgiving? Merry frowned. Yes, it's late November, of course...Thanksgiving.

Nick smoothed a strand of hair that had escaped from her fleece hat. He handed her Rita's set of keys. "Drive slowly. That spare looks pretty bald to me. I'll be right behind you." He grabbed the flat with one hand and tossed it into the back of his truck.

He'll be right behind me.

~ * ~

The snowfall last night had been heavy and wet. As she'd trudged to Cassandra's this morning, new snow grabbed at her boot treads until she was stumbling on top of two inches of packed snow piggybacking on the bottom of her boots. She'd pulled her feet free at the door and walked into the quiet, warm room in her wool socks.

The air has weight today. She looked out of Cassandra's windows. As the studio space warmed the glass, chunks of sloppy snow spun away from the piles mounded like white, bushy eyebrows over the tops of the window frames. They drifted down the panes, stopping and starting again in new channels, changing direction, unpredictable, breaking into smaller pieces as they descended.

Cassandra sat at the largest studio table, dipping a long soft-tipped brush into a jar of black underglaze. As Merry watched, she painted a squat black raven on the side of a pitcher, using only five strokes.

"I've never seen you paint figures on your work before." Merry sat down next to her.

Cassandra shrugged. "Just ravens. Just sometimes." She pulled another pitcher forward on the table.

They sat without talking for a few minutes while Cassandra painted. Merry thought about ravens. They were everywhere, fat inky black birds with shiny, curved beaks. Merry often heard them before she saw them. They made a bewildering array of calls, from harsh crow-like caws to odd hollow-bell tones. Nick had told her they were wily, that they worked together in groups to trick other animals to get food. One would distract a dog while the others stole the food out of its dish. Nick said...Nick. She sat straighter on her stool.

"Cassandra," Merry spoke, then hesitated. "I want to tell you something."

Cassandra didn't pause. Her brush continued to glide. Another raven appeared, this one poised for flight.

"Hmm?" Cassandra's eyebrows raised just a hair, but her brush continued its smooth swoop across the pot's surface.

"It's about Nick." Her own voice sounded thin and uncertain in her ears. She exhaled slowly. She knew she was going to sound foolish. She'd rehearsed this conversation in her mind, hoping to make it sound mature and matter-of-fact, not like they were both still high schoolers, but no magic words emerged. She'd decided just to blunder through this as best she could.

Cassandra's hand wavered for only a fraction of a second. "Nick?" Her voice was cool and neutral.

"It's just that...I wanted you to know...that I've been spending time with him." Another deep inhale and exhale. "I...just wanted you to know."

Cassandra nested her brush into the precise center of the towel folded next to the glaze jar. She stood and moved to the shelf of bisque-fired pots, choosing another two to bring to the table.

"I...I just..." Merry's mind buzzed. What else should she say?

"I know." Cassandra's voice was quiet. She put the two pots, another tall pitcher and a fat round bowl on the table, then she turned to Merry. Merry looked into her eyes. All the Cassandras flitted behind those eyes—the one who was aloof and unapproachable, the one who was haunted by the terror of a brutal attack, the one who loved Nick. And, too, the one who was her friend. They were all there.

Cassandra's mouth curved upward, not warm, not happy, but with the hint of smile, perhaps a sad smile, that seemed to say, It's okay.

"Do you want me to show you how these underglazes work?"

Merry swallowed and nodded. She understood. They would probably never talk of this. But her own heart tugged open and lightened, ever so little. She knows. It's one less secret. One less thing I'm hiding from someone I care about.

A chunk of icy snow crashed against a windowpane as the rising wind pulled it from the thawing roof. The sharp crack startled both of them, and Merry realized they'd leaned toward one another as they jumped, without thinking. The way friends do, she thought.

Twenty Nine

It was the third Thursday in November, but Merry thought the date was the only fact that linked this Thanksgiving to any others in her life.

Rita told Merry that Bess and Bill put on Thanksgiving dinner every year, because they lived in one of the few cabins spacious enough for everyone, but mostly, Rita said, because Bess missed her big family during the holidays. She'd left her brothers and sisters and cousins back in the "old country" when she'd emigrated as Bill's bride, years and years ago. "You'll see," Rita whispered to Merry, as they arrived. "That old Brit accent of hers gets stronger and stronger as the night gets going and the wine gets a-flowing, even though Thanksgiving ain't no Tory holiday, as far as I know."

The middle of the main room of Bess and Bill's cabin rose a full two stories to the ceiling, with the bedrooms and an office loft circling the sides as a partial second floor. An open staircase connected to a walkway with a polished fir bannister circled around the inside of the second story like a catwalk. In the downstairs space, Bill had linked mismatched tables of various sizes and shapes across the big room, then covered them with overlapping white paper tablecloths. Merry thought it looked like they would be eating off the top of the boxcars of a miniature train that Bill had driven across the living room. Folding chairs, deck chairs, kitchen chairs had all been called into service at the twenty or so place settings. Some settings sported plaid napkins, some had flowered napkins, some had plain bright-red napkins. Tall dark wine bottles stuffed with skinny short red candles graced the center of each table segment, along with glass jars of grocery store daisies, dyed in improbable neon colors. It was color and pattern chaos, and it screamed festivity. Merry couldn't help but laugh.

Rita and Merry had insisted on coming early to help, though Bess had protested that she would have everything under control. When they arrived, pots bubbled on all four burners of Bess's big woodstove, and the cabin windows streamed as the damp heat hit the icy glass.

"Whew, you were right," Merry murmured to Rita, as she shed her jacket and sweater and grabbed an apron hanging on the peg by the open kitchen. Rita had warned her to wear a light T-shirt. With the woodstove burning hot all day to cook the dinner, the cabin was already above eighty degrees, and they were only the first guests to arrive to add their body heat to the mix. Beads of perspiration popped out on her forehead and upper lip.

She smelled the huge pan of potatoes boiling on the stove, and the familiar dense scent of green beans topped with canned onion crisps baking in the oven. Bread too, yeasty and fresh-baked, and the sweet, warm waft from berry pies, cooling—as best they could—on the small kitchen table. But she frowned. There was no heady buttery smell of a huge bird sizzling and roasting in the oven. Could someone else be bringing that? Or, her eyes opening wide with alarm at a new thought, had Bess somehow gotten distracted and forgotten to put the turkey in hours ago?

But there was another scent, too, briny and a bit sharp. There on the counter, over three feet long, lay an enormous king salmon, headless, its orange flesh almost florescent under the iridescent silver-and-gray skin. It was an object of primal beauty.

She realized she was gaping at the fish. Rita cackled. "That's right, it's your first Alaskan Thanksgiving. No turkey for us. Just the finest fish in the world. Winter-caught King. Come on, there's work to do."

Bess filled mismatched glass jelly jars with red

wine, and they made a quick toast to Thanksgiving before turning to work, cleaning and chopping vegetables for salad, slicing the breads, whisking together a tangy lemon sauce for the salmon. The temperature in the cabin climbed.

More guests arrived. Nick first, his hair freshly trimmed and slicked back, toting four bottles of red wine, presenting Bess with a small bouquet of pink carnations and a kiss. He immediately offered to pitch in to help with the cooking, but Bill quickly diverted him to the small glasses clustered around the whiskey bottle near the fireplace.

"Don't worry. Boys get to clean up," Bess called out, her voice rich with Cockney burr. Merry grinned into the massive bowl of cooked potatoes she was struggling to mash with a very inadequate fork.

Nick was suddenly at her side, grabbing the bowl. He loomed over her and twirled an imaginary handlebar mustache. "Now you just give me that big bowl, little lady. Stand back and watch a real man at work." She chuckled at his botched attempt at a Southern drawl, and she leaned back against the sink to sip her wine and watch him attack the potatoes. There was a comforting clatter and bustle all around her in the kitchen as the various dishes were hurried along to meet together in perfect order at the finish line, but for the moment she was content to pause and look at Nick. He seemed so perfectly at ease, with the air of a man who knew where he belonged and was happy to be there. He noticed her watching and flashed her a huge, crooked grin.

"Happy Thanksgiving, Merry." His eyes were warm and direct and made her flush. She felt her breath catch in her throat, and she was glad the hot kitchen provided her cover.

"Happy Thanksgiving right back at you." Her voice sounded a little strange, throaty, in her own ears. She looked into his eyes and smiled. Her stomach quaked a little then, a hollow pang she hadn't felt in a long time. She wondered if she was going to have any appetite for the meal to come. "You are indeed a handy man to have around."

They could have been called a motley dinner crew. No one had really dressed up, though a few sets of flashier earrings and a couple of pressed shirts had made an appearance. The noise of their conversations and shouts of laughter rang through the hot and crowded cabin, as jokes and jibes were tossed from one end of the long string of tables to the other. Bill's two mutts, some blend of golden retriever and husky, quietly padded around the perimeter, staring at the steaming dishes, their eyes anxious and soft with hope. Merry looked around in wonder. It was so unabashedly jolly. Dickens, she thought. No goose, and no Mister Scrooge, but this is definitely Dickens.

Bess and Bill's ten-year-old daughter had cut out rather droopy brown paper turkeys (Why not salmon? Merry thought) for the place settings, each one scrawled with a name. Merry was pleased to find herself between Nick and Moira. She caught a couple of pointed dagger glances from Cassandra, who was seated far away at the other end of the table, but she was too happy to worry about it. Nick spent a lot of time listening to Harry, the mini-mart cashier, seated on his other side, but Merry knew from experience that was because Harry rarely stopped talking. For once, Harry had taken off his squashed ball cap, and his frizzy brown hair flew around his face as he talked, almost as if it generated its own wind currents. She just picked at her food. The flutter was still there, deep in her stomach.

Bill stood and tapped his spoon against the jar serving as his wineglass. He listed a little to the right, probably, Merry thought, as a result of those pre-dinner whiskeys. He made an effort to pull himself straight and hem-hawed. "Old friends and new..." he droned, slowly.

Bess tugged at his shirt. "Oh, get on with it, Bill," she said, giving him an affectionate poke in the ribs.

"Well, okay then." Bill had started to lean again.

"Let's do the thankfuls."

Merry snapped to attention. That was what she'd done at home, with her mother and father, every Thanksgiving. It had usually been just Mom and Dad and her, holding hands and murmuring their gratitude for being together, content with one another. She had never felt closer to her parents than during those celebrations. They were a small family and not usually sentimental. All three of them were quiet by nature, and they meshed well together, recognizing the often-unspoken love that existed among them without any need to find words for it. But at Thanksgiving, it seemed natural to craft those feelings into a few sentences that reflected the deep bond they shared. Then Dad was gone, taken by a stroke much too soon. She and Mom carried on the tradition for years, even after Mom had to go into the care home. But then Mom had started to forget, not just the thankfuls, but little by little, everything. Mom's memories drifted away first, and then years later her body followed. Merry felt tears prick the back of her eyes.

Michael had refused to continue the tradition. Thanksgiving was just another Hallmark holiday, he said. "Pass the turkey and keep the wine coming." She could hear him so clearly in her head. Why had she given up so easily? It had meant something to her, the holiday pause, the time to reflect and appreciate. It was just a little thing, but it had been important. Yet she had agreed, that yes, it was a silly tradition and its time had passed.

But today this was no contemplative scene. These thankfuls were raucous and thoughtful and funny and touching, but not quiet.

Bess was tearfully thankful that she'd just heard that her dear niece was going to pull through after a bad car accident. (Her accent had continued to regress during the evening, as Rita had promised, and now it was a bit difficult to understand her.) Medford was grateful for the "awesome summer king salmon season." ("Not that it did me all that much good, personally," he told the jeering crowd.) Cassandra's voice was quiet and subdued, but she said she was grateful that her work continued to go well. Harry, his fingers fumbling above his head for his missing ball cap, was thankful that his parents were still in good health, and that he was finally off the night shift at the mini-mart.

Rita rested her fingers lightly on Rachel's arm, as Rachel stared down at the table and whispered, "I'm just glad to be here." Rita jumped in right away and said, "And hell, I'm just thankful that Rick caught that big, old salmon for this dinner." Rick beamed and the rest of the table applauded. Zinnea, who taught meditation at the library on Thursday nights, intoned a Zen blessing: "In this plate of food I see the entire universe supporting my existence."

It was Nick's turn. Under the table, he took Merry's hand. "Well, I'm just glad to be here with old friends—and new." He squeezed her hand and didn't let it go. It was her turn.

She was just going to say thank you, something that simple, but suddenly she was speechless. She had so much joy, sitting here, eating this meal, holding Nick's hand. Somehow she had landed where she was meant to be.

Everyone was gazing at her, waiting, but no one looked impatient or even surprised. They were smiling, some maybe a little quizzically.

She stumbled over her words, but she got them out. "Thank you, everyone, for letting me be a part of this. You will never know..."

Her voice broke, and she couldn't manage any more, but it seemed to be enough. Attention turned to Moira, who was making some joke about being grateful that the gallery was still afloat, if barely. Moira's sparkling red hoop earrings bounced around her face as she talked. Merry could feel Nick squeeze her hand again, but otherwise he let her be. She leaned ever so slightly into his arm, drawn to him as if he had his own gravitational pull.

The party began to break up soon after the thankfuls, everyone seemingly mellow after the food, the wine, and the whiskey. The men made quick work of the dishes, only breaking one jelly jar. "A record," Bill announced, his words slurring into one another. "Remember the year we broke Bess's giant glass platter?" Bess punched him gently on the arm and sat him down in a nearby chair.

Rita and Moira left right after dinner. Merry saw the deep lines of fatigue in Rita's face, and knew she probably wanted to lie down somewhere. Moira waved Merry away and insisted on driving Rita back home.

Merry and Nick were two of the last to leave. They said their good-byes and set out into the crisp night, the fresh cold air splashing against their hot faces.

Nick held her hand and she let him lead the way.

~ * ~

When she first awoke, she didn't know where she was. She'd had that disoriented feeling before, but in the past it had always been unpleasant at best, blooming into a tiny ball of panic until she could anchor herself in a time and place. But this time, the small moment of disorientation didn't come with a flash of fear. She awoke deep in contentment.

Of course. She smiled to herself as she became fully awake. She was in Nick's bed. She was naked in the warmth of Nick's bed, nestled under the weight of the puffy comforter, opening her eyes to the morning sunlight that poured through the window next to her. She pushed her face into the feather pillow and grinned, remembering the night before. Nick. She nudged her mind away from any judgments about what had happened, or any thoughts about what came next. It was enough to have this time to savor the way she felt right now, her body warm and heavy and still, peaceful, cocooned in the deep mattress. It was enough to lie here quietly, staring up at the rough ceiling.

But where was Nick now?

Muffled sounds escaped from the kitchen nook, and she smelled fresh coffee. She sat up quietly and looked over at him. He was moving slowly, taking cups out of the cabinet, not wanting to wake her, she supposed.

"Good morning, Nick." Her voice rolled out throaty and low. She felt a jab of shyness. This was all new territory now. There was no going back after last night. He was wearing a heavy-knit sweater and jeans, but she now knew what lay beneath—the freckles over the skin of his arms, muscled from his work on the boat, the wiry, red hair that covered his chest, the way his neck smelled, clean and musky. She felt her face start to warm.

He turned and smiled at her. "Good morning? You've slept more than half the morning away. Coffee?"

She nodded, easing herself back onto the pillows.

He brought two cups over to the bed, sliding one into her outstretched hand.

"Merry..."

She looked up at him. His voice changed, and now it had an odd guarded edge. Something wasn't right.

"Merry," he said again, and cleared his throat. "We need to talk a bit. I need to tell you about some things. About me."

A pang of anxiety worried her stomach. She had no idea what he was about to say.

He ran his hand gently down her arm, then he stood and took a few slow steps toward the table. "Last night was wonderful—well, at least it was for me." He looked over at her, and she saw affection in his eyes, but something else too. Hard creases framed his eyes and mouth. What was wrong? Surely he couldn't regret what had just happened between them.

He took a deep breath and paused, as if he were trying to choose his words carefully. "You don't know very much about me. Well, I guess we could say we don't know very much about each other, really." Merry felt her body tense. Was he going to ask about her past?

Nick carefully placed his cup on the table and turned back toward her. Merry watched as he stared at a spot somewhere near his feet. He cleared his throat again. He still didn't look at her.

"You deserve to know," he said, "but it's not something that is easy for me to talk about." His blue eyes were dark and solemn.

"Nick, if there's something you don't want to talk about..." Did she want to hear this? They were just starting to really know each other, to care about one another, focusing only on the present. She had guarded her secret carefully, but he was going to share something about his past that was obviously important to him. It could change everything.

Nick crossed his arms and hesitated. Merry could only wait and wonder.

"It seems sometimes that I've been here forever. But it's only been about ten years." His voice was hoarse and gravelly, as if the words were reluctant to come out. "I'm from California, Merry, and would you believe it, I was an investment banker there." He chuckled, but it was mirthless. He walked away and stood next to the fireplace, staring down into the embers, before turning back to face her.

"I was a banker, and a damned successful one, and I was married and had a family. A wife and a little girl. She was ten when I left." He paused. "I haven't seen her since I left."

Merry's eyes flitted over his rigid face. Nick had a family? A family he left? A hole opened inside of her, and it was filling up with fear and apprehension. This was not what she ever expected to hear from a man she'd seen protect Cassandra and watch over Rita. Suddenly, she realized how little she knew of him. She pulled the blankets closer around herself.

He walked back to the bed and fumbled in the pocket of his jeans, then held out a scrap of paper—an old school photograph, creased and worn and faded. She tore her eyes from the little blonde girl's smiling face and looked up at Nick. "Cindy," he said, and grimaced.

Nick stared at the photo, running his thumb over its weathered surface. "Back then, my work was everything to me. It took all my time, my attention, all my energy. I didn't have anything left for Anya and Cindy. Anya loved it at first because there was lots of money in it. We didn't want for anything. She could buy everything she wanted. But she got lonely I guess, and decided to look for company elsewhere." He frowned. "I can't really blame her now, but it sure did set off a firestorm in me then. So we divorced, and it was just about as ugly as it could get. We fought, we were mean, and Cindy kind of got lost in the middle of it."

Nick looked over at her. She was riveted in place, absolutely still. A chasm opened before her, a deep frightening pit, and she didn't want to look down into it. What if Nick wasn't at all who he seemed to be? He must have noticed how rigid her body had become, motionless, as if poised for flight, because he started to talk more quickly, opening and closing his hands as if he were trying to get them to tell his story.

"I wasn't an abusive dad or anything. I just wasn't around much. Anya played dirty, and made it damned difficult for me to have any sort of relationship with Cindy. After a while, Cindy didn't even want to see me. She'd throw a tantrum when I went to pick her up for a visit. I got mad, really mad." He looked over at Merry, a sheen of perspiration dotting his forehead.

"I threw in the towel; I gave it all up and came up here. After the divorce, I wanted a fresh start and I was sick of the business world and of what I had become. I came up here and signed on a boat and found that fishing suited me." He shrugged. "Homer suited me. I could do clean, hard work here, and I could sleep at night." He was looking at her intently as he talked, as if he needed to see that she was listening, that she was understanding. She gave a slight nod. She could see that he was dredging every word, each sentence, from someplace very deep inside of himself, someplace where this story had been hidden and guarded. She was spellbound. She let his story wash over her, trying to hear every word, trying to understand.

"And I always paid child support and all that. I didn't abandon them financially. Anya made sure of that, but I would have anyway. She kept the house. But I didn't fight hard enough for Cindy."

He sighed, and the pain in his face was so raw she winced.

"Anya got married again, to the jerk she'd been seeing while we were married, and he moved into the house. Pretty soon he was Cindy's dad, not me." Nick's hands opened and closed, opened and closed.

"I got tired of fighting for visits, for contact, to make Anya stop bad-mouthing me to Cindy. So I stuck my feelings for Cindy away, justified to myself that she was doing fine without me and didn't really need me. Some nights I'd find myself crying..." He paused, his eyes brimming with tears. She wanted to comfort him, but she didn't move. How long, she wondered, had he held this inside?

"Anyway," he said, shaking his head, "after a while I didn't think about her every day, or even every week. Then about a year ago, I don't know why, I got a yen to see her. I wanted to see how she had turned out, I guess. Now that she was old enough, and Anya wouldn't always be in the way, I wanted to see if we could be some sort of family again."

He looked at her, and she read all the sorrow and regret in his eyes. "I called her. She's married now, of all things. Married at twenty, way too young." He shook his head. "And she wanted nothing to do with me. Nothing at all. Seems that Mr. Perfect Second Dad wasn't so perfect after all. Turns out that she blamed me all those years for not being there for her. Not being there to protect her."

He picked up his cup from the table and stared down into it. "I didn't fight hard enough, Merry, and I'll always regret it. I gave up because I didn't want to fight Anya anymore and Cindy paid the price. Would you believe it?" He looked at her, his glare direct and hard and angry. "The guy molested her. Molested her for months when she was fifteen before she convinced Anya that she was really telling the truth about what was happening. I left her and someone came in and hurt her. I never knew..."

The tears starting running down his face and his voice cracked. Merry felt his deep pain wash over her, and she stood and moved close to him, holding him, wrapping her arms around him. She could feel his body shudder with the sobs that erupted from the very center of him.

He took a shaky breath and pulled back from her, standing tall and straight and seeming all the more vulnerable for it.

"So now you know the truth about me, I guess. I gave up and I didn't fight for my little girl. I just ran away. I was a coward, and I just left and let the chips fall..."

Merry buried her head in his chest. His pain was so raw and deep, even after all this time. She felt his guilt about not taking responsibility, about running away from his life. Yet it was clear that he had taken that pain and become someone better. She saw it in his tenderness with Rita, and his need to shield Cassandra, as best he could, from the world that tormented her. And she realized something too, something that had been hovering around her consciousness that she hadn't wanted to know. But now she knew.

She loved this man, this man scarred and burdened by his personal failure to do the right thing, to protect his child, to be the man he thought he should have been. She loved him. In the middle of the muddle she had made of her life, she had fallen in love again. And, though he hadn't yet said it, she thought he loved her too. Why else would he have told her this story, so hard and painful to tell? The thought of being without him was unbearable, but all she had offered to him was a veneer shell of a person, a fake person built of lies and cowardice, who hadn't faced up to her responsibilities and who had run away, too, run away and left a lot of people to pick up the pieces and grieve for her. He had shared the pain of his story with her. He had dragged out the darkness of his past and displayed it to her.

She reached out, took his hand, and they stood together, silently. She needed to tell him, she knew she did. She needed to confess that she, too, had a secret past that she was ashamed of, a past of cowardice and avoidance and denial. But she couldn't, not now. For the moment, she could only hold his hand and stand next to him, wanting him and loving him.

But soon. Her world was tilting, and she had to tell him soon. She was putting down roots; she could feel it. She was forging new ties. She was becoming a part of this world. She couldn't pretend much longer.

~ * ~

They spoke only a few words on the drive back home, just agreeing about the fineness of the day, and making a little halting conversation about a "For Sale" sign on a boat parked along the road. He placed his hand over hers on the truck seat, and his body heat radiated through her hand, up her arm, and into her heart. She was giddy and bedazzled, still awash in memories from their night together, and the shared intimacy from Nick's revelations this morning. She understood that she had a mountain of confusion and deception to clear up, but now it all seemed possible. She could do it; she would straighten all this out, and soon, but not right now. Now she was enveloped in a comforting fog, and she wanted only to remain in this moment, with Nick beside her, fragmented images of last night still teasing her mind. Yes, there was so much to do, and the very heart of the work was telling Nick about who she was and what she had done. But for the moment, she needed to relish this time with him, to drink it all in, when the world seemed so new, fresh, and stunningly bright. Late morning sunlight sparkled on the tops of the snowdrifts by the road, and even the brown frozen mud of the rutted roadbed held its own charm, guiding the truck tires along like the steel rails of a roller coaster.

She closed her eyes and leaned back against the seat. This is what happiness feels like. I remember now. Nick squeezed her hand as they pulled up in front of Rita's cabin.

They sat for a moment in silence, the only sound the engine's low humming. Nick inhaled and turned to face her. When he spoke, his voice rumbled over her.

"I might not see you until tomorrow. I'm picking up Pete and driving to Kenai to get that carburetor." He glanced at his watch. "In fact, I'm late. I shouldn't be more than a few hours there." He squeezed her hand again. "But I'll be thinking about you. I'll come by as soon as I get back."

She leaned over and kissed him. They pressed their foreheads together for just one moment, and she tipped her head up to smile at him as she pulled away and opened the truck door. She lingered on the doorstep, her arms wrapped tightly around herself against the biting cold, and watched the truck rock its way back up the uneven road. Even after Nick was out of sight, she stood there, dropping down into her feelings, relishing the heat she could feel in the deep core of her body and the excited buzz in her brain.

When her feet went numb, she pushed open the door. Rita was sitting at the kitchen table in her rumpled bathrobe, her head bent low over a newspaper, holding a cup of tea. Merry felt a small jab of guilt. What should she say to Rita?

"Rita...ah...I hope you weren't worried. About last night..."

Rita's gravelly voice cut in. "Merry, it says here that Safeway's got a meat sale. Maybe you should go by and get some of those nice beef patties we like."

She didn't look up, but Merry could see the hint of a smile on her face as she continued to look with apparent intent interest at the paper.

"Oh, sure."

"And you better hustle up, girl. Remember Moira said she wanted to do some inventory or something like that today, and she's coming to get you in half an hour."

Rita was definitely smiling now, though she kept her face pointed directly down to the table as she turned the page.

"Oh my gosh, yes, I forgot." Merry turned and rushed toward the stairs. "I just...completely forgot." She bounded up the steps two at a time, her body almost weightless, as though she was being danced aloft by puppet strings.

~ * ~

The afternoon rolled along in a pleasant, confusing blur. Moira hadn't wanted to take a technical inventory after all. She just wanted to move around some of the displays and get some sense of the gallery's current stock since, she said, there was often a buying rush right before Christmas. The locals liked to send authentic Alaskan gifts to their friends and family. "They especially like those wooden moose that poop out candies when you move their tails. Goodness knows why." Moira rolled her eyes and arranged the pooping moose on a front table. "Not our most artistic offering, that's for sure, but they help pay the bills."

Merry grinned and trotted back to the storeroom for another box. Somehow she was following Moira's directions and answering her questions, though her mind was almost completely elsewhere. She couldn't stop smiling. If Moira noticed her constant goofy grin, she didn't comment about it. Merry thought she was too engrossed in the decisions of where to put the faux fur seal pups and the seaweed and starfish door wreaths to notice.

Cassandra's work, as usual, was displayed alone on

a table in the center of the gallery. Merry paused to stroke the long, smooth line of a swooning pitcher, glazed in a rosy plum hue. Her smile faltered for just a moment. Cassandra won't be surprised, but she will still be hurt. She stood a little straighter and took a deep breath. I love them both. I'm going to make this all work. She felt almost fierce, bold in her resolve. I know I can make this all work. I have to. She shook her head briskly and hurried back to help Moira with the stuffed seals.

They finished up at five o'clock, well after the weak winter sun had set. Moira gave her a lift to the last cutoff to the cabin before she hurried off to a late appointment. Merry reached the cabin door in just a few minutes, but she was already shivering from the icy tendrils of air that had slipped around her scarf and down her back. Even Rita's loaned fleece sweater and down vest, topped with her old jacket that cut the wind chill, couldn't keep the cold completely at bay.

Rita's truck was gone, but a very faint light leaked from the cabin's front windows. She must have left a light on for me. That was unusual, because Rita was passionate about not wasting money on electricity, but Merry didn't think much of it. It did make coming back to the small, cold cabin a little more welcoming. She shuffled up the front steps, stomping the snow from her boots. Her hands in her gloves were stiff and half-frozen, so she fumbled for a moment with the doorknob. She shoved her shoulder against the warped and stubborn door and heaved it open.

Thirty

Merry stood in the doorway trembling. The darkened hair, the mustache, and the low-set paunch made him look years older, but there was no question that it was Michael. He had found her.

"Meredith." He said her name in a flat, low voice, but she could hear a thread of satisfaction there too. He looked at her and his lips curled upward the slightest bit, but she never would have called it a smile. "My little dead wife. You know, until now, I really wasn't sure it would be you."

He moved out of the shadows toward her. She gripped the doorknob tighter, feeling her head swim. She realized she was holding her breath, and she forced air into her lungs. This all seemed so unreal. Michael, yes it was Michael, but he looked different. My God, he's wearing some sort of disguise. The icy cutting wind from the meadow gusted through the open door into the cabin, ruffling the curtains and snapping the cover of the magazine on the kitchen table. She shivered, but she didn't move. A deep dread grew in the pit of her stomach.

"Close the door, Meredith. It's cold outside." His voice was even-toned, unrevealing. She nudged the door closed behind her, but stayed near with her back at it, staring at him. Michael was here.

Her eyes darted right and left, then widened as a jab of fear prickled down her spine.

"Where's Rita?"

"The old lady?" Michael shrugged, not taking his eyes off her. "I don't know. She drove away while I was waiting for you outside." Meredith felt a brief moment of relief. Rita wasn't here. This was just between Michael and her.

She pressed the palms of her hands back into the rough wood of the door, glad for the solid weight supporting her. Michael hadn't moved, but she felt his presence pushing against her. She lifted her chin and took a deep breath.

"Michael, why are you here?" She took another breath and tried to pull her thoughts together. "I know my leaving probably made a mess of things, and I am sorry about that. But you made your choice, and that choice wasn't me, long before I left."

He cocked his head to one side and stared at her. It was as if he hadn't heard her. "I didn't believe that you could do that, just disappear. Just like that." He spoke as if he were talking to himself. The strange mirthless grimace stayed on his face. His eyes were hard and he squinted, ever so slightly. "You know, you actually look good. Backwoods living must agree with you."

Her words were awkward, tumbling out of her mouth. "Look, Michael, I'm sorry. I never meant to hurt you or anyone. It all just sort of happened, hour to hour, day to day, and then I was here and well, it was better for me here." She forced herself to stare straight back at him without flinching. "I'm not the person I was back home. I know it wasn't the right way to leave, but after the crash..." She knew none of what she was saying made a lot of sense, even to herself. Now that weeks and months had passed, she didn't spend long hours thinking about what she had done and who she had left behind. She was immersed in the new life she was making. But now, with Michael in front of her, the bizarre facts of her disappearance and the absurdity of her running away from her real life slapped her in the face.

Michael still didn't move. He kept his eyes focused steadily on her face. "Yes, well, but now we have a problem to solve, Meredith." His voice was low-pitched and cool. "I think you had better come with me."

Her eyes darted around the cabin. "Now? Oh, Michael, I can't come now. I understand that we have some messes to clean up—messes I made—but I can't just drop everything and leave." She realized she was babbling, but this unexpected collision between her old life and her new one was more than her mind could make sense of. "I can't just walk out of here. I have some things to take care of first, some people to talk to..."

He took a step toward her, and she instinctively tried to step back, but there was nowhere to go. "No, Meredith, you don't need to talk to anyone. You just need to come with me. Now."

Again, she felt that sting of fear run down her spine. She didn't know how Michael should be acting, how anyone would act in this situation, but something wasn't right. Why did he look like that? Why was his hair that dark muddy brown instead of blond, and why was he wearing those baggy, old clothes? She saw that Michael recognized the hesitation that must be evident in her face, and he took another step toward her. Something was definitely not right.

"Meredith, you need to come with me now." His voice was a growl that allowed no discussion or disagreement.

She tried to think straight. Rita wasn't here, but Merry didn't know where she had gone, or when she would be back. There was a cold, hard fury in Michael's eyes. She had to keep Rita out of this.

She tried to pitch her voice low and calming. "All right, Michael, let's go someplace in town to talk about this, but I have to leave a note for Rita. She'll wonder where I am." She reached for the pencil and pad on the counter by the door, but Michael strode the rest of the way across the room and grabbed her arm. She gasped as he pulled the door open and knocked her through with a rough push, slamming the door behind them. Outside, the wind was whistling through the tops of the spruces. Her body started to shiver, but her brain wasn't registering the dense palpable cold. Her throat closed as she gulped the frigid air.

Now she was completely terrified. Michael had never been physically violent with her, but his hold on her arm was so tight that his fingers were digging deep bruises into her flesh. They both slipped on the ice-covered mud as he forced her toward the road, but his grip on her arm never loosened and she couldn't pull free. She saw a dark car half-hidden by the thick stand of trees at the end of the driveway.

"Michael, stop...stop, please." She struggled with him, trying to wrench her arm away, crying now, but he muscled her forward, saying nothing, somehow getting the passenger door open, knocking her head against the doorframe as he shoved her into the seat. As he started to walk around to the driver's side, she banged her door open, but he was back at her side in an instant. She looked up, not believing at first what she was seeing in his hand. A gun. A gun pointed at her.

"Sit still, you little bitch," he hissed, his glare radiating pure hatred. "It will be more complicated if I have to shoot you right now, but I'll do it, damn it, if you give me any more trouble. Just shut up and sit still."

He kept the gun pointed at her as he sidestepped to the driver's side and climbed into the car. This isn't happening. It can't be happening. A strangled sob rose in her throat as she heard the door locks clunk. Michael slammed the car into gear and it lurched forward.

"Michael." Her voice was a scraping whisper now, frantic and wild. "Michael, what are you doing?"

He seemed deadly calm again, as he drove slowly down the bumpy road. He nudged the gun next to him into the window side of his seat, where he could reach it easily, and his eyes looked straight ahead.

"Well, Meredith..." Once more, that awful humorless smile. "I can't trust you to stay dead. For some reason, Ellen is convinced that you're alive, and the meddling bitch is determined to look for you. And wouldn't you know it, the latest coroner's report managed to identify some of the remains from the crash." He squinted and glared into the shadowy gloom ahead. "But not yours, Meredith, not yours." He turned left onto another pitted track of a road, one that led toward a rocky beach concealed by a surrounding dense grove of scrub spruce. Tree branches grated and scraped over the roof of the car as the wheels thumped in and out of ruts.

"And if I can find you, who knows, maybe Ellen can too. It was pure luck that an old bag at the Fairbanks Airport recognized your picture. She even recalled that you—Mary, she called you—had gone back home to Homer. Said to tell you hello if I saw you."

He glanced her way, and his eyes glittered in the light reflected from the dashboard.

"You have to stay dead, Meredith."

She stared at him, not making sense of what he was saying. She tried to form words, some words, anything to make him stop. Her mouth was so dry that her voice sounded cracked and broken. "Good God, Michael. Stop. Please stop."

His eyes darted to her, and the tone in his voice was almost nonchalant, as if they were back at home, discussing what restaurant to go to. "After all, this is really your fault. You made this happen when you decided to pursue this little charade."

She forced herself to talk, although her dry throat was closing up. "Michael, I am sorry, I'm sorry I hurt you and everyone else. I'll go back with you. I'll make it right. We'll sort it out." She hardly knew what she was saying, but she had to say something, the right thing, anything to get him to stop and let her out.

He gave a harsh bark of a laugh. "It's too late, you have to know that." He looked over at her, his face contorted into an expression of cruel amusement. "When you 'died,' you took care of a lot of problems. No wrangling with divorce lawyers over how we split the property. George was easy enough to get out of the way, but I still wasn't sure that I could get you to use Syd. And I just couldn't have anyone digging into our accounts. There would be questions about where all that money's gone, why there's that second mortgage you don't know about." He leaned forward and squinted at the road ahead. "But now, the life insurance payout is going to arrive at just the right time." He lifted his left hand off the steering wheel and fingered the gun nestled next to him. "You didn't know, Meredith, but I've had some big money issues for some time. The kind of money issues that involve a lot of pain if they don't get fixed. But your death is solving them all." He glanced over at her again. "I just can't have you coming back from the dead. I think you understand."

A scream of terror was rising in her throat. Michael was going to kill her. This couldn't be happening. He had found her, and now he was planning to kill her. Her breath came in jerks, almost like hiccups, and she tried to think, to not panic. They bumped down the tiny road, and she knew there were no houses nearby and most likely no one around. He was strong, too strong for her to break away from him. Michael had a gun. And soon they would be at the beach.

Her brain wasn't working right. She couldn't think. She wanted to run, but there was no way to run. How was she going to get away? She forced herself to talk, to say something that would make some sense, but her breath was coming so quickly it was hard to speak.

"Michael, think. This is stupid. They'll know, someone, the police...they'll know because of the plane. You'll be on the list of passengers on the plane, the one you took to get here, and when I turn up dead, they'll put it together. You won't get away with it." Her words tumbled out, carried on bursts of terror, but she had to convince him, to make him listen. She jabbed at the door lock, but it didn't budge. "People know me here. I know it's just been a few months, but I have friends, a job...they'll come looking for me. Cassandra even knows who I really am." Damn, she thought. I shouldn't have said that. I'm putting her in danger. But as panic strangled her chest, she realized that nothing she could say was going to make a difference. Michael was hardly listening to her. He was only focused on what he planned to do.

He barely glanced in her direction. "Meredith, you don't think I've taken care of everything? It isn't that hard to get a new identity, especially when you're in my business. Hanging out with all those big-time crooks has its advantages. And I don't exactly look like myself, do I?" He kept his eyes on the road, slowing slightly as the car lurched over the gaping potholes sunk into the roadbed on the final turn to the beach.

She realized it was true. The way he looked now, it had taken her a moment to recognize him,. It was unlikely that anyone who didn't know him well would see blonde, svelte Michael in the overweight, dark-haired man in drab and dirty clothes sitting next to her.

"And besides," he continued to talk, almost lazily now. "You are just going to disappear again, Meredith. The people here will think you left just as mysteriously as you arrived."

They pulled up on the bluff overlooking the beach. A sliver of moon escaped from the clouds and she saw the wide low-tide flats reaching out to the sea, gleaming dimly in the darkness. Michael turned off the ignition and slowly lifted the gun from his side. It was pointed at her again.

"Get out," he said.

Thirty One

Michael had parked the car on the last few feet of road, right before the ground broke into a jagged cliff with a three-foot drop to the rocks below. He dragged her from the car by one arm and shoved her down the steep slope, pebbles cascading around her as her slipping feet pulled them loose.

Dark lurking spruces hemmed the tiny pocket beach. Piles of tumbled driftwood mounded against large, black, angular rocks, sharp-edged and jagged. The reek of ocean-shattered rotting seaweed burned her nose. She stumbled as Michael pushed her forward, dropping one knee into the ragged end of a slimy log. The pain made her cry out. Michael pulled her roughly to her feet and knocked her forward.

"Keep going."

Ahead, through the gloom, she glimpsed the smooth humped bank of a stream, and just beyond, a wide wash of water silently draining into the bay. A boxy white shape bobbed gently on the water. A boat. A small, white boat with an outboard motor.

She tried to slow down, but Michael hustled her onward. She barely felt the gash in her shin, but the blood running down over her foot made her slip again. This time she fell full forward. As she tried to break her fall with her outstretched hands, the splintered wood of an upturned stump opened gritty punctures in her palms.

"Get up, damn it."

She struggled to her feet. They were almost at the boat. She knew now what he must have planned. He would take her out in the boat and drop her somewhere in Kachemak Bay. She might be found, but probably not. The currents would most likely take her out to sea, or her body would end up in some deserted cove to be eaten by bears and ravens. And even if her body were found, how would anyone connect her death to Michael? As far as the world knew, he was nowhere around here and he thought she was already dead. It might be a mysterious death—maybe even a suspicious one—but no one would tie it back to Michael.

She felt the hard bubble of a scream rise again in her throat. Michael was stronger. What could she do? Beg for her life? She forced herself to think. Don't panic. What's the best thing to do? Suddenly, she remembered Nick's words after she had panicked and run from the grizzly. Never run from a grizzly. Don't act like prey. And Rita's advice, later. But you have to know your bears. You play dead with a grizzly, because then you aren't a challenge and it's likely to lose interest and walk away. But black bears are carrion eaters, so if you play dead with them, they'll just look at you as their next meal. With them you have to fight back with whatever you've got. This was no bear attack. But...she knew Michael. She knew what kind of enemy he was, so she had an advantage. And he didn't know the new Merry. He would be confident that he was stronger and in control, and that she wouldn't have the courage to stand up to him. He wouldn't be expecting her to resist. He was like a carrion eater, looking for an easy meal. She had to fight for her life, but how?

They would reach the boat in a few more steps. She feigned a stumble. "Just a minute, Michael, just a minute." She pitched her voice high and breathless. He loomed above her but let her pause. She huddled low as if she were catching her breath. Her hands scrabbled beneath her for something, anything to use as a weapon, but nothing was in reach except a few small rocks, worn smooth by the sea. But in her deep crouch, something was pushing, digging into her stomach from the inside of her jacket. The compass. Ellen's compass key ring and Ellen's key, forgotten in the tiny zipped pocket, along with the wedding ring she had taken off that first night after the crash.

Merry forced her breath out in shallow puffs and curled in closer to the ground. "Just one more second, Michael. I'm just so out of breath." She heard his hiss of impatience, but he didn't grab her. Not yet. He was probably confident that the end of this was near.

She stole a quick glance upward. He was scowling, his eyes scanning the beach right and left. He held the gun loosely in his right hand with the barrel dropped low, almost as if he'd forgotten he had it. Yes, he definitely thinks this will be easy. She slipped her hand into her jacket and found the tiny pocket. The zipper pulled open only a bit but it was enough. She grabbed the compass tightly in her right hand, letting the serrated edge of the key poke out between her index and middle finger. She took a deep breath.

"Okay, Michael, if you could just help me up..." He reached down to pull at her arm and she moved. With all the strength and speed she could muster, she twisted her body and raked the key across his downturned face. She felt his skin tearing, ripping right under her hand, and his terrible shriek as he dropped her arm and grabbed at his face almost stopped her. Almost.

The gun clattered onto the rocks as he dropped it. She knew she had no advantage except surprise, and she dragged herself upright. In one fluid motion, she grabbed the gun and started to run across the beach. The beach debris battered her ankles and feet, but nothing was going to stop her.

Michael cursed and started after her. If he caught her now, there would be no escape. "You bitch!" His raspy labored breathing was right behind her. She pushed ahead, clambering over the stinking logs, forcing her feet through the gravelly wet sand. I'm faster now. I'm strong. I can make it. She heard a heavy thud and realized that he must have slipped and fallen, but she didn't look back. It wasn't likely that he would stay down for long.

The gun was heavy and awkward. She didn't know how to use it, and who knew if it was even loaded? Slowing for a fraction of a second, she heaved the gun into the water of the bay. One splash and it was gone.

It took only a minute or so for her to reach the road. He was still coming after her, stumbling and cursing, but she didn't know how far behind he was. She took the briefest glance behind her. He was moving fast, but he was limping, and he was holding one hand over his eye. She must have raked his eye too. Good.

She forced herself to think. She would never outrun him on foot when he reached the road. The car. She had to get to the car.

Her feet scrabbled and skittered on loose dirt and rocks on the climb up from the beach to the road, but she snatched at patches of wiry beach grass to heave herself up. She jerked open the driver's door and threw herself into the seat. The keys were there, still in the ignition. Door locks, door locks... The eruption of panic was rising again, threatening to blast away her control, but she pushed it down and away. It took only a moment to find the lock switches and engage them, but he was upon her then, wrenching at the door handle, screaming at her. Blood was coursing down his face, streaming from a jagged rip that tore across his face from his hairline to his jaw. He pounded on the door and windshield with both fists, smearing blood on the glass, screaming her name, a look of absolute hatred on his face.

She twisted the ignition key and the engine roared to life. Michael dashed behind the car as she slammed the gears into reverse and floored the gas. He dove out of the way a split second before the car lurched backward. Her breath was catching in her chest, heaving and shaking, but she didn't stop. The car rocked and bucked as she drove backward over the ruts and potholes. Soon there was a slight pullout on the side of the road and she slid into it, turning the car, and shoving the gears into drive. But then

Michael was there again, somehow, this time with a massive tree branch that he smashed into the windshield. The glass shattered but held together in a web of a thousand shiny pieces. She dug her foot into the gas pedal and screeched away, feeling more than hearing the dull thump of Michael's body against the hood.

She was gasping in shallow huffs as she gripped the steering wheel, rocking wildly with the car as it careened from side to side on the narrow roadbed. The windshield's splintered safety glass was a glittering blanket of opaque cells, reflecting the light from the dashboard back at her. She craned her head out the side window, steering as best she could down the dark and mangled mud track. Police. Go to the police. She would hit the main road soon and could be at the police station in less than ten minutes. Oh God, this will be over soon. But...

Suddenly she remembered Rita, most likely home by now, sitting in the cabin just minutes from Michael. Rita, all alone. Michael was probably lying in the pitted snow and frozen mud at the side of the road, but still... Rita had no idea what was going on. Rita could be in danger because of her. She would be defenseless.

At the junction, she swung the car to the right toward the cabin. She would get Rita. She would get Rita out of there and they would go to the police together. Then it would be over.

Thirty Two

The car creaked and groaned, knocking against tree roots and rocks, struggling back up the dirt road to the cabin. Get Rita, get to the police. She muttered the refrain over and over, forcing herself to concentrate on the road ahead, each twist and turn, refusing to let her mind return to the beach, to the furious bleeding wreck of Michael chasing after her. Get Rita, get to the police. It was less than a mile, but it seemed endless.

And yes, Rita's truck was pulled up in front of the cabin in its usual place. The kitchen lights were on. She jerked the car to a stop and almost fell out of the car. She banged open the front door.

Merry yelled as she rushed inside. "Rita! Rita, where are you?" Her eyes scanned the cabin. The lights were on, and the door to Rita's bedroom was open, but she wasn't there.

"Merry?" Rita's voice descended, soft.

Upstairs. She was upstairs.

Merry leapt up the stairs, two at a time. Rita was nestled in a crooked heap on a pillow on the floor, her cane lying beside her, in front of the old bureau. The bottom drawer was open, and half the contents were spread across the wooden attic floorboards. Rita held up the picture of Annie in her plaid shirt, grinning into the camera, holding her shining salmon. Merry saw the bright line of tears as Rita rubbed her knobby hand across the skin of her cheek.

"Hello, Merry, I was remembering..." Rita stopped short as she looked up at Merry. "Oh my God, girl, you're bleeding. Was there an accident? Are you hurt?"

Merry shook her head, her breath still coming in short strangled gasps. "Rita, we have to go. Now. No time.

Please. Right now."

Merry grabbed Rita's arm and yanked her upward. "No questions. No time. We have to go right now."

Rita's face contorted with confusion and fear. Merry snatched the cane from the floor.

"I'll explain in the car. Now, Rita. As fast as you can, downstairs."

Merry's arm cinched around Rita's waist as they stumbled together down the stairwell.

"It's going to be all right. We just need to go now. Move, Rita. As fast as you can."

Get to the police. Get to the police.

They struggled off the last step, and Rita leaned heavily on her cane.

"Okay, girl, what—"

The front door slammed open. The crash of the door hitting against the wall was as loud as a gunshot. And Michael, covered with blood, his chest heaving and his mouth twisted into an evil snarl, standing between them and the world outside.

"You bitch."

He spit the words, staring at her, his face wild with rage. His eyes swept quickly over Rita, now holding onto the far wall for support, before he turned his glare back to Merry. Merry backed away from Rita.

"You stupid, stupid bitch. You know you can't get away from me. You just made it a little more complicated, that's all."

His voice was a growl, brimming with hate and fury. His eyes never left hers as he started toward her, limping hard on one leg, wiping the blood leaking from his torn face and gashed eye with one hand. She held her breath, she couldn't breathe, she was backing up, but there was no way out. And Rita, he would kill Rita too. Terror pounded in her head. He was going to kill them both.

"Michael, stop. Please stop. Stop this," she whispered, and she held out one hand, palm forward. She tried to take a breath, tried to unscramble her thoughts. Her words worked their way out of her mouth in clumsy lumps. "Look, let's just leave. Leave Rita alone, she's harmless. She's...old and senile. She doesn't even know what's going on. I'll go with you. Now. Let's just leave." Her whisper had a desperate hard-high edge. She had to convince him.

"Her?" He glanced behind him at Rita, huddled stiff and silent, hunched over her cane. "I'll take care of her later. Right now, Meredith, you're going to die."

He was almost upon her. He lifted his hands up, forward, toward her throat. She pressed back against the wall. There was no way to get away from him.

"Rita, run!" she screamed. "Run—"

A sharp crack reverberated through the room. Michael's eyes went wide. His face winced and slackened as he crumpled to the floor, dropping slowly and heavily as if his joints were disconnecting from one another. Falling and then lying still, in a heap of dark muddy clothing and blood. As Merry watched, horrified, the void he left was filled by a vision of Rita, standing unsteadily behind Michael with her feet set far apart, holding up with both hands the cane she had just slammed into his skull.

But then the picture changed again as Rita slumped forward, almost in slow motion, and collapsed to her knees behind Michael's unmoving body, like a drooping rag doll that had been tossed aside. Merry peeled herself away from the wall, shrinking away from Michael, and dropped down next to Rita, who was trembling, and her skin was ashen gray.

"Merry." Rita's cane clattered against the floor as Merry's arms encircled her and pulled her in close.

"Merry, I don't feel so good."

Merry held her tight, while Rita's eyes fluttered and closed as she slipped into unconsciousness.

Thirty Three

Time flowed and stopped and pieced together in a jagged rolling nightmare, disjointed and confused. Rita floated in and out of consciousness as Merry dragged her onto the truck seat, leaving Michael in a crumpled heap on the floor. She had bent over him to see that he was still breathing, but she had left him untouched where he had fallen. All her attention was focused on Rita, who was slipping into another place, her breath coming in short, shallow pants, her eyes only opening for fragments of moments before fluttering closed again.

Merry talked to her in a desperate low voice as she slammed her foot down on the accelerator, forcing the truck, rolling and bucking, as fast as she dared down the rutted road. "Hang on, Rita. We'll be at the hospital in a minute. You're going to be fine. Just stay with me, Rita. Please, please stay with me."

She jammed the gears into park in the hospital lot and dashed for the door, yelling as loud as she could. "Help. Someone please. Right now." Her lungs were heaving, starved for air, and the room was reeling. She could only point toward the truck as she hung onto the counter at the check-in station. It took only moments for the two orderlies to sprint from behind the swinging doors with a gurney. As Merry stood shuddering and sobbing at the door, they whisked Rita away. As they passed Merry, she could see that Rita's face was slack and white. One of her hands splayed partially open on her chest, crab-like and immobile.

At first, Merry was alone. She heard footsteps and urgent voices behind the swinging doors. She wanted to go through, to be with Rita, but she didn't want to be in the way. She leaned back in her chair and pressed her head hard against the wall. Images from the last few hours clattered in and out of her brain, not making any sense. Michael. Michael was here. How was that possible? He had tried to kill her. And he now lay bleeding and unconscious on the floor of Rita's cabin.

Her eyes popped wide open. Oh my God, Michael. The nurse from the check-in station whipped through the double doors and walked toward her with quick precise steps. Merry stood and grabbed her forearm and tried to speak, though her voice seemed stuck and broken. "The police. We need the police. Rita's cabin. Michael...a man. On the floor there. He's injured. He tried to kill me. The police need to go there now."

The nurse blinked hard and stared at her for a second, but then she grabbed the phone and punched in a number. She talked in a low grim voice while Merry sank back into the chair, shaking. After the nurse hung up the phone, she pressed a paper cup of tea into Merry's hands, patted her quickly on the back, and hurried back behind the white doors. Merry held the tea in both hands, rocking back and forth in the plastic chair.

She lost all sense of time. Her shin throbbed now, and the cuts on her hands prickled and stung. She huddled in the chair, holding her paper cup, until she looked up at the sound of clicking crisp footsteps to find a state trooper towering above her. He looked clean and efficient and very tall in his pressed blue uniform and shiny black shoes, and he cradled a small notebook in one hand while holding a pen in the other. He opened his mouth to say something to her, but then Nick was there. Nick was somehow there. Nick sat down next to her and pulled her into his arms, encircling her, holding her. She sank into the solid weight of him.

Nick. Oh my God. Nick. She exhaled with relief, and felt her stomach unclench just a bit.

"Merry, are you all right? Merry?" He pulled back

and looked down at her. His face was contorted into a mask of worry. "Trooper Richardson, he just called me on his radio from Rita's cabin. There's some guy there, out cold on the floor, pretty banged up. What happened? Who is that guy?"

She struggled to pull her words together. "Nick...Rita is in there." She pointed to the double doors. "Rita..." She started to sob.

Nick's arms went rigid when she blurted out the next words.

"The guy...is my husband."

Thirty Four

Merry gazed out across Kachemak Bay. She sat bundled in a fleece blanket at the top of the cabin steps, her feet tucked under her for warmth. A new sprinkling of snow had fallen overnight, and the early morning sunlight draped a spread of sparkling diamonds across the open meadow in front of her. All the colors were clear and true, from the deep navy blue of the bay, to the sharp outlines of the black and white peaks in the far distance. It was bitterly cold, so cold that it bit at her face as she turned to look for the source of the rhythmic crunching of footsteps she heard coming up from the road.

Cassandra walked huddled over against the cold, holding a shopping bag in her mittened hands. Merry smiled at yet another of the woman's wild outfits. Her long turquoise parka was belted with a sash of shiny hot-pink satin, and her gold-threaded hat sported twin poms like ears of fake pink fur. It was totally outrageous and yet…somehow she looked, as usual, elegant and beautiful. Wild and exotic and beautiful.

Cassandra settled down on the porch next to her, first pulling out a corner of the blanket to sit on. "Brrrr…it's a cold one," she said, as she opened the bag. She retrieved two paper cups of steaming coffee and a thin paper box of what smelled to be fresh doughnuts.

Merry sipped the hot coffee as she looked out over the bay. Cassandra poked into the bag of doughnuts and began nibbling on a jelly-filled roll covered in powdered sugar. They sat in silence for several minutes.

Merry sighed. "I've been thinking about what comes next." Her voice sounded oddly stiff, and she cleared her throat.

"Some of it I know, of course. Moira will rent the house after Rita's cousins come and get her things, though I don't think there's going to be much they want. Maybe some books and pictures." She shrugged, then smiled. "I think I'll take care of Rita's collection of bodice-rippers before they get here, as one last favor to her."

She felt a deep pang of grief then, right through her core. It had been hard to stay in the cabin these past few nights with Rita gone. But she had wanted to do it, to keep watch over Rita's few things, to feel her lingering presence in the worn, tattered furniture and her salvaged beach treasures, strewn through the cabin. Rita's cane leaned against the kitchen door, its beaked handle nudging into the doorjamb. Perhaps the cousins would let her keep the cane.

She leaned against Cassandra as she felt the lump of grief grow stronger, deeper. She didn't know if she could cry any more tears. She heard Rita, as clear as if she'd been sitting here right next to them. Rita would have tapped her cane impatiently against the worn porch floorboards. "Now stop it, girl. Pull yourself together. I was an old bird and I was going to go anyway, soon enough. Don't you get all weepy now. Just figure out what you're going to do."

The sun had finally reached the porch stairs. It offered little real warmth, but Merry tipped her face up toward it, enjoying the light.

"Have you made your flight plans?" Cassandra asked. She was rooting around in the box for another doughnut. Merry reached over and pulled one out for herself.

"Yes. I'll go tomorrow." She took a tentative bite through a thick slab of pink icing. "The district attorney wants me to come by to sign my formal statement sometime today. Michael's trial won't be scheduled for a long time. The DA said unless he pleads guilty, which tells me he doesn't yet know much about Michael." She smiled grimly. "Michael will get the best defense lawyer he can buy. This whole mess will probably go on for years." She stared out at the far mountains, so distant but so clear.

"And I have my own mess to clean up. I have a lot of explaining to do." She paused then, and took a deep full breath of the bitter winter air. The air stung in her nostrils and constricted her throat. Her feet were getting numb, but she hated to move away from this perfect frozen peace.

"And what then?" Cassandra asked, turning toward her. "And...what about Nick?"

Merry glanced sideways at her, not knowing what to say. Cassandra's mouth curved into a tiny thin smile. "Stop it. Don't worry. It's okay." Cassandra took another doughy bite. "I still have strong feelings for him, you have to know that, and I probably will for a long time, maybe forever. I think I would be dead now if he hadn't been there to take care of me..."

Her voice broke and trailed off. "But Merry, you and I both know that he doesn't love me, at least not in that way. And so it's not going to happen. And if it's not going to happen for me, well maybe it should happen for you."

She smiled her crooked little smile. "We can't waste a good man, you know."

When Cassandra mentioned Nick's name, Merry felt such warmth and longing for him. From the moment he had arrived at the hospital and found her in the waiting room, he had done everything possible to help her, and to take care of Rita's affairs. He had sat and grieved with her, cried with her, when the doctor brought the news about Rita. He had made sure that she was eating, and he'd driven her back and forth from the cabin and the funeral home. He had called Rita's cousins and made all the necessary arrangements. She had told him only a fragmented version of her own story, all she could manage, and he in turn hadn't asked many questions. His expression of stunned shock as she mumbled the words, as she tried to make him understand, made him look years older. He listened in silence. And all that had been growing between them, the new feelings they shared, somehow faded into the background as they dealt with the terrible blow of Rita's death, and the gritty reality of Michael and the life she had fled. He had been kind to her. He had taken care of her. But he hadn't said to her, "Stay." He hadn't said, "Don't go." Her past was a chasm between them, and he hadn't offered up a bridge over it.

Merry stood, her legs stiff and clumsy from sitting so long in the cold. "He is a good man." She shifted her weight back and forth, trying to pump up the circulation in her legs. "He is a good man and he deserves a good woman."

A raven croaked from high in the spruce trees, then glided across the meadow in front of them. Merry's eyes followed its path as it slipped silently into the shadows of the forest beyond.

"And I'm coming back, Cass, once I get everything straightened out at home. That may take some time, but I'm going to come back. And when I do, there won't be any loose ends or unfinished pieces holding me back. No more secrets. No more running away. And then we'll see what happens next."

Cassandra pushed herself up and brushed the sprinkles of powdered sugar from her parka. She put her hand over Merry's on the porch railing, and Merry felt that they were holding on to the world together. Merry wrapped her blanket around them both, and they stood side by side on the porch in the sunshine, staring at the distant glaciers, now polished a brilliant blazing white by the rising sun.

About the Author

Stephanie Joyce Cole lived for decades in Alaska. She now lives in Seattle, in a household that includes a predatory but lovable Manx cat named Bruno, and a young standard poodle named Rusty, who is in perpetual motion.

Visit Stephanie Joyce Cole at **www.stephaniejoycecole.com** or on Facebook.

Tantalizing Tidbits

Gardens, a short story by Stephanie Joyce Cole can be found in **Tantalizing Tidbits**, an eclectic collection of short stories written by bestselling authors, representing an eclectic mix of styles and genres. In a word, this book is a smorgasbord; an opportunity to try a bit of everything.

In the spirit of the smorgasbord, the collection is presented as a menu and authors have shared recipes which accompany each story—some fitting, some funny, some simply old favorites.

Ranging from ultra-short but spine tingling, to meatier tales that are nearly novellas there is a little something for every appetite including comedy, tragedy, fantasy, werewolves, at least one ghost, life, death, and of course love.

Made in the USA
San Bernardino, CA
02 May 2016